Other Books by Richard Donze

Dinner Music: How to Compose the Permanently Perfect Diet

The Natural Order of Things

The Secret Saint Anthony Prayer

a novel by

Richard Donze

Cover art and illustrations by

Joseph Cairone

Finishing Line Press
Georgetown, Kentucky

The Secret Saint Anthony Prayer

Publisher: Leah Huete de Maines
Editor: Christen Kincaid
Cover Art and Illustrations: Joseph R. Cairone
Author Photo: J. Paul Simeone
Cover Design: Nate Adams, Matthew Evans

Order online: www.finishinglinepress.com
also available on amazon.com

Author inquiries and mail orders:
Finishing Line Press
PO Box 1626
Georgetown, Kentucky 40324
USA

Contents

To the 1966 eighth grade class at Our Lady of Perpetual Help school
in Morton, Pennsylvania
"God's blessing sends us forth."

"[T]he problems of the human heart in conflict with itself...alone can
make good writing because only that is worth writing about, worth
the agony and the sweat."
William Faulkner

Originally Delivered Address Accepting the Nobel Prize in Literature
December 10, 1950
Stockholm, Sweden

Author's Note

While *The Secret Saint Anthony Prayer* is a work of fiction, novelists often draw on their own backgrounds and experiences, and this author did attend a Roman Catholic elementary school in Philadelphia's western suburbs in the mid-1960s. So even though the names of the school, students, teachers, priests, church, town, streets and businesses that figure most prominently in the narrative are all invented, many may have characteristics of real people and places the author knew at that time in that setting and still knows. In other instances, the actual names of area/regional towns, schools, churches, etc. that are part of the story's backdrop may have been retained. No character is based on or named after a single individual from the author's past or present, but instead all are composites that may incorporate (to one degree or another) some of the sensibilities, personality traits, physical characteristics and/or other pertinent aspects of two or more actual people, plus or minus imaginary elements and embellishments. So, while it is not entirely correct to say, in the usual way for fiction, that "any resemblances to persons living or dead is purely coincidental," it would be appropriate to assert that any reader who suspects or feels strongly that he or she knows what real person a particular character represents will likely bump into pieces of at least one and possibly more other people making up that aggregate, and frequently some persistently mysterious fabrications.

I

Summer Slips Away
(August 15th to Labor Day)

Summer was slipping away as usual in September 1963 as we got ready to start our eighth-grade year at St. Anthony of Padua elementary school (named for the 13th-Century Portuguese Franciscan priest and patron saint of lost things), and there was no way to know that in early November a death would occur in the school building that at least one of our classmates thought and may still think was a homicide, or that a few weeks later that same month President John Fitzgerald Kennedy, America's first (and as of September 2018, only) Roman Catholic President, would be assassinated in Dallas, Texas by somebody or somebodies that may or may not have been or included Lee Harvey Oswald, or that in January 1964 Father James Galvin, a diocesan priest, the assistant pastor at St. Anthony's and director of the altar boys would be yanked out of his assignment by Philadelphia's archbishop and diocesan leader (some might have said "autocratic ruler") John O'Brien for allegedly celebrating an illegal Mass in a motel room with street clothes, guitar-led folk songs, and a loaf of store-bought Friehoffer's bread on the leading edge of the incipient liberalizing ferment of the barely-year-old Roman Catholic Church's Second Vatican Council and banished to a distant parish in north central Pennsylvania somewhere west of Williamsport (I never knew or don't remember where exactly, but a year later when *Hogan's Heroes* was on TV and week after week we watched Colonel Klink threaten the physically massive yet emotionally fragile Sergeant Schultz with his worst Nazi campaign nightmare we used to say Galvin had been sent "to the Russian front"), or that in February the Beatles would come to America just as I was (and probably had been for months, maybe even years) falling in love for real for the first time with Mary Elizabeth Albarelli, a girl in our class with the names of the mothers of Jesus and John the Baptist who in October of that school year attended the same Friday night dance as I in the darkened gym of St. Eugene's Elementary School in nearby Primos when I wanted so much to ask her to slow dance to the Marvelettes song "Forever" but never summoned the courage, who in late December gave me a Christmas gift when I didn't know we were exchanging presents and so had to scramble to find the money and the idea to reciprocate, whom in late March at classmate Nancy Kendrick's 14th birthday party in a local neighborhood twin home's knotty pine paneled basement I kissed for the first time (I could sense her lips trying to open while I kept mine tightly shut, something for which I would later chastise myself repeatedly as a missed opportunity to "get some tongue" and with that the accompanying bragging rights) during a game of Post Office behind the closed door of the cellar bathroom while on Nancy's fold-down turntable record player with the hinged swing-out speakers John Lennon and Paul McCartney played and sang "It won't be long, yeah, yeah, till I belong to you" and "Whenever I want to kiss you, yeah, all I've got to do..." to McCartney's throbbing Hofner electric bass guitar on their recently released debut American album *Meet the Beatles*, who disappeared mysteriously right after Easter (or at least was absent from school for weeks) missing all of April, all of May including the May Procession when she would have almost certainly been in the running for May Queen although by no means a shoe-in since the nuns had serious questions about her chastity and didn't return until mid-June when the class was rehearsing for its graduation ceremony, or that later the next night at the graduation party I would be fighting for her heart with another boy in class, my scholastic and athletic rival Ronald Biggs whom we called "Biggsy" (one time in sixth grade at recess for no obvious reason other than it seemed to amuse him he decided he would start calling the Saint Anthony's community Bongo Congo after the recently released TV cartoon series Leonardo Lion, and rather than wanting to play the inept king he said I should be Leonardo while he wanted to reserve for himself the role of Leonardo's archenemy Biggie Rat who was always trying to overthrow the kingdom, and I didn't care because I thought it was stupid anyway, so he referred to himself as Biggie but I had the distinction of changing Biggie to Biggsy because of his actual name, so we called him Biggsy Rat and, after a time, just Biggsy) when Mary Liz and Biggsy were like the two poles of my existence and I was like a charged subatomic particle, forever bouncing between them, but never really striking either, and even before that first kiss I wanted to be near Mary Liz, around Mary Liz, seeing her anywhere I could, in the classroom, out on the recess yard where she and Nancy Kendrick and Dolores Kolowski and some other girls would stand in a huddle, talking, laughing, sometimes pushing each other, and every so often glancing quickly, furtively, over to where we stood—me, Biggsy, Robbie Hannum and Gerry Giordano—wondering maybe hoping maybe just maybe she is talking about me or wanting to see me as much as I wanted to see her anywhere everywhere after school in the magazine section at MacNamee's Drug Store where I went to read *Hit Parader* to get the words to the songs we were all listening to (such as the Beatles' "P.S. I Love You," trying to solve the mystery of whether they sang "*and* till the day I do, love" or "*un*til the day" or the Searchers' "Needles and Pins" and whether it was

"THAT they'd go away" or, ridiculously, "BACKache go away"?) in the days before artists included lyrics inside their album covers, wondering if maybe just maybe she might be there too, getting some aspirin for her mother or a prescription for her father maybe even coming over to the magazine section where I was to browse a copy of *16 Magazine,* always looking up at her house on the other side of Cedar Street across Timberline Avenue whenever I walked past the church to MacNamee's in case she might be outside walking to the family car or maybe raking leaves or pulling weeds or just sitting on the front porch, listening in the choir for her soaring soprano in "Tantum Ergo" or "O Salutaris Hostia" looking up from the altar where I was serving Mass or Stations of the Cross or Benediction, in case I'd see her at her usual spot on the right end of the front row in the choir loft, half standing, half sitting on the half wall, sometimes fanning herself with her songbook (it must have gotten hot up there with all the 13- and 14-year-old post-menarche girls in those heavy cotton uniforms), and after the kiss all of that was even worse, and coming into the Biggsy field toward the Biggsy pole repeatedly just in the normal course of competition for grades, book report contests, recess games, memorizing altar boy Latin and, finally, at the graduation party when he was slow-dance-close to Mary Liz where I should have been.

Interesting year.

The Reunion Idea

"Why do we need a reunion?" Nancy asked Paul. "We see each other practically every week as it is."

"And why a 50th reunion?" Gerry chimed in. "Hasn't it been more than 50 years?"

Nancy Kendrick, Dolores Kolowski, Gerry Giordano, Robbie Hannum and Paul Perdu were former classmates at St. Anthony of Padua elementary school in Springhaven, Pennsylvania, a sprawlish smallish (population around 5000 in 1956 when they entered first grade) Delaware County suburb about 12 miles west of Philadelphia, had remained friends since graduating in 1964 (Nancy, Gerry and Paul all attended Bishop Keenan high school as well, while Dolores and Robbie went to Springhaven High, but they all still stayed in touch) and did, in fact, see each other very regularly, most times weekly and almost always at Buddy's Tavern on Taylor's Mill Road in the center of the oldest section of Springhaven, for happy hour on Fridays between 4:00 and 7:00.

"It's actually been 55 years," Paul said, "but that could be part of the joke. Like, 'Welcome to the 5th anniversary of our 50th reunion,' or 'Welcome to the 50th reunion' then in parentheses 'Okay, it's been 55 years, but we figured "What was the hurry?"' or we could put '50th' on the invitation, then cross out the '0' and write a '5' above it. Or something like that. It would be hysterical."

Buddy's still reeked of stale cigarettes and beer even though it had been smoke-free for five years, but obviously not enough time for 70+ years of those baked-in odors to depart the old wooden everything—paneling, bar, tables and chairs. Everyone who smoked now had to do it outside, which Paul said made going in the front door like running the secondhand smoke gauntlet, although of course it wasn't beer-free so that smell never had a chance of dissipating. The guys still preferred their brews, often sticking with domestic mainstays by Bud and Miller or more local and regional Pennsylvania favorites such as Rolling Rock and Yuengling and more recently Victory out of Downingtown, while in recent years the girls had been leaning more toward white wine ("not too oaky" Nancy always said whenever she was thinking of trying a new chardonnay) or now and then even trying cocktails and altered martini concoctions using fruit, chocolate and other embellishments, the one with apple AND chocolate referred to as "the Buddy-tini."

"Hysterical?" Gerry asked. "More like *lame*."

"We have obviously already figured out who we like hanging out with from grade school," Nancy added, "but I guess it would be nice to see some of the others."

Getting together was easy for this classroom subset since besides genuinely liking each other they had all continued living in the general Springhaven region and no farther away than Robbie's 10 miles in the eastern part of Chester County which was still plenty close enough. And Friday late afternoons-early evenings at Buddy's meant they started and ended early enough to avoid disrupting work schedules too much or interfering with later-evening spousal commitments (Paul and Robbie were divorced but the others still married, Dolores twice, although sometimes husbands and wives attended as well and started their own separate conversations as the "aliens" leaving the St. Anthony alums to their memories) and even still allowed attending kids' after-school events, although with the parents now being in their late 60's none of that really mattered anymore unless there were grandchildren in recitals, playing soccer, or just needing to be babysat. There were other more formal occasions to get together as well, such as planned Christmas house parties, being invited to each other's and later their children's weddings, and more recently parents' and even two classmates' funerals.

Fifty-plus years was a long time to stay so close, but their bonding had deep roots, simply and organically related to the amount of time they all spent together in grade school. Unlike public schools that divided the first eight years of post-kindergarten education into five of elementary and three of junior high, at St. Anthony's and at all the other diocesan parochial schools in the area it was eight solid years in the same building with the same kids.

The idea itself—to organize a 50th elementary school reunion—wasn't as odd (other area Catholic grade school alumni were doing it) as it was that it was a little late—55 years after their actual graduation—but mostly that it was Paul's idea. So part of Nancy's challenge was related to the source and how totally out of character it was for him, leading her to wonder "Where did THAT come from?" even though it was less a formal construct than a more spontaneous, organic "Why don't we…" that emerged at that late-August-2018 session after a few beers and some of the usual memory swapping they enjoyed. No one could remember Paul ever having an original idea about anything involving socializing. He was the consummate passive friend; and even though he would eventually respond to calls and emails and even text messages, it was often many hours and sometimes even days later, and he rarely started any of those conversations. He would show up at parties and smaller get-togethers or just at Buddy's for the standing weekly assembly and be very engaged once he got there, but he would never initiate or organize anything. None of the others really minded—he was divorced and living alone and had no kids, but he had always been that way. He hadn't even chosen his career—his parents had done that, at least indirectly—and these days he could barely organize his life. But now here he was, presenting this concept and saying not only that WE should do this reunion but that HE would take the lead in planning and organizing. It was kind of interesting and actually even a little heartwarming for the others to see him so enlivened after the way his life had gone up till then.

"Exactly," Paul said. "It would be very nice. But there's another kind of pressing reason, actually a kind of urgency to do it now, this coming year. Yeah, we're late acknowledging the 50th anniversary, we dropped that ball in 2014. But after next summer, no more St. Anthony's."

It was true. As they all knew, St. Anthony's as a building and a local parish would no longer exist after the summer of 2019. The Philadelphia Archdiocese had been closing schools and consolidating parishes for several years due to severely dwindling enrollments which were part of lower 21st-Century birth rates and undoubtedly out-migration from Catholicism due to the ongoing fallout from the diocesan priest sex scandals, and at the beginning of the next school year in September 2019 St. Anthony of Padua was merging with Our Lady of Sorrows in nearby Taylor's Ford to form the new, consolidated Prince of Peace parish on the Taylor's Ford/Sorrows campus. A new housing development was slated for the post-demolition lot/footprint where the St. Anthony's school building, convent, recess yard and football field stood (the parish church a half a mile away would remain) and had stood since 1948, in the ongoing exercise to eat up every square foot of available space in Delaware County for new housing construction. After that, St. Anthony's would disappear into the Springhaven neighborhood of which it had been a part for 70 years.

Those were the ostensible reasons. But at least Nancy (and probably the others, too) wondered if there might be something else going on with Paul, something below the surface. Where did all this energy and enthusiasm come from? What itch was he trying to scratch? Paul usually kept his cards pretty close to his vest when it came to overt expressions of affect or intent, but sometimes his silence could actually be fairly transparent. Paul's usual joking fueled by his astounding memory for events that occurred between 1956 and 1964 almost seemed a cover up for some deeper desire to keep revisiting that mental and emotional place that in many ways he had never really left. Spouting the memories kept him in the figurative locus of those feelings and times, and being with the other four of them made some of that literal. But now he seemed to want to take that literal in-the-flesh part to another level. The most likely explanation in Nancy's mind was that he was simply creating a pretty complex and convoluted excuse to try to see Mary Liz Albarelli (his eighth-grade crush) again, or at least setting out a pretty elaborate piece of bait to see if it might attract her. Although it was by no means clear that they would even be able to find her. Whenever her name came up inevitably someone would share the latest story about where she was or had been heard from: Boston. Chicago. L.A. No recent sightings though, nor had anyone heard that she was or had been back anywhere near Springhaven recently, not even when her dad died in 2016.

All that aside, Nancy and the others finally conceded that it actually wasn't such a bad idea. And doing it soon, now, this year, before the planned demolition the following summer did make sense.

"If not now, when?" Paul said. "And the timing is perfect: summer is almost over, so we can start planning right after Labor Day, right around the time school always started, and things will gradually take shape over the following nine months almost like it's our project for the school year, then we have the party in June on a Friday or Saturday night around the time of the actual date of our 1964 eighth grade graduation party. I'll check the calendar, because it would be crazy if it were the exact same date. So between now and Labor Day it will almost be like we are getting ready for school—making sure we have enough pencils and erasers and loose leaf notebooks copy books and a pencil case…"

"Okay, okay, enough" Nancy interrupted. "Fine. Everybody think about it, and we'll discuss it some more after Labor Day. Right now, I need another chard. And Paul, if another beer will shut you up for a while, I'm buying."

"And Paul, if another beer will shut you up for a while, I'm buying."

II

School Year Starts
(Day after Labor Day to September 30th)

We called it a school *year* but of course it was really only nine and a half months between early September and mid-June. Not a full year by the usual 12-month January-to-December calendar, but its own calendar, one of many we moderns conveniently employ to mark the passage of days and months and the movement of the seasons in a particular context. Not really like fiscal years in the business world that are still 12 months but out of phase with the January-to-December cycle; maybe more like fashion years, when fall clothes fill up store shelves and racks in late summer, and spring clothes arrive in winter; or sports years with their two seasons—In, and Off—that also must conform to the seasonal weather as to whether the athletes compete indoors or outside and what kind of uniforms they can wear (there's a reason why ice hockey jerseys were originally called "sweaters," linking them to literal and figurative teeth-cutting time spent on northern-hemisphere frozen winter ponds); or agricultural years that affirm the Ecclesiastes passage about there being a time to plant and time to reap.

At St. Anthony's, as presumably at all parochial elementary schools in our area and maybe in the whole state and country for that matter, the calendar was a mix/blend of the conventional lineup of months and 3-month seasons and the Roman Catholic liturgical calendar that starts with the season of Advent usually in late November or early December (in America it's typically 3-10 days after the secular feast of Thanksgiving) then moves through Christmas, Lent and Easter, also called "seasons" with connecting glue-like intervals between each of those called, inauspiciously, "Ordinary Time."

I have no memory of how I measured time before I started school, although I imagine (and presumably it was) a purer more pristine pre-conscious connection with the weather, lengths of days and nights and intensity of the sun. On a larger scale, perhaps it was the experience of noticing that I could wear shorts and tee shirts and swim in pools, lakes, and oceans and experience bare feet on sandy and pebbly beaches and eat frozen treats from the neighborhood ice cream truck and get mosquito bites in one season, but had to wear hats and coats and gloves and boots and could sled and build snowmen in another; but on the smaller scale there must have been nuances, subtleties, perhaps subconscious—sights, smells, textures, a sense of a rhythm in plants trees skies and temperatures, a movement from cold and seeming death to warmth and fecundity and growth, through maturation and desiccation and ultimately back into death before the whole cycle started up again. Who knows? Whatever notions I had of time and seasons before I started going to school had either disappeared or more likely were obscured and perhaps even buried by the school experience once that started.

Although it has been 62 years since I started and 54 years since I stopped attending St. Anthony's, its Catholic school calendar still runs inside my head, occupies my thoughts and influences my moods. How could it not? It came so early in life, imprinting itself on my plastic childhood brain, lasted eight solid years and got reinforced another four in high school. It makes me want to resist and resent the obligation to return to work on July 5th because 54 years ago I would have been off; fills me with hard-to-describe feelings of loss and longing as I sense summer slipping away in late August; whips up waves of nausea and dread on Labor Day and New Year's nights when back then I contemplated starting and restarting school the following days after enjoying precious time off; traps me in limbo the whole month of no-longer-summer but not-quite-autumn September, boosts my energy on October's cool and poplar-leaf-yellow-colored days, increases my excitement and simultaneously distracts me from work as Thanksgiving and Christmas approach, makes me feel hopeless in the bleak winter desert after New Year's, then reestablishes that hope after Ash Wednesday despite the usual deprivation of "giving something up for Lent" because it means Easter and Spring and warmth can't be far behind; lifts my soul and spirit as Spring blossoms and blooms and spreads green grass and crocus and grape hyacinth and daffodil sights and smells everywhere, and suffuses me with the delicious and delirious sense of liberty as I get ready to dive headlong into summer.

Old calendars often have pictures, but as I think about and look at this one, at the images in photographs and memory and inside the figurative lined graphic boxes that house the dates and sometimes the short scribbled notes about what happened on those days, as I not just look but smell it and taste it and listen to it I say hello to an old friend, chuckling a little as I realize that because of that calendar that rhythm I am perennially challenged managing my responsibilities in the 12-month 4-season 3-months-to-a-season adult world of work where the weeks before and after Labor Day or Christmas or Easter or Flag Day are more or less the same except for the clothes I wear and whether or not I drive to work with the windows up or down, the heater or A/C on, and admit that at various times of the year when I see certain people or buildings or smell certain flowers or trees or floor wax or sweet decay walking near woods or hear certain songs on FM or satellite radio oldies or decades stations it is still in my reflexes head ears nose skin tongue an itch a beep click hum or flash that whispers or shouts St. Anthony, Biggsy, Mary Liz.

St. Anthony Seasons

On the first day of the 8th-grade school year Paul Perdu, Gerald Giordano (Gerry), Robert Hannum (Robbie) and Ronald Biggs (whom the other three, at least, called "Biggsy") were milling around in the schoolyard waiting for the dreaded first bell that would silence and freeze them in their whatever positions and conversations and gesticulations, even mid-stride if walking, and somebody (usually Biggsy) would teeter and totter and over-dramatize the challenge maintaining balance on one leg, making one or two or a few of them have to suppress their laughter which only made the freezing and silence harder. The second bell that followed was the signal for each grade to start moving again, in silence except for the rustling of their shoes on the schoolyard blacktop and form a line by the door, and finally when the third rang they would file inside the school, the shoe rustling more concentrated and louder now sounding like marching or like what they remembered or imagined from movies and TV sights and sounds it must have looked like and felt like and sounded like when captured soldiers were herded onto and into troop trucks or ships or POW camps. It had been that way for the last seven years, and they expected and got the same that day.

If they didn't feel summer's abrupt end the night before when their stomachs turned anticipating the return to school, or when they actually entered the schoolyard at 8:15 or 8:20 to have at least a few minutes to talk to each other before the first bell at 8:30, that third bell officially shut summer down. Walking up the steps sliding their hands on the early September early morning cool still-dew-damp iron handrail and past the building's outside brick walls and the cement cornerstone engraved with *Anno Domini 1948* (until Paul studied Latin more formally in high school, not from the altar boy Latin in grade school that was just the prayers and responses at Mass, and was able to translate the phrase into "year of the Lord" and realized it was the A.D. in historical dates he had always thought it was somebody's Italian name and always wondered who "Anno Domini" might have been and if her real name was actually "Anna" and the engraver had misspelled it or his chisel had slipped trying to make the final "A" and what she might have done in 1948) and into the dark hallway redolent of some unnamed disinfectant and floor wax that only made the stomach turning and mild nausea even worse was like walking away forever from the summer of 1963. No more freedom; no more languid dreamy mornings waking up slowly in the July haze to a bowl of corn or frosted flakes when it was too hot for eggs or pancakes in the days before any of their homes had central air conditioning (if they had air conditioning at all it was only a window unit or two, and if two usually limited to one in the living room where the TV was and one in the parents' bedroom, while the kids would sweat through the night with window fans circulating the sultry night air, forcing them at times to sit in the darkness directly in front of the fan and reverse the flow from sucking out to blowing in so they could at least feel some air movement but making sure they didn't speak too loudly into it their lips on the grill to make that odd vibrating sound they found briefly entertaining before remembering how hot they were); no more weekday pick-up hardball games on the dusty fields of Grove Avenue Park that was close enough to walk or bike to, each of their army school bags stuffed with a glove, a bat with its skinny end sticking out (Paul's was a Louisville slugger 34-ounce Hank Aaron model with a thin, easy to grip handle), a light brown, scuffed Rawlings hardball or two whose red thread was usually trying to escape the seams, and in Paul's case an empty Sealtest glass milk bottle from one of the empty ones his mother dutifully placed in the small grayish insulated box where the delivery man put the fresh ones and picked up the used but rinsed and filled with tap water and chilled in the fridge (long before the days of sports-top water and energy drinks); no more endless afternoons playing army with machine gun-shaped fallen tree branches in the small wooded area that sat between the backyards of the houses on Clover Lane and the small shopping center on Springhaven Road that had a dry cleaners, a hobby/pet shop where they used their allowance and/or lawn-mowing and/or birthday and/or other summer job money to buy small turtles, H-O miniature World War Two Africa Korps army men, and model battleships and airplanes including the balsa wood type with the weighted metal piece on the nose that were either gliders or had a propellor attached to a rubber band that invariably got wound so tight (hoping it would add speed and height and flying time) it snapped the fragile fuselage, and an A&P supermarket whose air-conditioned comfort they would seek and enjoy when they walked in from The Woods to grab quick drinks at the Oasis water fountain before the black horn-rimmed bespectacled manager, Mr. Kane chased them out because they were dirty, sweaty, and of course not buying anything; no more mosquito-swatting nights outside till well after 9:00 playing flashlight tag or walking to the 7-11 to buy cupcakes and sodas with that same shrinking cache of hobby shop money talking about how queer somebody like Michael Moylan was (a boy in their class with a soft white pudgy face to match his soft white pudgy body who might be called a nerd today but back then they used "queer" when it just meant odd or different as opposed to homosexual, although Michael may indeed have been gay as well) or how "nice" (their post-puberty word for pretty and/or attractive and/or large-breasted) Mary Liz and Nancy Kendrick and Dolores Kolowski were.

No more shorts and sneaks and tee shirts, but back to stiff collared button-down white shirts with blue ties and shined stiff shoes that would take until sometime in October before softening and picking up a few scuffs. They might rush home from school after that first day hoping it had all been a bad dream and wanting to wake up to recapture the free spirits they'd had only one or two days earlier, but it was already gone. It was still plenty hot, but the swim club was closed. They might don the summer "uniform" and go back outside hoping to ride bikes or play ball, but it wasn't the same. Outside looked the same as it did two days earlier, but tasted different, like a garden vegetable whose outside appearance is unchanged but inside has already committed its machinery to making seeds, and so tasted bitter. And there was already some homework and books to cover and pencil cases to resupply. And even though the first couple of weeks were transitional and the teaching and learning wouldn't get much traction until later in the month or even October, summer had definitely slipped away.

Before the first bell rang Gerry, perhaps overcome with the sense of loss at having to start school and leave summer behind blurted out, "I hate the fall."

Biggsy snapped right back, "This isn't fall, you imbecile. Fall doesn't come for another couple weeks and it's gonna be 80 degrees today."

It was already in the low 70s at that early hour, not at all unusual for that time of year in southeastern Pennsylvania with August only a few days gone, and still very humid—the thunderstorms that had ended so many neighborhood Labor Day cookouts the afternoon and night before hadn't really cooled things off or lifted the wet-blanket feel in the air—a reality that was easy to confirm since they were, after all, already sweating in those long pants, collared shirts and ties.

"Well, it sure isn't summer anymore, asshole," Gerry fired back; "we're back in school."

Biggsy said nothing but stared off to the left, as he always did when he was thinking, making a connection, putting something together. Then the first bell rang and that was the end of the talking.

They were dismissed before lunch, as the first day of school was always a half day when they'd get their general orientation to the school year ahead including instructions on how many black-marble copybooks, loose leaf tablets and small spiral notepads (for writing down the list of homework assignments) they would need (and the "approved" brands they would only be able to buy from the school store, like the ones with the times tables on the copybook back cover along with avoirdupois weights whatever the hell they were) and the teachers would distribute the textbooks the students would have to cover that night, using the brown paper covers printed with local business ads, including one for Paul's father's appliance store in town and Gerry's dad's 5 & 10, and having to cut up and use A&P, Penn Fruit or Food Fair grocery store brown paper bags when the printed covers were gone.

As they were walking outside to go home, Biggsy called Paul and Gerry and Robbie over and announced, "Mates, we've got some work to do on the calendar. Tomorrow. Second recess."

Paul would later find out that Biggsy had read *Treasure Island* over the summer, so for the first few weeks of school he called everyone "sea dog" or "old salt" or "mate" (or, more familiarly, "matey"). In seventh grade, when Biggsy was reading one Hardy Boys novel after another, for the longest time his small circle of boys were all his "chums" and everything they wondered about and got into was "the case of" or "the mystery of" or "the secret" this or that.

The next day, another hot humid one, they used their after-lunch second recess (the 30-minute break they called "long recess" to distinguish it from the 10-15 minute first or "short recess" they got mid-morning) to begin the "work" Biggsy had alluded to the day before, taking refuge from the noon-time heat under the shade of the huge northern red oak tree in Robbie Hannum's backyard that bordered the school's football field. St. Anthony's sat on about four or five acres on Sycamore Road, a street that eventually crossed Springhaven Road, the main artery in the newer part of their little town that itself crossed Taylor's Mill Road that ran through the oldest part of town (named for William Thompson Taylor, the founder of Springhaven in the early 18th Century and whose old stone house still sat near the trolley tracks and was used for town meetings and various photo ops—everything from weddings to little league group pictures).

The school had been built in 1948 before there was much in that part of town besides the two old houses (one with a brown cedar shake shingle exterior, the other white wavy stucco) that dated back to the 1920's where the Martins and Crandells lived, and the neighborhood kind of grew up around the school, homes added here and there, not suburban sub-development cookie-cutter style but a series of one-offs so that eventually the schoolyard and football field abutted and were contiguous with a large number of backyards.

Doing "work" with Biggsy almost always meant simply listening to one or another of his ideas. So it was Biggsy who usually did the actual work; his "mates" had the job to listen and participate in whatever game, scheme, or other project he'd dreamed up. This time, though, it was more of an intellectual exercise, and Biggsy was just looking for an audience, something a modern marketer might call a focus group off of which he wanted to bounce his latest idea, although it was more a participatory autocracy since Biggsy typically ended up declaring that this or that would be thus and such.

"Our mate Gerry got me thinking about the seasons," Biggsy began, and the work on the calendar he had done in this case was based on his newfound sense that the conventional division of seasons was all wrong. Biggsy was starting one of his soliloquies, a little monologue about what he had been thinking and as usual they let him go and followed along, either because they agreed or just realized from experience that disagreeing was pointless since he would just keep going anyway when it was clear he had already figured something out and/or already decided on something and didn't want any input or feedback other than unchallenged acceptance.

"What Gerry said made me remember what I saw when I was working at the swim club snack bar a few weeks ago," Biggsy continued. "I had to get there pretty early some mornings to start getting soda cups and hamburger and hot dog buns ready for the day, before the lifeguards had skimmed the pool, and I saw a few dropped leaves, all brown and curled up, floating on the water."

"Yeah, so?" Paul butted in.

"So," Biggsy went on, "it was an end-of-summer, coming-of-autumn sign, mates, but as early as mid-August. I don't remember ever noticing that before."

He then put that together with other observations he could easily make walking the three-quarters of a mile from his house on Jefferson along the

...if they had cared to notice they would have seen similar evidence in some brown, dry poplar and oak leaves...

mostly-wooded (and aptly named) Timberline Road to the swim club.

"The next day I noticed other things, like dropped yellow leaves and more and more acorns along the curbs. So we think of seasons according to the calendar. Gerry said he hated the fall and I told him it wasn't fall yet, but that's just the calendar seasons. What I was seeing made me think that fall isn't a calendar thing, but a nature thing that starts a lot earlier than the date for autumn on the September calendar."

Sitting there in Hannum's backyard, if they had cared to notice they would have seen similar evidence in some brown, dry poplar and oak leaves scattered on the ground around them.

"I tell you, mates, summer starts slipping away into fall as early as late June," Biggsy told them.

"What are you talking about," Gerry came back, as he always did. Paul used to think that Gerry saw his position as linebacker on the school's CYO football team (he was a natural since in seventh grade he had already reached his adult height at about six foot one with broad shoulders and huge Popeye forearms) as a role that extended to all his interpersonal dealings and interactions—he would follow someone who was running with an idea or a conversation then pursue and try to eventually bring him or her down. "June and July are about as 'summer' as you can get. The days are hot and long."

"Are they long?" Biggsy retorted. "Tell me the longest day of the year." Biggsy knew he had him, but he let him fall of his own considerable weight first.

"I don't know," Gerry responded. "Sometime around the 4th of July I guess, or maybe after that.

"It's June 21st, you knucklehead," Biggsy came back, "the first day of summer. The days get shorter after that, and that's a meteorological and astronomical fact. But mates, our old salt Gerry here isn't completely wrong, because we don't really notice the days getting shorter until about mid-August, when if we open our eyes we see a lot else going on, like I did at the swim club and walking on the way there. That's what I wanted to tell you all. There's so much happening. It's not just leaves coming down; it's acorns, too, and all kinds of plants losing their flowers and making seeds to drop into the ground so they can grow again the next year. And it's the squirrels and crows going crazy because they know the time is growing short and they have to get ready for what's coming, to put on some fat, to bury some nuts."

"What? What's coming?" Paul blurted out, and as soon as he said it he knew he had given Biggsy another in a long series of opportunities to best him."

"What's coming?" Biggsy repeated. "Why, it's winter, me sea-dog mateys. The death of the year. The squirrels know and the flowers know and the trees know, and they all know they need to get ready."

So a brief and seemingly insignificant conversation the first day of school that eighth-grade year about calendars and seasons created a little epiphany for Biggsy that was enough to make him recognize the inadequacy of trying to apply the vocabulary and timing of the conventional months and seasons to what was happening around them in the natural world, but also inadequate relative to what was going to be happening at St. Anthony's over the next nine-and-a-half months. Biggsy further realized that while calendar seasons have hard starts and hard stops on specific dates and were all generally about 90 days long, composed of 3-30'ish-day-long months each, the seasons as reflected in and measured by weather, school, church and life activities and what was growing (or not) in their fields and yards and woods have more incremental emergences and retreats, and are not all of roughly equal duration.

"Think about it, chums (now he was back to The Hardy Boys again). Summer doesn't begin at a solstice in June and end at an equinox in September, but as an actual season it starts appearing in May and slipping away in August, maybe even earlier. Like, when does summer start for us?"

"That's easy," Gerry said; "as soon as school is over."

"Exactly," Biggsy responded. "Near the solstice, but not right on it."

So Biggsy decided to revise the calendar and rename the seasons, replacing the conventional hard starts and stops by acknowledging the actual environmental risings and fallings and integrating the starts and stops more relevant to their St. Anthony microcosm. Part of the exercise included recasting the seasons' dates accordingly, mixing up church and secular and natural world events and holidays. That was the work, and he wanted the guys all to agree and start using the newer nomenclature.

There were several things they were sure of at St. Anthony's—certain ritualized activities related to their Roman Catholic religion and the liturgical year such as going to Mass every First Friday and Stations of the Cross during Lent and having a May Procession to honor the Blessed Virgin. But they also always knew when school would begin (always the day after Labor Day) and end (on or around June 13th, the feast day of

St. Anthony of Padua, and when June 13th fell on a Saturday they'd get out Friday the 12th, but if on a Sunday they'd go one more half day to Monday the 14th). So those dates would define the boundaries of summer, closely related to solstice and equinox and the natural world emergings and slippings away he had noticed, but not exactly.

But Biggsy also wanted to name that time from around August 15th or so (the Catholic feast of the Assumption, when Mary the mother of Jesus was "assumed" up into heaven, but also when according to the old world "blessing of the sea" custom Paul's Italian grandmother always asked Paul's dad to drive her to Atlantic City so she could put her feet in the ocean) to Labor Day, when those few leaves would start showing up on the surfaces of pools or alongside curbs or in backyards, or there might be a powerful thunderstorm to end a humid fortnight of dog days and leave the next morning crisp, clear, and full of Arctic breezes. Biggsy asked them for suggestions, but it was perfunctory, since he already knew what he wanted to call the season that had just ended two days ago: Summer Slipping Away: August 15th to Labor Day.

In keeping with what he and Gerry had verbally sparred about the day before, Biggsy didn't feel that September and the time after Summer Slipping Away was really autumn, but felt more like a transition zone, an interval between, a time of adjustment to the new school year. So he decided to call it simply and descriptively, "School Year Starts": The day after Labor Day (the 1st day of school) to September 30th.

"How can 'School Year Starts' be a whole season?" Gerry protested. "It's only a day. Like we started yesterday. Yesterday was one day!"

"I understand your concern, matey. We do have to report to school on a particular day, the day after Labor Day, which was yesterday; but the feeling of school starting seems to last a few weeks, at least to the end of September. Like we're getting off to a slow start. Now that I think about it, it doesn't feel to me that we've REALLY gotten started until October. It takes us a couple of weeks to feel comfortable. Sort of like warming up before a football or basketball game. Don't you all agree?"

As usual, if anyone disagreed he didn't say anything, as they had learned it didn't make any sense to argue further after Biggsy had already made up his mind. Taking their silence as tacit agreement after about 15 seconds he simply said, "Great" and then "So here's what I've come up with for the names of the rest of the seasons following 'School Year Starts,' why I think we should name them that way, and the dates":

- Autumn: October 1st to October 29th (Biggsy said that October, with the leaves reaching their peaks of color change before dropping along with the cooling temperatures and shortening days feels the most like fall, certainly more than late September, November and early December which are technically all part of the usual calendar autumn season.)

- Season of the Dead and Dying: October 30th to the Wednesday before Thanksgiving and encompassing the 4-day holiday of Halloween—10/30 (Mischief Night), 10/31 (Halloween itself), 11/1 (All Saints' Day) and November 2nd (All Souls' Day)—when the Church celebrates the departed and the world is brown and leafless, getting darker and colder and just generally feels dying and finally dead, although Thanksgiving Day with its harvest bounty filling up cornucopias was a kind of relief for the gray and brown and chill and the first step into the season of light that followed.

- Christmas: Thanksgiving to January 2nd. Christmas break from school usually began with the half day on December 23rd and ended on January 2nd when they returned to school after Christmas break (unless adjusted slightly when the holidays fell on weekends), but Biggsy argued that the Christmas season starts as early as Thanksgiving which was not just a holiday-related eating extravaganza but the day St. Anthony students (and arguably the rest of the country, especially businesses optimistically awaiting the busiest and highest revenue-producing time of year) aimed their sights on the holiday season before the Thanksgiving turkey and other leftovers were in the refrigerator. What Biggsy called the season of Christmas would include the church season of Advent with its sense of waiting for Jesus, waiting for the light.

- Winter: January 2nd to Ash Wednesday (a frozen desert with little or nothing to look forward to until Lent and the promise of spring, and similarly not too much to say about it).

- Lent: Ash Wednesday to Holy Saturday/Easter Eve (a season of penance and waiting for the promise of thaw and spring, similar to the way Advent was a church season of waiting for light, only Lent was longer and the sense of waiting and longing more intense).

- Spring: Easter Sunday to June 13th (Feast of St. Anthony's & the last day of school, delivering the rebirth and Spring promised by Easter and being sprung from school into summer).

- School Year Stops (June 13th*) (*or 12th or 14th if 13th falls on Saturday or Sunday)
Unlike the "School Year Starts" season, which Biggsy felt actually lasted a few weeks to give them all time to fully adjust to summer being over and school having begun, he felt the stopping of the school year was something they could do instantly, as soon as school was declared done for the year, and therefore represented a 1-day season.

- Summer: June 13th to August 15th (the last "official" day of school was a day to physically be in the school building and the classroom, but not really a school day—it was actually simultaneously the last day of school and the first day of summer).

Sensing that recess would be over any second Biggsy wound it up. "There it is, mates; the new seasons. And a hearty, happy 'School Year Starts' season to all of you."

They all got up saying nothing, brushed off their pants, and headed back to the schoolyard as the first bell started ringing.

Getting organized

To double down on the way he had surprised his friends with the reunion idea in late August, Paul showed up at Buddy's the Friday after Labor Day with evidence that he had actually thought more about it over the intervening two weeks. After they somewhat grudgingly agreed to move forward, the first order of business was to name the five of them the "Reunion Committee." It seemed a tad pretentious, as if the current principal or some director of alumni relations (which role didn't exist) might have charged them with the task, but they went along with it, and in fact that's what they were or at least would be once Paul started delegating and assigning.

Next they would need to pick a date and venue and find the rest of their former classmates and contact them. Paul said he could start texting those whose cell phone numbers he already had, which was a little funny and actually a bit pathetic, because it would have been a pretty short invitee list if Paul had just reached out to the few people in his phone "Contacts" list (probably just Gerry and Nancy and Dolores and Robbie). There was the possibility of using social media to look for classmates and get the word out, except Paul didn't participate in any social media. A cell phone was as about as modern and high tech as he got; he had only switched from flip phone to smart phone six months earlier, but considered himself very connected just because he had learned how to text. So he would need some help, which was fine. The rest of them were on various social media, and despite Nancy's initial assertion that the five of them already represented all the reunion participants they would ever need, she had a number of "friends" that shared grade school memories and/or pictures from time to time. She had also been posting grade school pictures for several years and had about 15 or so former St. Anthony's classmates following her (not all from their grade, but some of them might know how to reach others or even be their siblings). So between followers and friends and family she could probably start assembling a list with contact info. Maybe the school could even help with last known addresses and such if they were willing and able to share for a school-related function.

Paul volunteered to handle the music, and also gave himself the job of creating a memory booklet, an assignment he could probably handle and even complete, especially if he approached it like writing a paper which in high school and college he could almost sit down and create in the moment as if by fiat—*Let there be essay*. Paul was certainly smart; he wouldn't have gotten into a good college and later medical school without the brains, and his disorganization was never an impediment because his memory was not just good but remarkably good, astonishingly photographically good. He consistently seemed to remember the most from what had happened those eight years (some memories even going back to first and second grade when they were only six and seven years old), usually to the shared amazement and entertainment of everyone else. So the booklet was actually a natural for him, and after writing and memorializing it on paper, it could be distributed at the reunion party. Paul thought he would call the memory booklet just that, then subtitle it grandiosely: "A collection of factoids and trivia from our eight years at St. Anthony's on the occasion of the 50th anniversary of our graduation plus five years." "Way too long" was the predictable response from everyone at Buddy's, assuming they even took it seriously; but again, after the beers and wine and Buddy-tinis and hearing Paul recite it over and over they realized it was perfect.

One of Paul's memories was of something their classmate Ronald Biggs (whom they called "Biggsy") had proposed just as the eighth grade was starting—a re-naming of the seasons according to what happened during the nine-plus months of the school year. Paul recalled that there was something like nine of what Biggsy called the "St. Anthony Seasons," and with a little effort he could probably name them all or most of them. He thought maybe he could organize the booklet the same way, maybe not exactly, but along those lines, with nine chapters to correspond to each season. On the other hand, he realized that probably not enough people knew about this even at the time so the whole thing might be kind of lost on the majority of attendees. Plus, he wanted the booklet to be his own creation, to not have anyone else's fingerprints on it (and especially not Biggsy's), chuckling to himself to realize and admit that he still felt the need to compete with Biggsy even 55 years after they had slugged it out in and out of the classroom in various academic and athletic arenas. Still, whether his erstwhile classmate attended the reunion or not, or didn't attend but heard about it or not, in light of all their prior school-time interactions Paul thought he probably didn't want to give Biggsy that satisfaction.

He thought he could complement the booklet with an interactive trivia contest, perhaps in the game show answer-question format, with category titles such as "Things that happened in Church" and "Songs we learned in Music Class," along with simple subject categories such as "Geography"

(Answer: "Leading export of Chile?" Question: "What is Guano?" Seagull poop. [Groan]), "Arithmetic," and on and on. There could even be an impromptu sing-along rabbit hole based on what was in the "Music Class" category, where Paul could once again showcase his memory since most of the lyrics to those early American folk tunes (such as "The Erie Canal Song") were still rattling around in his brain.

The more he talked about it, the more contagious his excitement and enthusiasm became for the other Committee members. This could be fun.

III

Autumn (October 1st to October 29th)

When the temperatures started to drop a little and the days were getting decidedly shorter, the CYO football team started playing its Saturday league games and maybe you'd come home from the game and smell someone burning leaves in the neighborhood (before there were any clean air concerns and township ordinances prohibiting it) and pumpkins started showing up in farmers' markets and even outside the A&P it was easy to tell we had entered another season. While it was never really easy in the absolute sense to get into schoolwork and studying and taking tests and doing homework, I can grudgingly admit it was a little easiER in October. And the lunchtime recess got a little more active when it was cooler and we didn't sweat as much (in eighth grade most of us were at least 13 so instead of our boy sweat having a kind of sweet prepubescent smell it could get a little rank by the end of day, so cooler temperatures were welcomed by all).

The day we gang-tackled Biggsy during our usual second/long recess game of Fox Chase the Geese on the football field one October afternoon, nine or ten other guys saw what I had been staring at for weeks. To this day I don't know if any of them had seen it prior to that since we never talked about it, but I probably had the most opportunities since at the beginning of the eighth grade year and for two months after that Biggsy sat right across the aisle to my left, and we occupied the last seats in Rows 1 and 2 so no one sat behind us. Biggsy acted as if he was seeing it for the first time, too, but I found that pretty hard to believe. I mean, come on, he put on the same pants every day. And even if he did it blindfolded or with his eyes closed his pinky toenail would likely have felt it or even gotten caught in it at one point or another. So it was just more of Biggsy's usual attempts to obfuscate reality if it meant elevating his status; just more of old Biggsy's blowhard bullshitting, which always annoyed me. It was so pretentious, always making him seem better or cooler or smarter than everyone else, especially me, and especially since we had been engaged in a kind of unofficial competition, probably going back as far as first grade.

It started with our physical appearance: We were both about the same height, and in eighth grade at 13 pushing 14 that was close to 5'10", but he had a leaner look, a thinner face, sandy brown hair and blue eyes, while I was overall rounder—not fat, just rounder edges to my face and shoulders--with brown hair and brown eyes and a somewhat darker complexion. It wasn't exactly like chocolate and vanilla when we stood next to each other—when we were both tan as we were near the beginning of the school year before our summer color had completely faded we were more like beige and bronze—but he liked to say that girls really liked his Scotch-Irish blue eyes. I knew that I was of Italian descent which gave me my darker eyes and darker skin and a faster richer tan but didn't talk about it much because my name didn't sound Italian, but as usual Biggsy made the blue eyes comment so convincingly and of course there was nothing I could do about that.

Then there were the report cards we got four times a year, and seeing who got First Honors, Second Honors, or no honors, corresponding to the highest and second highest grade ranges, and everything under that. We also competed for the scholastic awards that were handed out at the end of the year at a formal evening ceremony on or near the last day of school and always in the Church to combine it with a prayer service and some music by the choir at the same time the 8th grade graduates were being given their official send-off. There were two main prizes awarded in each grade—one for the highest average (obviously a very objective measure), and one for "effort" (obviously a much more subjective teacher assessment). The latter didn't necessarily correlate with native talent or ability, but was intended for someone who really seemed to try the hardest, perhaps overcoming some life hardship or just beating the odds and maybe had improved the most by sheer exertion and overcoming some natural tendency to poor performance and perhaps even sloth. The teachers cultivated our class's competition every day of the week and every week of the year, well before the end-of-year honors, rewarding successful achievement with placing familiar gold stars on tests that also had a large "100%" at the top and/ or a big red capital C (for "correct," not the grade between B and D), then hanging these prizes on the cork bulletin boards next to the cloakroom doors for all to see, every day, every season (and in all their seasonal variety such as when the lines for the spelling tests' words were incorporated into drawings of pumpkins, cornucopias, or Christmas balls that we later got to color in Friday afternoon art class after the tests had been graded), every time we hung up and retrieved our coats.

Biggsy was smart, I'll give him that; he won the award for the highest average every year, so, I mean, if anybody in our year had a chance to go to medical school, he was the one. I was always right behind him, the perennial number two man. But he also had some irritating habits, in addition to kind of talking down to people. Like the way he'd slap down his pencil forcefully enough to generate a loud high-pitched wood-on-wood sound as it struck the pencil holder groove on the top of his desk whenever he finished an exam first, which he almost always did and usually a good 10-15 minutes before everyone else. When the teacher saw him just sitting there staring into space while the rest of us scratched madly on our papers, invariably she would say something like, "Be sure to check your work." But Biggsy never even flinched, which infuriated me even more because it meant that either he had been able to review every answer before the rest of us had even gotten through the test once, or was so confident that he didn't feel the need to check anything. And in sixth grade, while I couldn't ever prove it, I felt that Biggsy had played a little loose with the intent of a book report contest with the winner the one who had turned in the most reports, which he did, but I suspected he was able to win by reading shorter books and even some soft cover booklets (the kind you might get in a museum bookstore, like the ones our dad bought us at Independence Hall along with Declaration of Independence and colonial money replicas on a weird smelling stiff brown paper) while I stuck with longer hardback books such as Hardy Boys and Chip Hilton novels.

I never won the top award, but I never got the "Effort" award either, because I never expended any effort. Doing well on tests came fairly easily to me; since I had something of a truly photographic memory I never really had to study much or sometimes at all, and it never looked as if I was expending effort because it was truly effort-LESS for me to do at least well enough to be a close #2 to Biggsy. As easy and involuntary as breathing. (This continued into high school but hurt me in college when for the first time in my life I received an ego-slamming D on a Calculus exam, and afterwards had to actually study and work hard to get good grades). If Biggsy was the first to slap down his pencil into the pencil groove at the top of the desk indicating he was finished, I was the second. By seventh grade I was so frustrated that I'd never won any awards, I actually started an intentional, active campaign for the "Effort" award by always seeming to be working extra hard. So when Biggsy was the first one to finish a test and did his pencil slamming thing and looked around to see how everyone else was doing he would have seen me still working, seeming to be struggling, screwing up my face as I looked at my paper, writing something, then shaking my head and erasing it, then writing something else, then another head shake and erasure then finally I would write something I liked and nod and smile as if saying, Yes, all that effort and perseverance and stick-to-it-ness were paying off. It didn't work though. I guess Sister Placida didn't buy it. That year I got the second highest average, again, so no top award, and no Effort award either, so as usual I bit my lip when Biggsy walked away with #1. But he didn't walk off the football field #1 the day we tackled him unless #1 meant being the first person at the bottom of a heap, so at least for once he would know how it felt to be a loser and under everybody else, while I would know what it felt like to win (and more importantly, beat Biggsy).

Memory booklet

Paul continued fleshing out ideas for the memory booklet content almost immediately after the post-Labor Day meeting at Buddy's; since he worked three 12-hour shifts a week in the Springhaven Community Hospital's ER and was single it left him a fair amount of free time. He could have probably done it all from his own memory alone, but he didn't think it would hurt (and might help) to solicit input from other classmates and also consult some original source material, especially since there were probably some fuzzy details that could use clarifying and refreshing. Case in point—the subjects and behavior categories of their report cards, which he thought would be rich fodder for the trivia quiz, hence a good place to start.

Paul's mother had saved all of his grade school report cards (high school, too). She was a bit of a pack rat, an older term that in the 21st century would be replaced with "hoarder." Paul had some of those same qualities himself, although after his divorce and moving into an apartment and not having the attic, garage, basement and closet space he'd had in the house and the necessary purging that accompanied the move he liked to say that most of the clutter was now between his ears. Fortunately getting his hands on the report cards would not be a complicated mission involving unearthing some hidden cache of artifacts: when his mother passed away and he and his brother had cleaned out their childhood home where their mom was still living when she died (his father had died in a nursing home a few years before that), he simply picked up the shoebox that housed these school relics and some old pictures from where it sat on the cellar bookshelf (luckily about three shelves up from the bottom because some books and records on the lowest shelf were damaged and in some cases ruined in a little flood down there after a heavy rain—their high-water-table town was called Springhaven for a reason) and transferred it to a closet in his apartment.

He never even opened it during or after the transfer, since he had a fairly good idea of what his mother originally put in there and would likely still be there if and when he ever wanted to look at it. And now in preparation for the reunion and putting together the memory booklet he took the box off the shelf to look for the report cards and there they were—the same old yellowish-brownish thin cardboard documents about eight inches by six inches folded with his name printed on the light brown envelope housing each one. Randomly opening the card from 5th grade he saw the behavioral traits on the left and the academic subjects and numeric grades in rows and columns on the right, with enough columns for all the grading periods of the school year. There were spaces on the back where his parents had signed and where the teacher had written a number in the box next to "assigned to grade X" with the final report card of the year, all of it in the partridge-blue cartridge ink that held up just fine after 50+ years. Paul recalled how he always looked at the "assigned to grade" box on the final report card, even though he knew he would be moving up to the next grade as would almost everyone except for the few that "flunked" and had to repeat a grade. (Mostly that happened in first grade, probably with kids that weren't ready intellectually and/or emotionally to start school at a time when kindergarten was not a given the way it eventually became and learning disabilities not recognized, because after he went to second grade, the four kids who didn't move up and had to repeat first grade were right behind his class one grade back all the rest of the way through school, although it was rumored that Charles Popewicz had failed first grade three times, accounting for some of the cruel but patently false jokes about that being the reason he was shaving by third grade and driving by seventh.)

As Paul continued examining his 5th grade report card his eye went to the behavioral traits because there were narratives there that might make good trivia quiz material. It seemed dated of course, but as he read through them again he remembered reading those same words all those years ago.

- **Cooperation**: Respects rights of others, willingly joins others in work and play, is courteous and considerate toward others.
- **Self-Control**: Usually thinks before acting; restrains hasty impulses.
- **Perseverance**: Puts forth best effort; keeps on trying in spite of failure.
- **Courage**: Attacks difficulties with confidence, is ready to acknowledge mistakes and make amends; does what is right regardless of remarks of companions.
- **Obedience**: Cheerfully obeys rules and regulations both of Church and school; is at the right place at the right time ready for work; has work completed on time.
- **Orderliness**: Keeps desk, books and other materials in good order; prepares and arranges work neatly.
- **Health Habits**: Keeps face, hands, nails and teeth clean; is clean in habits of dress; sits, stands and walks correctly.

Such simple, almost quaint concepts: respect, being courteous and considerate, thinking before acting, not being hasty or impulsive, being courageous, always doing what was right despite what friends did (something parents used all the time whenever a request was accompanied by "But everyone is doing it" to which the elders might respond, "Well if all your friends jumped off a bridge...?" etc. etc. One time Paul the wise-ass came back with, "Depends how high the bridge was"), not just obeying but doing so "cheerfully," being orderly, neat and clean. At first Paul wondered what the teeth and nails must have looked like in some of those schools to have to specify that requirement in the report card, although he also recalled that there were some very poor and very dirty (and even very smelly) kids in St. Anthony's, from the far end of Sycamore Street. Even Biggsy had some challenges in that department as one of six kids, despite being as smart as he was.

Too challenging for a trivia contest? Maybe; although it wouldn't hurt to include those descriptors or at least parts of them, just for the fun of reading them aloud. Remembering the academic subjects would be a little easier: Religion (of course); English (composition, grammar, reading); Spelling; History and Geography (using the little dark blue McLaughlin series books and somewhat larger workbooks of the same color); Civics; Arithmetic; Science; Handwriting; Art; Music; Health. There were also grades assigned for "Thoroughness in daily work," "Attention during class," and "Home Study," along with spaces on the back for attendance near the area where teachers and parents signed.

Report cards at St. Anthony's were probably distributed quarterly, although at the time the students never really figured out the pattern, other than knowing for sure they would get one after mid-term exams some time in January, and again at year's end before school let out for summer. Other than that, the exact days and times were a complete mystery and ultimately a surprise. Usually the pastor Father Ellis would just show up at school one day (it was his job to distribute them), a vague-black-garbed man-shape outside the translucent upper glass pane in the classroom door, knock lightly two or three times then without waiting for the teacher to answer he just hustled in as we all jumped up and said "Good morning, Father" in varying degrees of sing-songy unison unanimity after which he said "Be seated" and we all sat. He may have actually been no older than Paul and his reunion-planning friends 55 years after graduating from eighth grade, but Fr. Ellis looked absolutely ancient at the time with his bald crown and rim of pure white hair. The teacher (lay or nun) who was usually already standing as she taught stayed standing after we all sat, so she could let Fr. Ellis sit at her desk where she placed the stack of report cards in front of him. It always seemed so mysterious—like, where did they come from? Where had she been hiding them?

After a couple of distribution cycles good students such as Paul and Biggsy (officially Ronald Biggs, Paul's sort of best friend and definitely archrival since they competed for everything—scholastic honors, athletic prowess and achievements, and eventually women) looked forward to getting their report cards because they usually both got First Honors, corresponding to a numerical grade average of 90 or better and accompanied by a 3X5 index-card-sized certificate with gold Gothic lettering and the student's name written in flawless Palmer method penmanship with an ink pen. Second Honors (average 80-90) came with the same kind of card but lettered in silver. They were like Olympic medals, and there was no secret about who got what because Fr. Ellis announced it to the whole class as he handed each one out, often making some positive or negative comment, such as "Very good, Ronald, First Honors as usual," or more bluntly, "Very poor," to Charles Popewicz," or horribly, cruelly a head-shaking "Leonard, I don't know why you can't be more like your older brother Robert; what a good student he was when he was here and I hear he's doing even better in high school." Then, after going up to the desk where Fr. Ellis sat, receiving their report cards and walking back to their seats students typically held open the card to scan the results and the honors cards were visible to anyone sitting nearby who cared to look. Once in the higher grades Paul started keeping an unofficial mental accounting of where he and Biggsy stood in the "medal" count—always either even or Paul one back or having gotten second honors rather than first.

Paul also looked through some of the photographs in the shoebox, stopping when he got to the one of him and a few other classmate actors the time St. Anthony's staged a production of *Peter Pan*. Of course Biggsy was cast as Peter, no surprise there, feeding the flames of their perennial competition. And even worse, it was after all the noise Biggsy had made about how theater was a waste of time and for pussies and faggots, and how he would rather be living his life than acting in a pretend life. And then he waltzes in at the last minute and gets the lead. Just like that. Paul didn't even want to audition but his mother more or less forced him.

Every year the Community Arts Center in nearby Wallingford put on a children's show and when Paul was in the fifth grade St. Anthony's asked the Wallingford Drama Class Director Mrs. Gravesly if she would direct a show at their school. St. Anthony's didn't have a theater or even an auditorium so it would be performed in the church basement (where the overflow 12:15 Mass was said for all the people who had been out late Saturday night and so couldn't make any of the earlier Masses, and Paul remembered when he used to serve that Mass as an altar boy how Mr. Galloway whom everyone knew was an alky used to come to the altar rail and open his mouth to receive the host and the smell of booze could almost knock over the priest and altar boy and the communicants on either side so people used to say he had probably just come straight to Mass from wherever he had been the night before or maybe he had slept an hour or two somewhere because his clothes were always a little rumpled too) which at least had a stage and a curtain, and she agreed and they decided to do the theatrical version of Peter Pan (as in, not the musical version Paul and many of his classmates had seen on TV that starred Mary Martin, the one Paul saw when he was about five and during the song "I'm Flying" while trying to imitate Peter without the benefit of the support harness and cables they couldn't really see in black and white he took a header off the top of the couch cutting his head on the stairway spindles and taking 4 or 5 stitches at Dr. DiDonato's home office around the corner and leaving a little scar right in the middle of where he parted his hair that he always called his flying Peter scar). But since he had to try out anyway he thought he might as well hope for the part of Peter, but Biggsy got it and didn't even seem as if he cared (as usual).

Paul was cast as Toodles, one of Peter's Lost Boys, whose only distinction was that his was the arrow that brought down Wendy when she and Peter and her brothers were flying to join them. After the parts were handed out, Mrs. Gravesly may have sensed the disappointment clearly evident on Paul's face, because as he was waiting on the church steps to get picked up one afternoon after rehearsal (his mom was always late so he was always last) she apparently tried to elevate Paul by saying he was perfect to be one of the Lost Boys. When Paul shrugged and said nothing she kept going, "I assume you know that's what your name means, right? In French?" and then she pronounced it with the flair she often used when coaching them how to recite their lines and in what Paul assumed was French, "Pare-DOO! Lost!" He had no idea what she was talking about, but that night he told his parents about it and after his mother said, "Hmm, that's interesting," his father said pretty casually that actually Perdu wasn't really even their real name, that they were of Italian descent and their name had originally been Perduzzi—that they had cousins upstate with that name, but somewhere along the line Paul's grandfather had changed it, or had it changed for him.

Paul just said "Oh" and dropped it, not really being interested at that age. But a few years later the topic surfaced again when his paternal grandfather died, and at the funeral he read the names on some of the flower arrangements and met a few distant cousins (distant as in southern New Jersey and Hazleton, Pennsylvania). Driving home from South Philadelphia Paul's father felt a more expanded explanation was in order for his two sons, so he turned off the radio and explained that his father, their grandfather whom they called "Pop Pop Lou" (to distinguish him from their mother's father, Pop Pop Frank) had actually been born "Luigi" near Messina in Sicily in the late 19th century, and that "Perdu" had actually originally been "Perduzzi," although it wasn't clear whether or not that change occurred at Ellis Island if and when Luigi had said "Perduzzi" and in the common fashion that creates Italian dialects (such as when pizza became beetz and the lunch meat capicola became gabbagoal) he simply swallowed or even totally dropped the ending "zi" and said something like "per-DOOTZ" and maybe it sounded like "Perdu" to the immigration official or was the closest Anglo match in his own head.

Or maybe Lou had changed it himself (Paul's dad wasn't really sure) deliberately, volitionally attempting to assimilate as also commonly occurred back in the early 20th century when he came over as a teenager with an older teen brother—the two of them, kids really, on a huge ship alone, on the ocean all that time, finally glimpsing the Statue of Liberty in New York Harbor, having heard of her and even seen a picture once, sent to meet an older cousin who had already arrived and started a life and they too looking to start some kind of life after leaving the tiny mountain village where they barely subsistence farmed and to preserve the one pair of shoes each of them sort of owned before it would be handed down to another brother or cousin or neighbor they would actually take off their shoes before walking down the mountain (Paul's dad said that the first time he heard this he asked his father, "What about preserving your FEET?"), but of course such an assimilation attempt would have only worked on paper since anyone who ever heard Lou speak would know instantly he was foreign-born (and more like a Luigi than a Louis), and anyway he was barely literate. Paul's dad went on to say when he (Paul's dad) was growing up they only spoke Italian in the house and he (Paul's dad) didn't really learn English until he started school when the Irish used to look down on them and call them dagoes and wops, and by the time he (Paul's dad) could read and write his name had always been Perdu.

Paul had never questioned the name or his grandfather's accent, but learning he was Italian when he himself was about the age Luigi had been when he came from a different country to a land he had only heard about but never seen and whose language he couldn't speak but unlike Luigi not going anywhere except Springhaven or nearby Media or Upper Darby where the closest shoe and clothing stores were and maybe Philadelphia to visit his grandfather in the late 50s and early 60s when testosterone was starting to drip out of his glands but not yet flowing and certainly not yet the torrent it would become in eighth grade but enough to quash the nascent priesthood aspirations that had been awakened when he was studying Latin to become an altar boy in fifth grade and awakened instead little wisps of hair that sprouted under his arms and on his upper lip and when his voice seemed to be experimenting with low and high at the same time and sometimes in the same sentence and the girls in his class who suddenly didn't seem as revolting as they had only a few months before when he and his friends might have been inclined to call them "cooties" seemed very interested in young men of Italian descent from Philadelphia, some of whom made hit records and could be heard on the radio and seen in movies or on TV shows such as *Bandstand* and *Ed Sullivan* with names such as Frankie Avalon (whom Paul learned later had actually taken trumpet lessons from his father's sister's husband who had worked at the Philadelphia Armory but played a little horn during the war and continued gigging and teaching afterwards and, by the way, Frankie Avalon still owed him some money) and Bobby Rydell (originally Ridarelli) and Fabian (last name Forte but no one knew that then) who all had good-sized pompadours with maybe a little twist of hair tumbling onto the upper forehead that Paul practiced trying to make happen himself, maybe skipping the hair styling cream those days when he was thinking it was kind of cool to be a young man born in Philadelphia (which he had been, since there were no hospitals in or near Springhaven in 1950) and a dark-haired dark-eyed Italian like Frankie and Bobby and Fabian so maybe, just maybe, if this little thing he was starting to feel about girls ever developed into anything more, as an Italian he was probably well-positioned, and certainly better positioned than Biggsy who bragged all the time that he was Scotch-English-Irish and had relatives in America as far back as the Revolution.

Even better was that Paul had always known his mother was Italian—her maiden name was Cavallo and when he was in eighth grade both of his maternal grandparents were still alive and living in South Philly—which meant that he was not just Italian but 100% Italian. Paul filed this away, not realizing at the time that when he got to eighth grade it would give him something—an important something, whether or not he ever decided to try to leverage it—in common with Mary Elizabeth Albarelli.

Biggsy's Hole

St. Anthony's was co-ed, but when Paul and his classmates returned to school that September in 1963 they learned that the nuns had separated their two eighth-grade classes into one each of all-boys and all-girls. Neither the principal nor any of the other teachers ever said why, at least not on the record, but a number of the boys and girls (including Paul) that Biggsy collectively referred to as "the clique" all assumed it had to do with reports that filtered back to the convent about some wild goings-on the second semester of seventh grade at Mary Elizabeth Albarelli's birthday party. Paul had been there, and some prior and newly-established boyfriend-girlfriend couples had indeed paired off and were making out as usually happened at parties, plenty wild for nuns that while not literally cloistered were at least somewhat sheltered. At that particular party it took those duos a little longer to get around to it because everyone knew how strict Mary Liz's parents were, and they were afraid her folks might come down and check on them at any minute.

Paul and Nancy and some others were surprised they even let Mary Liz have a boy-girl party; that apparent softening and the fact that the coast stayed clear for a good half hour after Mr. and Mrs. Albarelli laid out the food and beverages—cold cut sandwiches (roast beef, bologna and American cheese, and ham and American cheese, and since they were of

Italian descent also capicola and provolone cheese [the roast beef, bologna and ham all intentional nods to their American assimilation] all of them on round Kaiser-type poppy-seeded rolls), plus some potato chips and pretzels and soda pop in big glass bottles with paper cups and an ice bucket—may have led to some distraction and complacency, because nobody was even guarding the staircase. That allowed Mrs. A. to tiptoe right into the basement unannounced, and hit the light switch at the bottom of the stairs just as things were getting kind of steamy. Paul, romantically unattached at that particular time and uncoupled at that particular moment witnessed all the scrambling and confusion with Mrs. A. screaming, "Get out! Everybody, out of my house! Now!" as they partygoers clambered up the stairs, with maybe a boy hastily and clumsily tucking a shirt into pants where a girl's hand might have recently been, and maybe a girl fumbling to rearrange a blouse where a boy's hand might have recently been on top of or even inside it and outside into the light whichever way they could—kitchen or front door, and for those who knew the way, via the side door of the house's addition. Those who lived close enough to walk home started walking fast and even running, but a lot of the kids lived too far to walk (or run) and would need rides, except their parents or older siblings weren't expecting to pick them up for another couple of hours. Mrs. Albarelli was too distraught to do anything as controlled and sober as calling those kids' parents, so Mr. A told each of them to call his or her own home and say the party had ended a little early and no other details. Most of the kids were gone after 30 minutes or so, but those who couldn't reach anyone at home or didn't try sat outside on the curb waiting—not right in front of the Albarelli's, but a couple of houses down.

After Mass the next day Mrs. A. went to the convent to talk to the principal, Sister Bernadette Margaret (whom many in the class called "Bernie"), and either Mrs. A. embellished the account herself or Bernie's inexperienced, fertile mind imagined and invented something way beyond what a bunch of 13-year-olds were capable of with respect to sins of the flesh, even with their pubescent glandular surges, because the next year the classes were split up. Bernie also decided to teach half the classes herself, going back and forth between boys' and girls' rooms high-school-style while the kids stayed put (perhaps to avoid mixing in the hallway) to personally see to it that they all behaved.

Biggsy wasn't at the party, although not only didn't he seem bothered by that he actually used it to articulate his opinion and occupy some kind of intellectual or maturity high ground. The day before at recess he told Paul, "Of course I was invited but I'm not going. I'm not going to fool around with girls till after I'm out of medical school."

That was typical of the kind of inflated thing Biggsy would often say, making it seem as if it were his choice, that he had declined the offer, bullshitting his way around the embarrassment that he hadn't been invited (and Paul knew he hadn't because Nancy Kendrick had told him). He could have worked his way onto the list; some of the girls thought he was cute with his blue eyes and sandy brown hair, even with that small cowlick clump sticking up at the back of his head. He was tall, too, a real advantage when the boys played pee-wee touch football at recess, since with Paul just as tall as quarterback he could just throw the ball high into the end zone where a crush of defenders stood around Biggsy and watch that long arm emerge from the pack and snag the little pimply pigskin. Paul and Gerry and Robbie had also passed along to him a few "So and so likes you" as written or verbal correspondence the prior couple of years, usually from

Nancy who was kind of like the default messenger from the girls' cohort of the clique, but Biggsy never paid any attention to any of it. If he got notes from girls, he tore them up, and usually in front of whoever delivered them, usually saying he had more important things to occupy his attention.

So if the scholastic competition wasn't irritating enough, Biggsy's too-cool attitude about girls and every other pursuit he deemed unworthy of his attention really aggravated and frustrated Paul. But unfortunately, the more Paul wanted to avoid the source of his frustration, the more it seemed he and Biggsy were thrown together, forced into a false closeness. Even before eighth grade when they sat across from each other the first couple of months, Father Galvin, the assistant pastor who supervised the altar boys, used to regularly pair them up to serve the 9 o'clock Sunday Children's Mass, do weddings, funerals, High Masses, Stations of the Cross, Benediction services, etc. Galvin said they were very professional and about the same height which just looked better on the altar and they were better at the Latin than most of the other kids (this was the early 60's, before the Vatican II Council brought on the change to English), and they didn't mind getting out of school to do Friday Stations of the Cross during Lent or the weekday funerals any time of year (in addition to earning a couple of dollars for those), and Saturday weddings usually meant five bucks each.

They liked Fr. Galvin for the most part, since after hanging around with nuns and female lay teachers all those years it was refreshing to have a little male influence, and he was a lot younger than their seemingly-ancient pastor, Father Ellis, so it seemed he was a little cooler or at least a little more modern than Ellis, maybe even hip. And he would sometimes address them as "Gentlemen" or "Mister" as in "Mr. Biggs" for Biggsy, which felt kind of cool (although it got pretty old in high school when they had priests doing this all the time). Father Galvin was tall and thin, around 6'3" or 6'4" or more (and he sometimes referenced playing a lot of basketball at the seminary which enhanced the youthful vibe he seemed to give off), and although ostensibly clean shaven he had the kind of five o'clock shadow that usually made its appearance around noon and thereafter looked the way the boys' faces did as older Halloweeners when they rubbed their cheeks and chins with stubble-simulating burnt cork and went out as hobos. Father Galvin also had close-set eyes, almost making him look even a little cross-eyed, so much so that when their class got to high school Biology and studied the freshwater Planaria that had what looked like crossed cartoon eyes making them seem either a little drunk or a little confused or both, the first time their class saw pictures of this teeny flatworm in Bio lab Biggsy laughed out loud while picking up his textbook and pointing to the photomicrograph saying, "Look; it's Galvin."

Paul didn't mind getting frequent altar boy assignments, since he enjoyed the performance aspects—being up on the altar was kind of like being on stage, wearing the cassock and surplice costume, handling special tools such as the paten, the cruets, the censor, and the candle lighter (for which it was pretty important to adjust the wick so just the right amount of flame emerged from the tip—a real art) along with all the bowing, genuflecting, kneeling, and other scripted prancing around in front of a pretty captive audience of their peers. Paul also had a flare for the Latin pronunciation (which he sometimes attributed to his Italian roots once he had found out about those), while his usual partner said he didn't care about any of that, but was more interested in actually understanding what they were saying and in some cases making the links between Latin roots and modern English words well before anyone else had any idea about the etymologies they would learn in high school.

When Biggsy articulated his long-term dating plan that Friday before Mary Liz's seventh grade party, he also added a little gratuitous sarcastic slam.

"You can waste your time in the clique if you want, but I'd rather be an individual." Whenever he used "the clique" to describe the group of boys and girls that hung out together, it made him sound really old to Paul; like he was the grownup, chastising his much younger charge.

"We're all just friends" Paul had told him that time and a number of times before; "we have fun; we listen to music; we walk around; what's the big deal?"

"You're setting your sights too low," Biggsy retorted, and that was the exact phrase he used, again making him sound like a parent or teacher. Paul assumed he probably stole the expression from something he'd heard his own parents say or something he'd read, which he was always doing.

Still, Paul couldn't stay mad at him consistently, because he was also very funny, maybe even certifiably nuts. One day in early November when they were in seventh grade Biggsy was standing by himself on the football field during recess, looking down at the ground and yelling, "Oooh! Gross!" over and over. Paul and a few of the other boys ran over, thinking it might be a smashed turtle or a dead mouse or something cool, but when they got there and saw what he was looking at Denny Higgins said, "It's just dog shit." Now that Biggsy had assembled an audience he took over.

"Maybe," he said, "but let's make sure." He bent over and picked up a piece.

"Biggsy! What are you *DO-ing*?" Paul yelled.

"Feels like dog shit," he said, then held it under his nose and screwed up his face, saying, "Whew, it sure smells like dog shit." Then before anyone could even say anything else he plopped it in his mouth and said, "Yep, tastes like dog shit, too."

Paul started to say, "Biggsy, Christ!" but Biggsy kept rolling so Paul couldn't step on his next line.

"Guess it is dog shit; sure glad I didn't step in it." He got off with only a few solid punches to the shoulder for jerking their chains that way; turns out he had hit the mother-lode of fudge candy bars on Halloween a few days earlier, so he got the idea to take some of them to school, roll and shape them to look like little turds, and put together that little one-man show.

A variation on this theme occurred one day in eighth grade while they were eating at their desks (their lunchroom on the ground floor of the school building had long ago been converted to classroom space for all the young boomers getting cranked out of those good Catholic circa-World War II marriages). Paul had a store-bought single-serving lemon pie for dessert, and Biggsy asked for a piece (as he often did) and Paul obliged (as he usually did, since he and everyone else knew the Biggs family couldn't afford such luxuries on a regular basis), but this time Biggsy only ate a little, then dug out some of the gooey lemon filling, hid it in his hand, went over behind Theresa Moore (who was kind of skittish anyway) when Bernie was out of the room, and pretended to sneeze a huge, long, stuttering Aah, Aah, Aaaaah, CHOO! kind of sneeze, convulsing forward as he did and simultaneously throwing the mucus-simulating lemon glop onto Theresa's desk, right onto the waxed paper next to her tuna fish sandwich (it was a meatless Friday, naturally). She jumped and almost screamed, but was too quickly distracted by Biggsy once again scooping up the mess and putting it into his mouth which caused her to clamp her hand over her own mouth and almost drove her to the girls' lavatory.

Some of the stupidest and silliest things Biggsy did were also some of the funniest, since they happened during class and the laughter had to be contained. Like Paul, he was a very quick study so he didn't really have to listen to whatever the teacher was saying, instead amusing himself with little games, and often pulling in Paul's gaze from his nearby desk. For instance he'd use the tip of a sharpened pencil to cut out pictures of people's heads from their readers or spellers and then place them on top of other pictures of people in the same books. He wouldn't even have to say anything: Paul could feel him staring from across the aisle, until eventually Paul would turn to see some grotesquely large man's head on top of a much smaller young girl's body, or something similar. Once a small guffaw popped out of Paul and, not willing to reveal the source of his mirth, it cost him some time staying after school. Biggsy also liked to draw sneakers on the illustrations of people in their textbooks; if there were no legs, he'd add those, too. As many in the class said, he was smart, but crazy.

And smart meant in every subject, but he was particularly good at Arithmetic; and not only good, but fast. Everyday the class did a math exercise from the back of their textbooks called *Drill and Mental.* It was a series of short calculations that each student was required to perform mentally (no pencil and paper), then bark out the answer, starting with the first person in the first row and progressing down one row and up the next in snake-like fashion until everyone had had a turn. That was the *mental*; the *drill* part involved shouting the response as quickly as possible, and often this was instantaneous such that a listener walking by the room would simply hear something like "six, 15, 32, one-third" etc. in rapid succession. If one person was having trouble or taking too long (and a second or two was considered too long) the student on deck was permitted to yell "Too slow!" and blurt out the correct answer. Everyone assumed the nuns thought this would inspire the slower students to bone up and get faster; unfortunately, the slow stayed slow and the fast just got faster.

Paul was very good at *Drill and Mental,* one of the best in the class, but of course, Biggsy was better; and because he was right behind Paul in the line (the last person in the second row succeeded the last person in the first) he frequently got the chance to "Too slow!" Paul. Compound fractions were Paul's undoing. If he saw something like three-sevenths over four ninths his eyes would glaze momentarily. He knew to flip the fraction in the denominator, remove the dividing line and multiply, but all of that took time, and he just couldn't process it quickly enough to get the answer before Biggsy, who seemed to be able to just see the solution all at once without having to visually go through all of the calculation steps. He never gave Paul enough time, but let his answer fly as soon as he had it. It was as if he sensed Paul's momentary weakness and confusion and pounced on it.

Even when Paul tried to count ahead to see which problem he would get so he could start working on it in advance, it wasn't consistently effective— either Paul was still Too Slow or someone ahead of him would screw up and throw off the count.

*　　　*　　　*

Paul didn't remember when he first noticed the hole, almost as if it had always been there. It was on Biggsy's right pants leg, just below the knee, so it was pretty easy for Paul to see from his vantage point across the aisle, and about the size of a quarter, but irregular, kind of ragged. The pants looked as if they belonged to a suit since they were kind of shiny; knowing how many older brothers Biggsy had it was a good bet that the pants had been handed down a couple of times. Paul saw the hole every day because Biggsy wore the same pants every day, and after a while it became kind of a routine, something Paul had to check off his list as having done it before he could get on with the rest of his day. If Paul got to school in time to talk to Biggsy in the recess yard before the first bell, he would look down quickly to make sure the hole was still there. If he missed that opportunity, he would steal a glance after morning prayers as the class was settling into its seats and say to himself, "Yep; there it is." Paul even looked for it when they served as altar boys together, in the sacristy before or after the service when they changed into and out of their cassocks and surplices.

After Paul had convinced himself it was the only pair of "good" pants Biggsy had, meaning for school or dress up, he felt bad. He knew the same thing could never happen to him, since if he'd had a hole in his pants his mother would have either fixed it or gotten him a new pair; as the son of a local businessman, they had the means but also wanted to showcase their economic security to some degree. Paul and many of his classmates all knew the Biggs family was poor, partly because they had so many children and felt strongly about paying for all of them to attend Catholic school. Biggsy's father did something at the big Westinghouse plant in nearby Lester they always passed on the way to visit family in South Philadelphia. Once while driving past Westinghouse Paul heard his parents discussing what Mr. Biggs did for work, and Paul's dad saying something to the effect it was a good job, in management, but it was just all those children. Some kids said there was a Biggs child in every class, an obvious exaggeration because Biggsy was in the eighth grade and had three older brothers and an older sister, and there were eight of them altogether, so there were only a couple in the lower grades, although it did seem like a lot of them whenever the whole family was at Mass, spreading out over a whole pew. Paul's mother used to say, "My heart goes out to that Biggs family; when I see them at church, all looking so shabby, I just want to cry. It's such a sin."

That eighth grade year she talked about taking up a collection for them at Christmas in her bridge club, but Paul's father said, "Don't bother; they won't take it. Remember what I told you about what happened at football practice in September?" Paul's dad was the assistant coach of St. Anthony's team, which was part of a CYO league that included some of the other area parishes. Biggsy had come to the tryouts and made the team, but something happened at the first practice. He had come with his father who went over to talk to Paul's father while Biggsy walked up to where Paul was standing with Gerry Giordano and tossing a football up in front of him and catching it again. They were supposed to get their uniforms that night, but Paul noticed Biggsy had no shoulder pads, so he asked him about that.

"I didn't bring them," Biggsy said; "I heard we were just learning plays and doing passing drills tonight, but no blocking or tackling." It was a ridiculous thing to say to Paul, since if anybody knew what was going to be happening at that practice it was the assistant coach's son, and Paul had his shoulder pads and was ready for some serious physical contact, possibly even directed at young Mr. Biggs. But before Paul could challenge him with "Where did you hear that?" Biggsy grabbed the ball from Paul and said, "Go long" as he backed up to throw a pass, like a quarterback stepping into the slot. Paul started running, since it's the only appropriate response to that combination of words and movements, and Biggsy hit him with a perfect spiraling high-arced bomb. Paul was the team's likely quarterback, but at that moment Biggsy threw the ball better and more accurately than Paul typically did. Biggsy had effectively distracted Paul and changed the subject, then Mr. Biggs called him and they left. Paul never knew exactly what happened until his father filled in some of the missing details when his mom had mentioned the possible holiday charity.

"John Biggs came up to me," Paul's dad said, "and asked if there were any extra shoulder pads Ronnie could use." Ronnie? His dad called him Ronnie? It sounded so weird to hear him called anything but Biggsy. They had gotten used to Bernie calling him "Ronald" and the occasional "Mr. Biggs" from Fr. Galvin, but hearing "Ronnie" made it sound as if Paul's father were talking about a different person.

"I told him the school provided the jerseys, pants, helmets, and footballs," Paul's father went on, "and each student was responsible for his own pads and spikes, but said I'd ask around, and see if anybody had anything they could lend or even let them have. He said 'Thanks, that's OK, never mind' or something like that then left with his boy. A shame, too. I saw Ronnie run at tryouts, and he's pretty fast; he would have made a good running back. But you see what I mean? They would be embarrassed if you tried to give them anything at Christmas."

Paul's mom just shook her head and repeated, "Such a sin."

Paul felt bad for Biggsy, but it didn't last long because, as usual, he started bullshitting his way out of the football thing. After he missed the second practice Paul went up to him at school and asked if he planned to come to the next one, or ever. "Nah," Biggsy said; "my dad and I discussed it, and after looking at the schedule of practices and games we decided I wouldn't have the time. I have to start working on my science fair project, because the medical schools will be looking at what I did and the grade I got so it has to be a good one."

Paul said to himself, "Bullshit, bullshit, bullshit! Discussed it with his dad! Like two grown men—just John and Ronald. Bullshit!" Of course Paul had no idea what medical schools looked at and how far back in someone's schooling they looked so Biggsy may have gotten that from his older brothers, but the science fair projects weren't due until January or February, so there would be plenty of time to play football into early November and get the project together later, especially for someone as smart as Biggsy was.

So their little competition continued, and even spilled out of the classroom and into the recess yard. At the end of seventh grade year when the eighth graders at the time relinquished their seniority rites to the football field, about twelve to fifteen or so of the boys in Paul's class had started to play a game called "Fox Chase the Geese." It was an amalgam of three other games they played at school and in their home parks and fields: traditional Tag; football; and the baseball-flavored Run the Bases. One kid started out being "It" usually by some sort of eeny meeny miny moe random process—he was the Fox—and everyone else represented the Geese. At the start of the game the Fox would stand at about the 20 or 30-yard line while all the Geese were behind one of the goal lines (each end zone represented a "base" where the Fox couldn't get them). Then the Geese would start to run for the safety of the other end zone, and it was the Fox's job to simply tag one of them before he got there. Then the Geese would run in the other direction for the original end zone, again trying to elude the Fox. Unlike traditional Tag, though, the one tagged didn't become the new It, the new solitary Fox, but joined the original Fox and the two of them pursued the rest of the Geese as they ran back and forth between the end zone bases until all the Geese were captured and turned into foxes, except that every goose after the first one had to be tackled instead of just tagged.

Paul's class had started playing it regularly at the end of seventh grade, and picked right up again that September of eighth. As it turned out, Biggsy wasn't only quick in Arithmetic, he could also run faster than any of the other boys as Paul's father had observed, and he showed off this prowess whenever they played that recess game. Invariably Biggsy was the last of the Geese to be captured, and not just because he could outrun them, but also weave, cut, change directions, head-fake, and basically get the Foxes so confused and bumping into each other that he had no problem scampering the rest of the hundred yards into the safety of the end zone. Michael Reynolds was usually the second to last to go down; and while he wanted everyone to think he was just about as fast and had as many evasive moves as Biggsy, the truth is that he went home for lunch and got to the recess yard about five minutes before the bell so he joined Biggsy in one of the end zones with the game in progress and almost over with very few Geese left uncaptured.

For the week or two before that October day, it seemed the Fox pack hadn't caught Biggsy once, meaning the recess-ending bell would ring before they had tackled him. Paul couldn't remember if they had ever even laid a hand on him during all that time. When Biggsy was the last goose in the end zone he had the annoying habit of waiting a long time before he would run again. He'd look at the assembled gang waiting for him to make his move, then start wagging and wiggling his index finger as if counting them and making them think he was plotting out an ideal safe passage. Paul thought he was bullshitting again, assuming he couldn't really figure out what might happen over the course of 100 yards, so he was probably just trying to slow things down so he could remain uncaptured when the bell rang. This may have actually been part of his downfall that day, because the frustration of the Foxes had been building.

Usually they'd scream, "Come on, Biggsy," or "Come on, you asshole, the bell's gonna ring," or something like that, as they were doing over and over again that day.

It didn't affect him, though; he just kept that finger going, first to the right, then left. Paul was really boiling, anxious that the bell would ring any second and he really wanted Biggsy to run more than he usually did. Out of nowhere and with no thought preceding it Paul heard himself bellow above the crowd, "Run, you pussy!" Maybe that insult hit a nerve, because right after that Biggsy took off, and Paul smiled knowing that, this time, they were going to bring him down.

Biggsy ran fast as usual, weaving and bobbing, and went the first twenty or thirty yards untouched. After that, though, the rest of the boys started to track him, with Paul in the lead. Like a swarm of animated bees they used to see in cartoons (the kind that would fly out of the hive en masse and roll itself into a boxing glove so it could punch someone) the pack moved as one, stopping when Biggsy stopped, and changing direction when Biggsy changed direction. They were on him, one angry skulk of foxes fixing on its prey. When they finally closed in on him around midfield, Gerry Giordano, a linebacker on the CYO team, ran up in front of Paul and dove low for Biggsy's ankles. Biggsy kept churning like the running back he could have been, and a couple of times was almost able to break out of Gerry's lock, so it wasn't until Paul came in high that Biggsy started to topple. Most everyone else fell in after that, and even though Biggsy wrestled and squirmed all the way to the ground, in another few seconds he was down and about ten guys were on top of him. It was over. There was no escape. They had him.

It was close, and hot, and smelled of the mix of sweet October grass and that peculiar male adolescent peri-puberty sweat. A few punches got thrown in the melee, then Biggsy started shouting from the bottom of the heap. "Get off! Get off, you assholes!" Nobody moved at first, but they felt him wriggling below them. "Get off, you fucking bastards!" Then one by one the boys started peeling away, either of their own volition or from the force of Biggsy's yelling and pushing and squirming. Paul was the last one on and Biggsy gave him a huge shove with his feet that propelled Paul back and off balance until he, too, was on his back. Paul and Biggsy both sat up simultaneously, Paul looking at him and he looking down at his pants leg and screaming, "*Look what you did, you assholes; you ripped my pants!*" Paul immediately felt the words forming and bubbling up inside him, the words that would finally reveal what he knew about him. "*You're* the asshole. That hole's been in your pants for *two months!*" But the bell rang first, and Paul said nothing. The recess yard din stopped cold as usual,

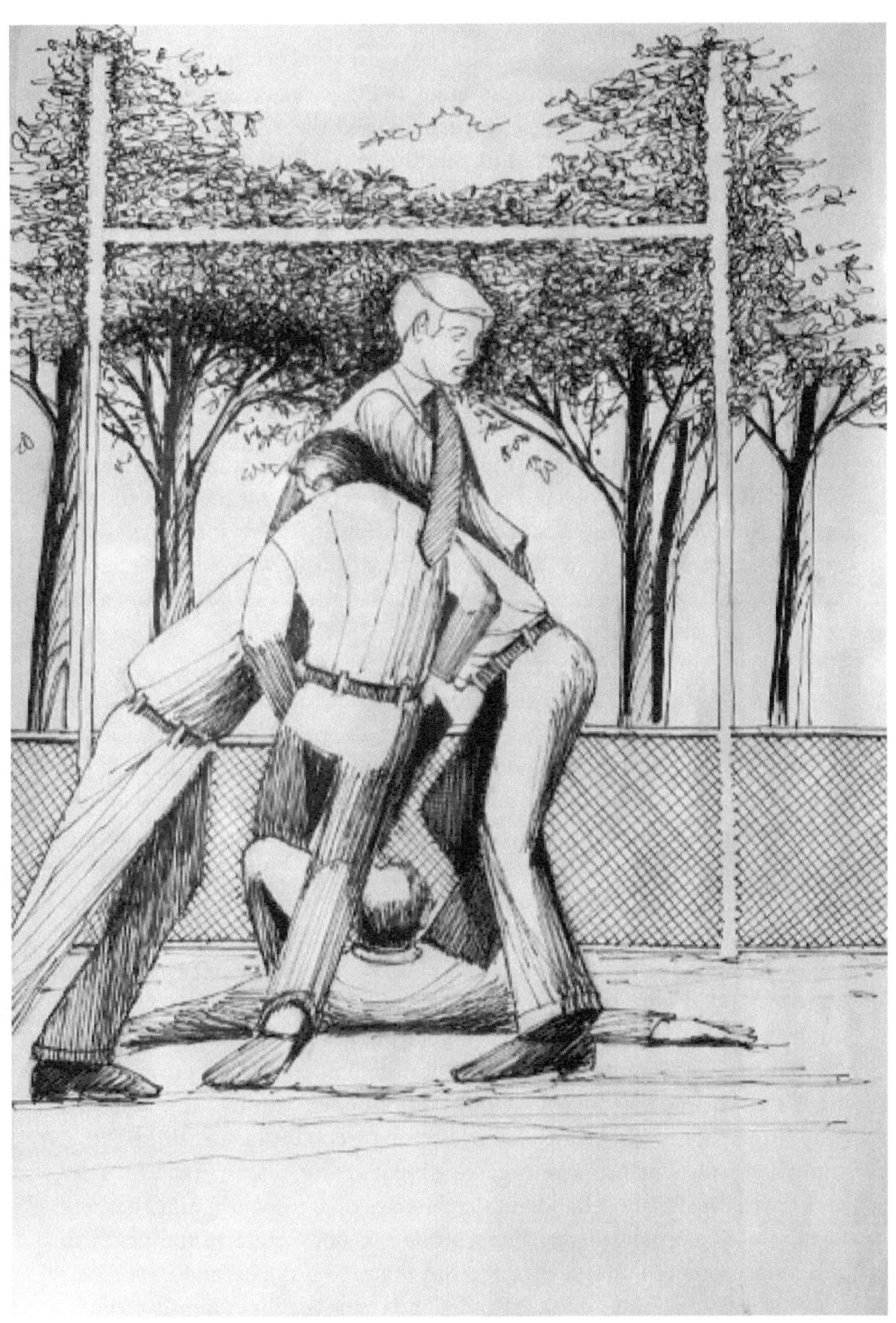

"It was over. There was no escape. They had him."

so it was easy to hear Biggsy's "You bastards; you fucking bastards" first as a yell, then incrementally more quiet as Biggsy stayed on the field and everyone else walked off and eventually joined their class in line. By the third bell when it was time to start walking into school, Biggsy silent now, had joined them. Back in class they stood to say their usual Grace after Meals, then blessed themselves and started to sit down. As they lowered into their seats Paul looked down and to his left for the hole; there it was, but with grass stains and dirt around it. It might have even been bigger. Maybe they did rip it a little.

*   *   *

St. Anthony's parish was in the middle of its annual Forty Hours Celebration, when the Blessed Sacrament is exposed on the altar off and on for three days for individual quiet adoration and a few formal services. Altar boys were the official "watchers" during the quiet times—assigned to kneel for an hour in silence, on kneelers up close to but not on the altar, in the center aisle of the church. Biggsy and Paul were scheduled for that night's last shift, 8:00-9:00, but Biggsy got there before Paul did and was already suited up and on his kneeler when Paul came out to relieve Denny Higgins. As in class, Biggsy was to Paul's left, so instinctively he looked over and down, but he couldn't tell what Biggsy was wearing because the cassock went all the way to the backs of his shoes. There were a few people in the church, but they thinned out as the hour dragged on, until it was just Biggsy and Paul.

Kneeling there in the silence and even getting a little drowsy Paul thought about their recess game that day; images of Biggsy's face just before he went down seemed huge and monstrous as Paul got sleepier and almost nodded off, and the noise of their shouting was distant, garbled, and rough. Paul thought of Biggsy's little picture people with small squat legs and sneakers and funny heads. He remembered his mother saying what a sin it was that Biggsy's family was so poor, and realized he didn't really understand that. Sin was something people did—stealing, lying, murdering, disobeying, coveting, cheating, cursing, making out at parties and trying to slip their hands under blouses or into pants; stuff that was against the commandments; that you had to enumerate to the priest in the confessional; that Jesus died for. Sin required a sinner, and Paul didn't know who had committed the sin that had made the Biggs family so poor.

Paul stared up at the huge crucifix above the altar with the larger-than-life corpus and noticed, as he did every time he looked at it, the sad look on Jesus' face; the shape and smoothness of the biceps muscles in his outstretched arms; the ribs sticking out; the small splashes of red paint near the nails in Jesus' hands and feet and at the hole in his side where the Roman soldier had lanced him. Paul thought about a conversation he and Biggsy had had the year before after they had served Stations of the Cross and were in the sacristy getting changed.

"Do you know what 'ignominious' means?" Biggsy had asked.

"What?" Paul responded.

"'Ignominious,'" Biggsy repeated; "the word in the Stations ceremony when the priest says that Christ died an 'ignominious death on the cross.' Do you have any idea what that means?"

"Not a clue," Paul fired back, putting on his jacket.

"You mean to tell me that you've been coming here for seven years, every Lent and must have heard that word fifty times and never bothered to look it up or even wonder what it meant?"

Yes, he had; and no, he hadn't.

"That's the difference between me and you," Biggsy said, sounding like the grownup again. "No natural curiosity." Paul had started to say, "Who gives a shit?" but Biggsy continued. "'Ignominious' has to do with names. I looked it up; it comes from the word 'ignominy' that sounds like another word you say whenever you make the sign of the cross in Latin. Do you know what that is? Forget it, I'll tell you. It's 'nomine' from 'In nomine Patris.' 'In the name of the Father.' 'Nomine' is part of 'ignominious.'"

Biggsy was losing Paul, who just wanted to get home, but Biggsy kept going.

"It has to do with names, and actually means not having a name, or not having a good name. Know what I mean?"

"Biggsy, why are you telling me this?" Paul had asked impatiently. "You're not my friggin' teacher."

"I don't know," Biggsy responded; "I just think it's a cool word. I mean, we call people 'assholes' and 'shit-heads' and all that, but 'ignominious,' that just seems so much worse. It's like there's so much shame and disgrace that the person isn't even good enough to be called an asshole; they've sunk to the level of not even deserving to have any name, not even a bad one."

Kneeling there Paul thought about his own last name, the one Pop Pop Luigi changed or had changed for him by an Ellis Island worker when he entered the country, and whether or not the name change meant he and his family were ignominious, and whether or not that meant Paul was lost as Mrs. Gravesly at Wallingford Arts Center had said when she learned his last name was Perdu. Or maybe Biggsy was the one who was ignominious, without a real name, since almost no one called him Ronald, and whether HE was the lost one, lost in the sin of poverty, fallen through that hole in his pants.

Mostly Paul still wondered what Biggsy was wearing under that cassock, and whether or not he had changed his clothes after school and before coming to church. He wondered what Biggsy would wear the next day at school. Now so many kids knew about what had happened and what some of the boys on the field had seen, and those who hadn't seen would hear, so Biggsy couldn't just come back to school the same way. Would the pants be patched and cleaned? Would there have been enough time to get that done or would he need to be absent that day? Would he be wearing another hand-me-down from an older brother, a pair that didn't fit him all too well, maybe the waist bunching up where he had tightened his belt so much the long end of it couldn't be contained in the loops so it flapped around, maybe the cuffs extending well beyond the edge of his shoe heels, or even possibly a new pair? For 7+ years Paul and Biggsy had been classmates, adversaries, competitors in the classroom and on the playground, so would the hole in the pants incident drive them even further apart, or maybe turn them into something they had never been—friends—maybe because Biggsy realized Paul must have seen the hole before and therefore could have said something about the pants but held his tongue instead?

Fr. Galvin came out onto the altar and genuflected in front of the Blessed Sacrament. Using the ends of his wide stole he was wearing around his neck and over his shoulders he removed the Host from inside the Monstrance, put it back inside the Tabernacle, genuflected again, closed the door, turned the key, and walked down the center aisle to where the two altar boys were kneeling, Biggsy staring straight ahead his gaze fixed on the altar and not even looking at Fr. Galvin and Paul practically asleep.

"Time to go, gentlemen; I think your dads are outside. Thanks for watching."

Biggsy got up right away and walked briskly to the sacristy; Paul roused himself and followed. Without saying a word or looking at each other they took off their cassocks and surplices, hung them on the rack, put on their jackets, and walked out into the cool October night to their fathers' waiting, warming cars.

IV

Season of the Dead and Dying
(October 30th to Wednesday before Thanksgiving)

Biggsy named this season thinking of the ghosts and goblins of Halloween at the end of October and the Church feasts honoring departed saints and souls at the beginning of November, but anyone living in the Northern Hemisphere with open eyes can see the multiple shades of gray and brown everywhere outside during November, and anyone who allows distractions to fall away even just a little bit can't help hearing and feeling the first really chilly pre-winter winds that blow down the last of the yellow or red or orange or brown curling leaves as stiff stems let go of branch attachments. But when the season started in 1963 we didn't know how much other death and dying and letting go we would soon be experiencing—first in the school's boiler room, and later in Dallas—but we found out soon enough.

A Mess Beyond the Power of Red Dirt

Paul wanted at least a little blurb in the memory booklet about Hiram, the janitor at St. Anthony's for as long as anyone could remember until he died on Monday, November 4, 1963. Actually he had started while Paul's class was in the third grade but he and his classmates had only vague recollections of the person in the job before that; to them, the word "janitor" was synonymous with "Hiram" for most of their time at St. Anthony's.

The seeming mystery about his death was an extension of the larger and more general mystery about his life. Paul recalled several distinct stories: that he had originally moved to the Philadelphia area from the South—for some reason North Carolina stuck in his head; that his mother had brought him north to accompany her when she joined Father Divine's International Peace Mission which was headquartered in the City of Brotherly Love, at which point her name was changed to Angel Love and she started doing domestic work (that last part was known to be true, since some years later "Miss Love" worked as a maid in Gerry Giordano's house—one of the few students at St. Anthony's whose parents had enough money to afford one—and occasionally she worked late enough to run into Gerry when he came home from school and would sometimes ask him, "How's my son doin'?" without ever mentioning Hiram by name); that at some point he ran away, ended up in Boys' Town, and their pastor Father Ellis knew one of the priests there and said Hiram could have a job at St. Anthony's as school and church janitor. Hiram was obviously African American, with a wide nose and short tightly-curled hair, but very light skinned with blue eyes. If he had a last name, neither Paul nor any of his classmates knew it—he was just "Hiram"—inscrutable but at the same time somewhat transparent since they saw him every day of the school year all over the school and church properties and he actually lived in the boiler room on the school's ground floor across from the boys' lavatory (Biggsy had seen his bed in there once or twice when he had been able to look in or even go in), but most of the time, once that door was closed no one knew what went on behind it.

The day Hiram died began inauspiciously, with Paul getting annoyed at Biggsy, a weekly and often daily occurrence, but this time because during one of the recurrent seat/desk shuffles the nuns and teachers liked to do from time to time (sometimes to break up a disruptive tandem) Bernie had recently moved Biggsy from the last desk in the second row across from Paul where they'd been since September up to the first seat in the first row (the row and seat closest to the classroom door). With that move (seen by some or at least by Paul as an elevation in status) Biggsy was granted and enjoyed and made the most of the privilege of being the official door opener whenever a visitor knocked and wanted to enter, again when that visitor or the teacher or a student had to exit, and even occasionally being assigned errands that took him away from classroom drudgery temporarily. Paul and Gerry and some of the other boys resented the fact that Bernie gave him that seat and privilege and, by extension, resented Biggsy, probably assuming he had sucked up to Bernie in some way, even though he cut her up behind her back as many of them did. Usually the person in that seat was someone smart enough to be able to miss a little classroom time doing errands and such and therefore Biggsy often eventually was placed in that position and role once he had earned enough good grades in the school year to predict he would once again walk away with the end-of-year award for highest average, although Paul had occasionally occupied that door-opener seat briefly in sixth and again in seventh grade, both times surrendering it to Biggsy who held it for months (in seventh grade from January till the end of the year).

Paul's irritation and even resentment grew when Biggsy would prolong the time in the hallway standing post by the door, waiting to close it when the visitor left, as if a professional doorman, or when the errand that should have taken 3-5 minutes (drop off something for the nurse, take a file to the principal's office or a letter across the parking lot to the convent, or go to the boiler room to get the janitor Hiram for some housekeeping chore—anything to get out of the classroom for however long) would end up taking 10 minutes and sometimes even longer. The boiler room trip was usually to ask Hiram to bring up what the nuns and eventually all the lay teachers and students called "red dirt"—the aromatic sawdust (was it possibly cedar?) to spread over some mess, usually where one of the students had vomited, which happened once in a while, anyway, but at least once a week for Mary O'Dougherty who must have had a very weak stomach to begin with, but was really challenged on Fridays when the pre-Vatican day of meat abstinence tuna sandwiches were sitting around at room temperature or even hotter in the cloak room all morning.

St. Anthony's never had a cafeteria, but they originally had a large lunchroom in the school basement where the students would deposit their labeled lunch bags and lunchboxes in the morning—lined up on the long green tables by grade and classroom—and find them at noon and eat there before heading out to recess, and on those meatless Fridays even though there might have been a variety of items in those bags and boxes such as cheese sandwiches, peanut butter and/or cream cheese and jelly (Paul's mom sometimes made him a triple-decker sandwich that had peanut butter and jelly on the lower deck and cream cheese and jelly on the upper), and peppers and eggs which was an Italian staple for Gerry Giordano such that even if his mom hadn't written his name in large cursive flourish on the brown bag perfectly placed so it would still be visible even when the top of the bag was folded over (some bag folds were neat and creased, others curled and uneven, often because the bulging contents of sandwich in waxed paper, dessert such as cupcakes or pies, and maybe an apple or banana prevented a neat fold), it was easy to spot his bag by the large grease stain that had bled through the sandwich wrapping. But far and away the most common Friday lunch was tuna, overwhelming not just Mary O'Dougherty's but all the students' noses as they walked into the room at lunchtime, especially in winter when the doors were closed and the radiators cranking.

Since the baby boom was dumping so many kids into the school systems in those days, the demand for space had long ago outstripped the size and number of classrooms so eventually there were two classrooms for every grade and the lunchroom was converted into two additional classrooms, after which the students simply ate in their classrooms at their desks and stored their lunch bags and boxes in the long closet that occupied the entire width of the room at the back—the nuns called it the "cloak room," a quaint and somewhat anachronistic term since no one referred to their windbreakers, rain slickers, or winter coats as "cloaks" anymore, so the Friday tuna smell bomb was transferred to the classrooms when those cloak room doors opened at noon.

Beverages were invariably white or chocolate milk delivered daily by trucks from the Wawa dairies outside Media in metal crates containing one 4-oz glass bottle for every student that had ordered their week's milk every Monday morning when they had to remember to bring their milk money, and which also created the need to form a "milk crew"—two eighth graders who would pick up the milk crates around 11:30 from where they had been dropped off outside the doors near the school office and deliver them to each classroom—another escape from whatever subject was being taught at the time, so like the door-opening position usually reserved for students that were smart enough to be able to afford missing a little class time, so once again a natural job for Biggsy and this time Paul because the "crew" required two boys, and another opportunity to "milk" the assignment, stretching a 15-minute job to one that took them just about up to lunch time at noon.

Eating at their desks did create some neatness challenges, as there were often crumbs and other debris on the desks themselves and on the floors underneath. The floors would get cleaned at the end of the day by the students assigned to be "cleaners" for the week (their names typically written in chalk on the side blackboards that were reserved for such messages while the front boards were used almost exclusively for teaching), who had to sweep the floors, clap the erasers outside, and even clean the blackboards with water to wash away the erased shadow remnants of all words spelled or misspelled, arithmetic problems solved or unsolved, and historical or geographical names and dates written out and underlined, but each individual student was responsible for tidying up his or her own desk, usually using the pinky finger side of the hand to sweep all the crumbs into the sandwich wrapper or onto the lunch bag itself that would then be rolled up and thrown into the tall wire trash cans in the days before plastic trash can liners (Hiram emptied all the trash cans after the student cleaners departed for the day).

Because a number of boys in Paul's class weren't meeting Sister Bernie's standards for cleanliness by leaving crumbs on their desks, she started inspecting the desks once all the kids had gone outside for recess such that on returning from the schoolyard they could see that Sister had written several names under the word CRUMBS on the side board, which drove Gerry Giordano crazy since his name was usually there once or twice a week, causing him to come in from recess, see his name, scowl and predictably say "Oh man, not again," then slightly under his breath but still with emphasis , "GET my name offa there; I'm not a CRUMB!" Gerry's family had moved to Springhaven from South Philadelphia, as had Paul's, but the Perdu family had moved there before Paul was born so he had never lived anywhere else and was therefore pure suburban. The Giordanos, on the other hand, had come to St. Anthony's parish in time for Gerry to start fourth grade, so he retained a little of what might be called the "edge" of having lived in an urban area where there were hoods who carried knives and even gun-wielding Mafiosi, and where the term "crumb" had a second and pejorative meaning when it referred to a person, hence Gerry's learned revulsion to being placed in that category, even if it only literally meant that some bread remnants had been found on and/or around his desk.

The frequency and regularity of Mary O'Doherty's vomiting episodes were such that in eighth grade she and Sister learned to communicate non-verbally: Mary would have that distressed almost terrified wide-eyed eyebrows-raised look on her first flushed-red then greenish face then spring out of her chair and bring her hand up to cover her mouth, and Bernie with her sternest possible face popping out of that starched stiff white habit so red it almost looked like a boil ready to burst would point quickly and forcefully and repeatedly to the door with her outstretched arm, her habited sleeve still swinging from those violent motions, sometimes adding "Move!" or if Sister was especially impatient and/or Mary moving too slowly for what seemed an increasingly imminent expulsion or desks were in the way she might repeat "Move!" then add "you poke!" and Mary would take off like a rocket.

Even though the boys and girls were in separate classrooms, since they were right across the hall it wasn't hard to hear Mary's shoes on the linoleum tile floor. So when Biggsy had the front seat assignment, part of the choreography included him jumping up from his seat to open the door so that whichever nun was in their class could go out into the hallway to either assist the girls' class teacher with tending to Mary, or else tending to the girls' class herself. This often left the boy's class unattended, so when this happened and Biggsy was still standing by the door after Mary had flown past, he would watch her run down the hallway heading for the stairs to the lavatory on the ground floor, her footsteps still echoing on the tiles, Biggsy looking after her, and if she made it to the stairs without vomiting in the hallway Biggsy, still staring into the hall, would start nodding his head and reaching his arm back into the classroom would give the "thumbs-up" sign to the rest of the class. If she didn't, Biggsy's thumb pointed down and his head shook rather than nodding, but the boys didn't need any "didn't make it" signals because they could all hear the familiar splat, then another, then often another. In that case, eventually one of the nuns would come back into the room and tell Biggsy to head for the boiler room to summon Hiram and his red dirt, while she or another nun took Mary to the nurse's office.

But this one Monday in early November when they'd just come back to school after a 3-day weekend (Halloween and All Saints' Day the previous Thursday and Friday) when the scene played out with Mary and it was thumbs down and Biggsy got to the basement door marked "BOILER ROOM" in black letters on a white metal sign on the top door jamb, he knocked but there was no answer. So he knocked again but still nothing.

Assuming Hiram must have been out in the building or on the grounds somewhere, Biggsy opened the door as he had been pre-authorized to do to get the red dirt himself (Sister really gave him a lot of responsibility), and as he was scooping it out of a huge heavy gauge cardboard barrel out of the corner of his eye he noticed a shoe on the ground over by the back room where Hiram actually lived and slept, and as he looked more intentionally he realized the shoe had a leg in it and that leg traveled up to a groin and on and on—someone was on the ground. Biggsy let go a brief high pitched "Aaah!" reflexively, and even dropped the scooper, but the shoe-leg didn't move. So after deliberating a few seconds with his heart pounding in his ear and the shoe-leg still immobile, he decided to walk over to it when he saw Hiram on the ground motionless, face up, eyes open and dull gray, with something like little black or dark brown particles around his mouth and down the front of his shirt.

Otherwise there was nothing else obviously out of place or knocked over or blood for as much as Biggsy could tell just looking quickly and being pretty distracted. He didn't hang around to inspect Hiram or the room any more carefully but wanting to get out of there as quickly as possible he forgot the red dirt and now it was HIS footsteps echoing up the stairs and in the hallway rather than Mary's and he was yelling, "Sister! Sister!" with other classroom doors opening and other teachers coming outside and Sister came out into the hall to intercept and he was saying, breathlessly, "Sister…there's…something…wrong . . with Hiram!" and she, "What do you mean 'something wrong'?" and he, still out of breath, "I think…he's dead…Sister."

Everyone in the classroom heard it as did Mrs. Lynch and Miss Howell in the classrooms next door and across the hall but Sister didn't say anything, walking hurriedly past Biggsy her rosary beads slapping against her habit, joined by Miss Howell, and now it was Sister's footsteps everyone heard and Biggsy had never seen her move so quickly, especially since everyone assumed she was old, their ages hard or impossible to decipher in those habits but looking back maybe she was in her 50s or even her 40s. Mrs. Lynch came into their classroom where everyone was murmuring trying to get more information from Biggsy, and eventually just telling them to take out their Arithmetic books. She asked Biggsy where they were in the exercises at the back of the book and Biggsy, although still pretty shaken by what he had seen and reported, collected himself enough to look at his book and saw that they had last worked on Chapter 14 so she told them

"...he saw Hiram on the ground motionless, face up, eyes open and dull gray..."

to do the exercises in Chapters 15 and 16, even if they hadn't done those chapters yet in class they could at least try the word problems. Then she left the room to tend to her own classroom.

They had a hard time concentrating and were still talking so Mrs. Lynch came back in and told Biggsy to stand in the front of the room and take names of talkers who would have to stay after school for a week. So he tried but it didn't do any good. The kids were buzzed, even more so when a car pulled into the school driveway and Robbie Hannum popped up to look out the window and recognizing the long black Ford Fairlane said "It's Ellis" for pastor Father Ellis, then 10 minutes later Randy Stanton in the patrol car (Randy drove St. Anthony's school bus but also belonged to the local and very small Springhaven police force; Mrs. Lynch had gone back to the office and made the calls) and finally an ambulance that pulled up close to the middle doors so Robbie couldn't see what they were doing because of the little overhang in the way, but no sirens or lights, and 20 minutes later they pulled out again, and everyone assumed Hiram was in there.

Maybe he wasn't dead as Biggsy thought. But he insisted "I know what a dead person looks like" and Paul shot back "You're so full of shit. What dead person did you ever see?" and Biggsy came back with "My Uncle Harry. My brother and I saw him have a heart attack and keel over and die while he was watching the Army Navy game on TV a couple years ago." And no one challenged him after that.

A week or so later in the schoolyard before the first bell Biggsy told Paul and Gerry and Robbie, "First recess, Hannum's oak." The other boys complied as usual, if for no other reason than simple curiosity to find out what Biggsy was cooking up this time. The huge northern red oak still had a few brown leaves hanging on when they got together, and since first recess was short (15 minutes) Biggsy got right to the point. "Chums," he began, and Paul closed his eyes and shook his head briefly realizing it was Hardy Boys Biggsy this time, "I was reading the blotter in the *Sentinel* (another in a long list of Biggsy's annoying traits was using terminology or jargon that, just because he knew it he assumed everyone did so he dove right in without explanations; in this case, the Sentinel was their local weekly newspaper, the *Springhaven Sentinel*, and the "blotter" was the regular column detailing recent police department activity, usually minor crimes, a few break-ins or store robberies maybe, and a few years back the bizarre community-rattling apparent murder-suicide involving the Jansens, an older couple on Harvey's Creek Lane, presumably because Mrs. Jansen was ill and failing and Mr. J was feeling rather hopeless) and noticed there was nothing there about Hiram."

"So," Paul said. "What did you expect to see?"

"Obviously," Biggsy continued, "you boys didn't notice that the police were here that day, and when I went down to the lavatory the boiler room door was closed but when I came out of the bathroom the door opened and Randy Stanton and his partner Bill Haverty walked out."

"So what," Paul repeated. "That doesn't mean anything."

"You don't think so?" Biggsy asked. "Well I do. I think it means a lot and I think the police are investigating and not saying anything right now which is why it's not in the paper. Keeping it quiet. I don't expect all of you to understand all this, but since I'm a little bit older than all of you…"

Paul cut him off, "Jesus Christ! Not that again! You are like two or three months older." (A child had to be six years old to enter first grade at St. Anthony's, and since Biggsy was born on November 7, 1949 and turned six in November 1955 he had to wait until September 1956 to start school when he was almost seven, so yes he was a little older than almost everyone in his class by a few months or more and a full six months older than Paul, and he lorded over everyone but especially over Paul as if he were 5-10 years older and 5-10 years more knowledgeable and wiser about the world.)

"Investigating what?" Gerry asked.

"Possible homicide. Murder."

"You're usually pretty crazy, Biggsy," Paul came back, "but this time you're really off your rocker."

"You guys weren't in there," Biggsy said, "but I was. I saw him! And I saw something on him that might be a clue."

There was nothing to do now but just let Biggsy continue sketching out what could be, in his mind, his version of a Hardy Boys case that might be titled, *The Clue in the Boiler Room*.

"Remember I told you he had these little dark spots or specks all over him? Well, a couple days later when my brother went over to Swarthmore College library (Biggsy's older brother John was a high school senior at St. James in Chester, but it was not unusual for high school students in the area to occasionally take advantage of the resources in the local college library) I went with him and looked up a couple of things. I had to dig and dig, into the medical books which I will have to do at some point later anyway, and I found out that those little specks can be a sign that someone was bleeding in the stomach. Sometimes it can be from something called an ulcer, which is sort of like a hole in the stomach, and sometimes it can be from drinking too much. I don't know about the ulcer, but I've never smelled any alcohol on Hiram," and the boys agreed that they hadn't either, and almost everyone had uncles or grandfathers or maybe even fathers that would have previously familiarized them with that characteristic aroma of booze on breath. Biggsy continued, "But sometimes it can be from being poisoned."

"Poisoned?" Paul blurted. "By what? And who would want to do that to Hiram? He never bothered anybody."

Biggsy replied, "Those the are questions we have to answer, but I have a couple of hunches and theories. One of the things that can do it is in rat poison, and I know Hiram kept some of that in the boiler room. But Paul is right—who would want to hurt Hiram, unless he was like Jimmy Stewart in that movie *The Man Who Knew Too Much*."

Just then the bell rang. Since they were far enough away from the school building and out of earshot of teachers and most other students, Biggsy broke the "freeze" rule to add one more thought:

"Maybe he knew something or saw something or had something on somebody who wanted him out of the way. This will be tough to solve, but we have to try."

*   *   *

Paul just wrote this in the memory booklet draft: "Hiram. Our janitor. A presence at St. Anthony's for most of our time there, although we didn't know much about him. His death in the school building—right in the boiler room on the ground floor—in November of our 8th-grade year was not just unusual, but even somewhat traumatic to a degree for kids our age at the time. It shook us, but not as much as what was about to happen later that month. Some people suspected foul play, but that was never proven as far as we know."

Are you a doctor?

Paul and Nancy went to the Locust Hill Tavern banquet hall to make the arrangements for the party. It was one of the oldest buildings in Springhaven, had been an actual food, drink and lodging tavern back in the 18th century, and there were still some locust trees on the property that the Springhaven Historical Society believed (or talked themselves into believing) had been there when some British troops had passed or even lodged nearby around the time of the battle of Brandywine in September, 1777. At one point there might have been a hill as well, but after a couple hundred years of development in the area surrounding the site there was no longer any discernible elevation in the land, if there had ever been much of one in the first place.

When the banquet manager came back with the contract she put it in front of Paul, but he slid it over to Nancy since she was handling the finances out of her personal checking account. While Nancy was looking over the paperwork the manager turned to Paul and asked, "So are you really a doctor?" Paul just said "Huh?" and she continued, "One of my waitresses recognized you from the Fast Care Center, said you stitched up her hand when she cut it on a broken glass a couple of years ago." Paul just said, "Yeah, I used to work there." The manager said, "So you really ARE a doctor then." Paul said, "No...I mean, Yes...I mean, Yes, I am a physician, or I was one, but No, I don't practice anymore."

"So what do you do now? Sorry if I'm being too nosy."

"It's OK. I work at the hospital, in the ER."

"So you're still a doctor then?"

"No, I gave it up. I'm a tech now. I assist the doctors and nurses."

"Why did you give it up? I mean, who gives up being a doctor?"

"Wow. You aren't shy, are you. You'd be surprised. A lot of people give it up."

"But why did YOU give it up?"

"It's complicated."

"Did you lose your license or something? Sorry. I'm REALLY being nosy. I just never heard of anyone who stopped being a doctor, you know, before retiring, or getting sick or in trouble or whatever."

"I still have a license. I'm healthy. I wasn't in any trouble. I just didn't want to do it anymore."

"Well, maybe you made the right decision because, no offense or anything, you look about as much like a doctor as I do, and I definitely don't look like a doctor."

Paul came back with, "What's a doctor supposed to look like?"

"I don't know," the manager said; "I just know that you don't. Although Janet, the waitress, she said you did a nice job on her. "

At that point Nancy chimed in, "Yeah, he's a real doctor, and a good doctor, but if he had a nickel for every time someone told him he didn't look like one or act like one or that he missed his calling…" and Paul interrupted, "…I'd have about $2.35."

"What?" the manager asked.

"Two dollars and thirty-five cents," Paul repeated; "you know, because I've heard it, like (quickly doing the mental math) 47 times."

"What?" she said again and Paul said, "Forget it." He hated clichés so much that he decided to supply a concrete response to the old "If I had a nickel for every time" line, just to keep himself interested.

Nancy was surprised that Paul had gone into as much detail as he had with the banquet manager. Paul had even surprised himself because he generally didn't like talking about the whole business of why he went to medical school and why he became a kind of peripatetic journeyman physician instead of the more conventional path of settling long-term into a stable specialty and practice, and why he eventually stopped practicing altogether. Complicated indeed, starting back to his college days at Villanova in the late 60s when he had no idea what to pick as a major and finally chose History because at least he liked reading and he had become interested in American history at an early age after his dad had taken him and his brother to Independence Hall when they were still preteens and he had come home with a replica of the Declaration of Independence and facsimiles of colonial paper money his dad had bought in the gift shop, both mementos printed on stiff, light brown parchment paper that actually smelled old, and maybe even more so because of all the social and political unrest in the country during his college years from 1968 to 1972 from the anti-war and civil rights movements which made him feel he was actually immersed in history as it was happening. His freshman year in college began the September after the 1968 assassinations of Martin Luther King, Jr. and Bobby Kennedy and the riots at the Democratic Convention in Chicago, so he took an elective senior-level course on Revolutions that examined the French, Chinese, and Russian revolutions looking for parallels between those and what was happening in America at the time. But he waited until the last minute in the second semester of sophomore year to declare that major, and when he told his parents they (especially his dad) kept asking over the last few weeks of the semester, "What are you going to do with a History degree? Teach?" and when he didn't have a ready answer they (mostly his dad) would say, "Have you thought any about our previous suggestions, like about being a doctor?" When Paul simply answered "No" his dad said "Well maybe you should. We keep telling you you're smart enough. That's what the smartest kids do."

It was true. Paul had scored almost 1500 in his SATs, and by the end of junior year in high school he was one of the top five on the boy's side of the school (Bishop Keenan, his high school, was co-institutional in that boys and girls were under the same roof, but not truly co-ed because the two genders were in separate classes and classrooms on separate sides of the building). He probably could have gotten into Penn or even one of the other Ivies, but at the time his dad said that Villanova was a very good school, was Catholic, was closer and suburban and therefore safer than urban schools such as Penn in West Philly (and closer and safer than other Catholic choices in the region such as St. Joe's out on City Line Avenue or LaSalle in north Philly), and he could get there taking the bus or trolley to 69th St. in Upper Darby and then taking the Norristown High Speed Line right out to Villanova's campus. When Paul had asked about living in a dorm his dad had simply said it wasn't necessary, given these convenient travel arrangements, not to mention it being less expensive to live at home. "If you want to pay for it, be my guest," his dad would say, "but if I'm paying for it you can live at home and commute." As a result Paul didn't really engage much in campus life. "What's wrong with that?" his dad used to ask rhetorically. "You're there to get an education, not go to parties and drink illegally," at a time when the whole notion of considering college an important socializing milestone in a young adult's life was not part of the cultural conversation, or at least not in his home. His older brother had gone to St. Joe's and lived at home and that was good enough for him so Paul's dad figured that same model would be good enough for Paul (Paul's older brother also had had a job and a girlfriend at home during his college years so he had never really pushed it).

While Paul's father pitched the idea of a medical career more for practical reasons (i.e., as an altruistic way to make a nice living and, as he had said many times, if someone were more or less gifted academically whether through hard work or natural ability or both, it was the logical career path to take), Paul's mother had softer, more emotional reasons for wanting her son to pursue that profession. She was born in 1916, two years before the influenza pandemic of 1918, and while she had no distinct memories of what was happening since she was only two at the time, she heard later about how the flu had taken her older sister and a cousin that also lived on Ritner Street in South Philly four houses down, she swore that she remembered the deaths, her mother and mother's sister crying, and even if she wasn't sure of those exact memories she used to say she thought she picked up the moods of fear and sadness and mourning "by osmosis" when that phrase was starting to become part of everyday conversations—or at least that was how she explained her morbid fear of fevers and respiratory illnesses. Just hearing the word "flu" caused goose bumps and her hair to stand up as she felt the adrenaline careening through her arteries and she started fidgeting to try and dissipate it simulating the "fight" part of the fight-flight response since she was usually not in a place where she could start running to flee. Having heard that her sister died at home unattended, without medical attention or support (obviously there was no 9-1-1 at the time) because the doctors at the time were running themselves ragged trying to care for all the hundreds and thousands who were ill and simply couldn't see everyone who needed seeing, she grew up wondering if her sister might have lived if only a physician had been able to get to their house.

Once after repeated coaxing and encouraging almost approaching badgering Paul actually asked his mother "Why do you want me to be a doctor so badly? What is it about being a doctor that makes you think and feel it's what I should do?" She replied, "Oh I don't know. You get to help people, which is enough, but it's also…it's just…it's just so pres-TEE-gious. You know, whenever you see a doctor out in a store, or at church or just driving by people say, 'There's doctor so and so.' And whenever a doctor walks into a room and someone says, 'There's doctor so and so' all heads turn to look." But Paul had his own hypothesis: That his mother, having pre-consciously absorbed the grief and mourning in their home when her sister and cousin died, and growing up with that family narrative and on some level knowing or at least believing that if only a doctor had made it to their house her sister might have lived, she wanted her son, her smart son, to be the one who would succeed in making it to some other person's house and just by showing up be able to stave off death. The doctor never made it to her sister's bedside, but Paul would have made it, and given the chance now he would make it to some other little girl's bedside and make things right.

She more or less confirmed his theory one other time they were having this kind of conversation. "Remember," she started, "when you or your brother were sick in bed and we knew Dr. Salatucci was coming over to the house to see you? Remember how that made us all feel? Like everything was going to be all okay. That he would take care of things. Don't you remember that feeling? And wouldn't you like to be able to make people feel that way?"

Paul responded, "That's not how I remember it. I just remember dread, being afraid he was going to give me a shot and it was going to be painful since that's what invariably happened when he came over."

As a result of the repeated and almost relentless pressure from his parents, and also his own grudging realization that he would need to do something with his life after college (and while he didn't want to admit that his dad might be right about something, he didn't think he wanted to teach History or even teach at all), Paul did look in the course catalog and learned that a student could be any major and still be considered "pre-med" if he took the courses required for medical school entry—Calculus; Biology; Chemistry; Organic Chemistry; and Physics. So when it came time to register for his junior year classes, he decided to start more intentionally completing the pre-med courses as electives. Since he had already taken Calculus and two semesters of Biology to fulfill his science and math core curriculum requirements, he was already a little ahead of the game and would still be able to get enough courses in to fulfill his History major and do all the medical school prerequisites without having to do summer school between junior and senior year (which would have also meant asking his dad to pay for it, which predictably would have been challenging although in support of a medical career maybe not so much), although that also meant there would be precious little space for any other electives, those little mind-expanding pieces of candy such as Philosophy or Anthropology that his friends were taking, although many of the History electives for his major (like the Revolutions course) were pretty satisfying.

Despite the political distractions on college campuses in the late 60s and early 70s, Paul did well academically—after his cake walks through St. Anthony's and Bishop Keenan where he relied mostly on his memory and a rocky start the first semester of freshman college, he was able to adapt, put his head down, and plow through his school work—both in the classroom and on the MCATs, so at the end of junior year he started applying to medical schools. His dad inserted himself into the process again as he had done when Paul was choosing a college. Applications arrived in the mail almost everyday, from as far away as Tufts, Pritzker, and Tulane, and Paul's dad just watched. But when the application arrived from UCLA, he'd had enough. Walking into Paul's bedroom holding the UCLA packet in his right hand and slapping the 8½ x 11-inch thick envelope against his left hand he asked, "What's this supposed to mean?" Paul responded with "What are you talking about?" and his dad came back with, "California? Are you serious?" Paul closed his eyes and looked away and said, "I really don't wanna talk about this now" but his dad said, "Well, we're GONNA talk about it now whether you want to or not, before this goes any further."

Paul said, "I stayed home for college; I even LIVED at home. So…I don't know…I just thought, maybe it would be fun to go away for medical school, or at least apply to see if I could even get in."

"Fun?" his dad said "You thought it might be FUN? Do you think I would have fun paying for it?"

"Jesus," Paul said. "I knew that was coming, sooner or later."

"Excuse me?" his father said.

"Look," Paul said, "I'm doing what you and mom want. Right? I'm going to medical school like you've always wanted. I'm 21 years old. I can drink legally. I'm going to be able to vote in the presidential election next year. Can't I at least choose where I go to graduate school?"

"Not if I'm paying for it," his father said, prompting Paul to close his eyes and shake his head as his dad continued, "If you want to pay for it yourself, be my guest. But if I'm footin' the bill, we have excellent medical schools right here in Philadelphia."

And that was that. Paul's dad predictably played the money card, and Paul didn't have the energy or desire to resist, since he didn't even feel strongly enough about attending medical school in the first place to force himself to work his way through at the school of his choice. He said to himself, "Fine. They want me to do this; they want to pay for it; I'll go where they say. I don't give a shit."

So he ended up applying to the University of Pennsylvania, Jefferson, Hahnemann, Temple and the Medical College of Pennsylvania—all the schools in Philadelphia where he might earn an M.D. Penn and Jeff rejected him outright, without offering an interview. He interviewed at Hahnemann, but they ultimately rejected him too. But Temple and MCP both invited him for interviews, and both accepted him. His parents would have preferred one of the other three schools, but they were still happy and proud, especially that he had two choices, which meant he would go SOMEWHERE and would therefore ultimately, become the doctor they wanted him to be. Paul was leaning toward Temple, since MCP used to be called the Women's Medical College of Pennsylvania, and even though the name changed when they started admitting men in 1970, a lot of people still referred to it as Women's Medical, and Paul worried that people might think it was still predominantly a school for women, but now also for men who couldn't get in anywhere else. Going to Temple would allow him to avoid carrying that baggage, even though any potential stigma was only his perception.

His parents had their own ideas, naturally, although now that Paul had been accepted and they knew that their dreams would become reality in only a few short years, their tone softened somewhat. Discussing the subject one night at the dinner table Paul's father opened with, "So what are you thinking?" Knowing exactly what the non-specific question referred to Paul said, "I don't know…Temple maybe?" His dad stuck out his lips, raised his eyebrows and nodded his head saying, "Temple…Temple… yeah, sure that's a good school. I don't know about that neighborhood, though. Pretty rough up there on North Broad Street. What about MCP?" Paul said, "Sure, I'm still thinking about that." When he stopped there his dad prompted him with, "And…?" and Paul said "AND I'm still thinking about it, that's all. Still thinking."

"What's there to think about?" his dad went on. "Is there any reason you WOULDN'T want to go there?" Paul didn't really want to get into it, as usual, but for some reason provided an honest answer with, "I don't know…something about the whole 'Women's' thing still bothers me."

"Oh that's just, silly" his dad said; "MCP is a fine school, with a great history and a beautiful campus. And close. You could get the Media Local train to Suburban Station, then walk a couple blocks to pick up the 32 bus to Henry Avenue…" but Paul cut him off.

"WHAT? Are you thinking I'm going to live home, like in college? And take public transportation to medical school? "

His dad said, "Well…I was…" and Paul cut in again, "That's NUTS! Do you think medical school is like college, a couple classes a day, long breaks between classes, home at 3:00 in the afternoon? Medical school is all day, every day, and some nights and weekends. It would take me two hours to get there and two hours to get home. And then when am I supposed to study? Reading on the bus and the train? No, that's it. I've had it. I know you're paying for it, you throw that in my face every chance you get. But if you want me to do it, you're going to have to get me an apartment near the school or buy me a car or I'm not going."

Somehow his dad understood that Paul was serious, so the compromise would be that Paul would choose MCP and live at home and his dad would get him a car. Actually, Paul was OK with the car vs apartment deal. Living on either campus—in East Falls or North Philadelphia—without a car would be pretty confining. And even though it wasn't new or fancy (his father had worked out a deal with his brother/Paul's uncle Arthur whom everyone called "Shorty" back in the day when such descriptive nicknames were common and not considered insensitive or politically incorrect to buy his old Tempest—Paul's dad had always been a "Buick man" while his brother preferred Pontiacs), the car was freedom, including the freedom to stay late at school and even occasionally sleep over in classmates' apartments, including a particular classmate named Melody Donnelly whom Paul had gradually become attracted to ("just saying your name is like singing" Paul used to tell her) whom Paul started dating and eventually married in 1976, the day before they graduated.

After a two-week honeymoon in California (Paul finally got there, financed by wedding gift money rather than his father), they settled into their residencies in July. Melody had chosen Pediatrics and did her training at the Children's Hospital of Philadelphia. Paul wasn't really sure what he wanted to do, but finally picked Internal Medicine and landed at Fitzgerald Mercy Hospital in Darby. They decided to live in an apartment in Lansdowne on Providence Road but near Lansdowne Avenue, close enough to the train for Melody to ride that to 30th Street Station and walk the few blocks to CHOP, and also close enough for Paul to actually walk to Fitz, which he was forced to do after the Tempest died (Uncle Shorty had sold him a junker to begin with but with almost monthly oil changes Paul had kept it going over four years).

Melody was all set for three years, but after one year of his residency—just enough to get a State license to practice—Paul quit, saying he was "tired of being in school" and wanting to earn more than a resident's salary, which he did after landing a job in Drexel University's Student Health Center in West Philly near CHOP, so sometimes he and Melody could take the train to work together or maybe have dinner in town before coming home. Melody went along with his decision initially figuring or at least hoping that he would eventually go back and finish, once he saw that he wouldn't be able to get very far without having completed a residency and getting his board certification. But as she finished and got a job in a pediatric practice in Media and they moved into a house in Wallingford, and she saw that he was staying in the Student Health job and never talked about going back into training, it became an ongoing source of tension.

Typically, on a weekend, she would start to sulk and brood and he would say, "What's wrong with you?" or "Is something bothering you?" and she would respond, "What do you think?" Then she would start to rant, egging him on to go back and finish his residency and get board certified and settle into a respectable practice instead of staying in and settling for a "going nowhere" job which she said "looks bad on your record." Paul would typically respond, "I don't care. For someone who never really wanted to do this in the first place I think I've done pretty well going against the grain all these years. And we live more comfortably than a lot of other people we know."

"But not as comfortably as I'd like" Melody would come back. "Look at the guys who were in our class. Are you doing as well as they are? Like Kevin who did Cardiology and Jack who did Orthopaedics? Do their wives have to work as hard as I do? I would like to start planning a family and work part-time, but I can't do that with you being so unsettled."

After years of repeatedly hearing these arguments and harangues Paul eventually said less and less and finally nothing (it takes two to argue he said to himself, so if I say nothing it's her monologue, but not an argument), which made Melody even more angry.

"Aren't you going to say anything?" she would often ask after she had ranted for several minutes, really boiling by that point. It didn't cool her off any when Paul would maintain his silence or say something snide such as "I would have answered a question but I didn't hear any interrogatory sentences in there; I believe they were all declarative."

So no one was surprised when they finally split; in fact, most of their family and many friends said they were amazed it had lasted almost 10 years, although it was actually Paul's inertia and foot-dragging that kept it going as long as it did. Melody remarried within a year to a pediatric cardiologist she'd known from residency (leading Paul to suspect they might have been having an affair prior to the divorce, but there was never any proof and it didn't matter anyway—in quiet moments of reflection he was actually happy for her); and despite getting a somewhat late start, she finally started that family she had always wanted—three kids in four years in her late 30's and early 40's—and continued working part-time in a general pediatric practice. Paul not only never remarried, he never again had a serious, long-term, committed relationship, just serial albeit infrequent dating, with five dates over three months his record for longevity.

Paul stayed at Drexel's Student Health until the spring of 1990 when the University decided to eliminate that Department and outsource the service to a local primary care practice. That was when Paul got his first job at an urgent care center which were just starting to crop up at the time, and where—as with the student health position—the hiring/credentialing threshold was having a Pennsylvania medical license in good standing. Board certification was not required, and Paul had heard the owners were fine with that because they could pay such docs a little less.

He had worked at two or three before finally settling at the Fast Care Center where the Locust Hill waitress had seen him, the last healthcare facility he would work as a physician, and ironically he decided to quit after a very successful encounter that probably saved someone's life. A woman in her early 20s had brought her boyfriend into the office saying he had a high fever and a headache and was "out of it." The nurse brought the patient back to an exam room, and while he walked mostly under his own power the nurse and the girlfriend were each supporting one of his arms. While he was lying on the exam table Paul lifted the young man's shirt to be able to listen to his heart while the nurse was checking his blood pressure, when he saw that the chest and abdomen were covered in a purplish red rash—as small as dots in places and larger splotches in others.

"How long has he had this rash?" he asked the girlfriend who was still in the room. "Rash?" she said; "I don't remember seeing any rash."

"He has to go to the Hospital," Paul said, then turning to the nurse, "Call 9-1-1."

"What's going on?" the girlfriend said, her voice more apprehensive. "Isn't it just a bad flu or virus or something?"

"Maybe," Paul said as the nurse left the room to go make the call, "but it could be something worse and he needs to be at the hospital."

"OK," the girlfriend said, "I can take him over. It's only a couple miles away," as if hoping the doctor's permission to send him by car would mean it wasn't as serious as he was suggesting.

"No," Paul said; "he needs to go by ambulance. *Now.*"

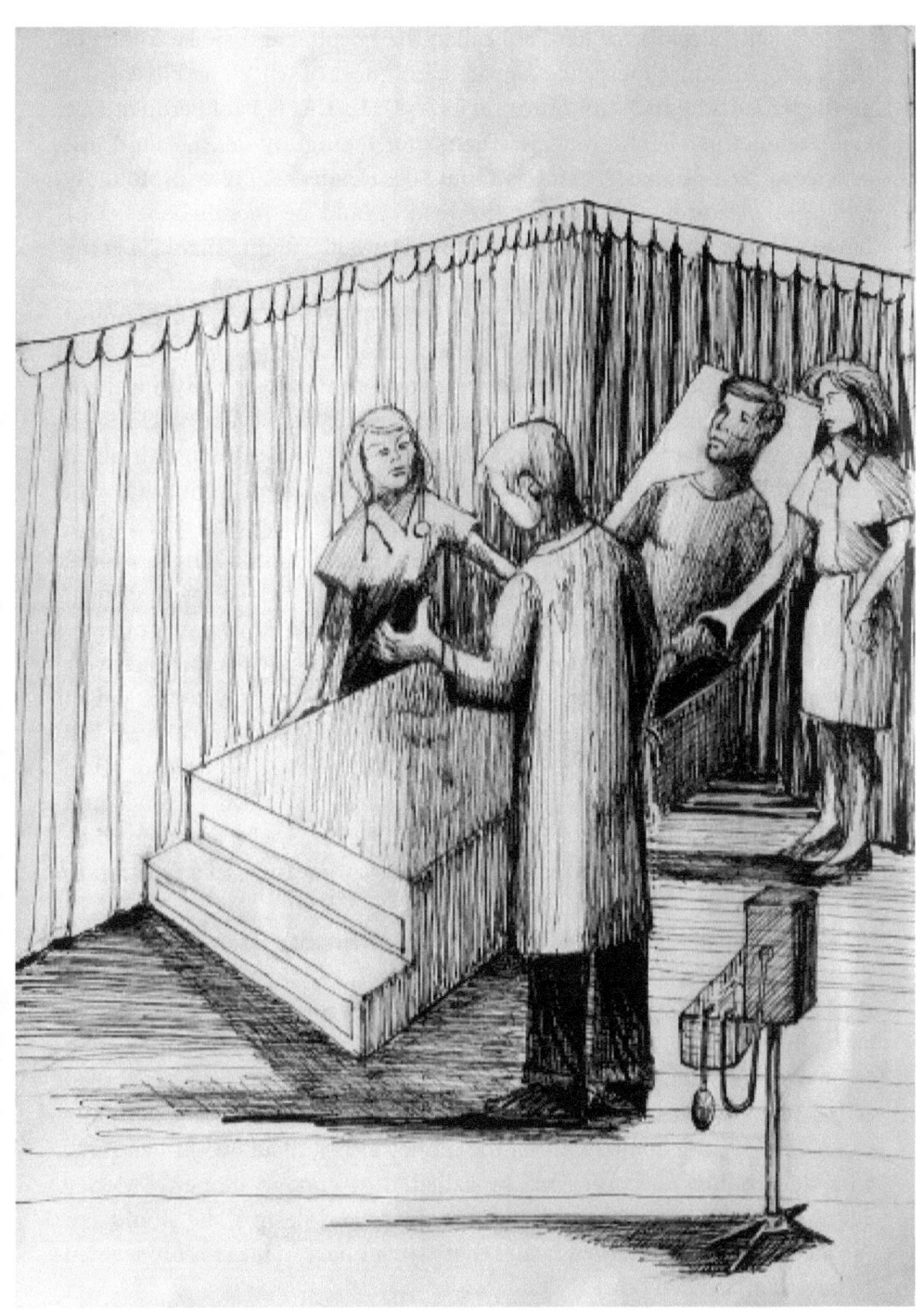

"He has to go to the Hospital," Paul said, then turning to the nurse, "Call 9-1-1."

After the ambulance left Paul called the hospital and spoke to one of the doctors in the Emergency Department, most of whom he knew from all the patients he had sent over previously. "Hi. This is Paul Perdu at Fast Care, who's this? Oh hi, Maggie. Thanks for taking my call. Listen, I just sent a guy by ambulance. Temp is about 104. Headache. Pretty profoundly lethargic, almost obtunded, but the rash…could be meningococcus…I haven't seen it much but…yeah, have to rule it out…Right. Thanks. Let me know…Oh, we put a mask on him."

As it turned out Paul was right: the young man had bacterial meningitis, and if Paul hadn't acted quickly the patient could have died. Instead, he not only survived, but made a complete recovery without losing any fingers or toes or organ function and walked out of the hospital several weeks later. The hospital Emergency and ICU and Infectious Disease doctors all called Paul at different times to say "Good pick up." The patient came back with a huge fruit basket one time when Paul wasn't there, but left a note saying, "You saved my life. Can't thank you enough." But just when he should have been feeling elated about what he'd accomplished—a lowly student health and later urgent care "doc in a box" physician, with one year of post-graduate training and not board certified had acted quickly and decisively and almost instinctively in response to someone's severe illness which may have been one of the reasons and maybe the key reason a 23-year-old man was still alive and well when he could have easily been dead—Paul decided he'd had enough. "Too much pressure," he told his friends and family. "That case could have SO easily gone the other way, and then I'd be moping around thinking I'd killed him. I don't want to be in a position to have to make those decisions anymore."

So he started working as the ER tech. At first it was awkward being supervised by and taking orders from nurses, physician assistants, and doctors that were increasingly younger over the years, but he got used to it. Actually, everyone knew he had been a practicing physician, so they often treated him as such and even solicited his advice on certain cases. He called it "respect and prestige without accountability." When friends and family often quickly added "and without the money either," Paul was just as quick to articulate his views on what he called "Just enough money." "Money requirements are relative to overall life needs and desires," he would say, "so all you need is just enough, and that's what I have." He certainly seemed to have it all figured out.

After Nancy had been reading a few minutes she said to the banquet manager, "Is it OK if I take this home and look it over?"

"Sure," the manager said, "but I can only hold the room another couple of days. June is a busy time of year for parties."

"I know," Nancy said; "I'll let you know for sure by Wednesday."

"That's fine," the manager said. "You and your husband talk it over" she added, nodding toward Paul, to which Nancy said, "Oh…you thought… No, we're not married" and Paul jumped in with, "That's right. I was married once, although not to Nancy here, but I stopped being married like I stopped being a doctor. Except my ex-wife is still around, but my medical school no longer exists, so that kind of nullifies my degree, don't you think?"

Paul wasn't kidding. In 1993 the Medical College of Pennsylvania merged with Hahnemann, and then in 2003 Drexel University absorbed both of them and subsequently closed MCP, whose East Falls campus was converted to a residential, shopping and dining complex.

The manager said, "I'm sorry I ever started that conversation."

Like our dads

Their eighth-grade classroom was the last one on the east end of the building with large north-side schoolyard-facing windows that extended from the waist-level sill/shelf that sat atop the radiators up at least six and probably eight feet. It was gray and dry when they walked into school that later November Friday morning, and with all that glass they could see it stayed the same through lunch and on after recess. It was the kind of day the sky seems to say, "I may make rain today, and I may not. Only I know, and all you can do is feel the threat and the gloom." Some said later they did feel that, with no idea how gloomy it would get. But when someone out in the hallway knocked on their classroom door late that afternoon when they were starting to get a little rammy with the day and week almost over and the short Thanksgiving week ahead, some sensed that something terrible had happened.

Sister motioned to Biggsy the door opener to stay in his seat and went to the door herself (perhaps because she wasn't expecting anyone) and opened it a crack, tilting her habit-encased head slightly down and to the right as she listened to whoever was whispering from the hallway, but very quickly she looked up at the person and into the hall, then immediately stepped out of the room without saying anything and without even closing the door behind her. No instructions to do any busy work or read, no admonition not to talk, she just left. That had never happened before. After they heard her footsteps in the hall and the familiar swish of her habit and rosary louder at first then gradually fading they started to talk, mostly wondering what was going on. While Biggsy had the job to open the door for visitors, whenever Sister left the room it was Gerry who stood by the door peeking into the hallway to see when she might be returning after which he would tell everyone to sit down and stop talking. So Gerry assumed his usual sentinel position at the door, five minutes later doing his whisper-shout "Here she comes!" as he scurried back to his seat and they all shut up.

Sister came back in holding something and still not saying anything (she hadn't said a word since she left the room and returned), but when she went to her desk they could see that she had brought a radio into the classroom, which was about as astounding as if she had walked in with an elephant or Willie Mays. They had obviously all seen radios before, but never in the classroom. Radios were home things, not school things. And

"...she had brought a radio into the classroom, which was about as astounding as if she had walked in with an elephant..."

it was even weirder and more incongruous seeing a nun with a radio since they all assumed nuns didn't have or do anything normal. They were nuns: they didn't eat or sleep or watch TV or use the bathroom (after the report a year earlier when they were in seventh grade that Tommy Cannon in eighth had opened the wrong door in the school office and found/caught Sister Camilla on the john and they all said No No No that's impossible nuns don't use bathrooms and it was just as impossible to construct that mental image of Camilla sitting on the toilet, her habit and cord and rosary all bunched up in her arms) and radios were part of normal life, not part of a nun's life. When the convent acquired a station wagon the following April and one of the younger nuns, Sister Anne Thomas started driving it, it was just as odd.

She plugged it in behind her desk and while still standing and leaning forward started turning the dial as it made those typical radio tuning sounds they had heard at home or in movies or on TV—those little snippets of talking or music that faded out and in with little squeaks as the dial was turned in search of a particular sought station. Finally she reached the desired spot and sat back in her chair. A man was speaking—his voice was deep and maybe just a little tremulous, and later they found out it was probably Walter Cronkite—and after a minute or two they heard him say clearly that President Kennedy had been shot and rushed to the hospital. A little nervous chattering started after that, releasing some of the tension, with Biggsy adding authoritatively that it would be OK, he would get taken care of and fixed up at the hospital. And still Sister didn't say a word or try to hush them up but just kept staring off to the right (the students left) in the general direction of the windows, but her stare was blank. Above her head in the corkboard that ran along the wall over the blackboards and where the nuns with help from some of the girls in class would pin seasonal decorations (at this time of year it was turkeys and cornucopias and a few leftover pumpkins and colored leaves from October that would soon come down and be replaced by Christmas trees and manger scenes) but two enduring images that never came down were picture profile silhouettes of Abraham Lincoln and JFK—one slain president from a century ago and another current one just shot but still, they hoped and some had already started earnestly praying, very much alive—also figuratively looking towards the windows.

Eventually the voice said the President was dead, and Paul remembered his stomach dropping and dragging his throat down with it. And for the first time anyone could ever remember the class was completely silent except for the radio—no talking, no rustling of feet or papers, no rattling of pencils in the little grooved pencil holder at the top of the desk. They listened. Sister stared. Paul thought of how much JFK's election had meant to Catholics in general and to nuns in particular. Of what he meant to Paul's family, remembering that time in the summer of 1960 when his father had taken him and his brother to a Phillies game at Connie Mack Stadium and before the game started there was some kind of stage set up at the edge of the infield behind second base that Paul found out later was for then-Vice President Nixon, campaigning to be president and about to make a speech. They were sitting along the first base foul line and while Nixon was speaking there was some commotion behind them in the stands and a few whistles and cheers, so Paul turned around and saw some men in the kind of green derby hats he had seen in St. Patty's Day parades and he might have even been able to make out their red noses and they were carrying a huge banner that read "Kennedy for President." Paul gazed up at his dad with an expression that must have looked puzzled as if saying "What's that all about?" His dad, wearing the black-rimmed glasses he always wore in the ballpark and movie theaters and driving at night that made him look like a different person to Paul probably anticipated his son's confusion, but realized he couldn't get into the whole notion of working-class families descended from immigrants or immigrants themselves generally supporting Democrats who generally supported "the working man" so while still looking out at Nixon but motioning with his thumb behind them toward the banner-holding green-derby-hatted marchers said simply, "We're with them" to end the conversation. Paul was only 10 without even a rudimentary sense of what was happening politically, but learned later about Kennedy and the Catholic thing and how that had trumped some of the occasional enmity between Irish- and Italian-Americans.

Paul looked out the window over to the playground, to the bike rack, and beyond that to the goal posts on the football field thinking he sees these things every day, but at this moment they all look different. All coated with gray as if the sky had released the clouds and they had drifted down and invisibly covered everything, except they weren't obscured as with a fog, everything was still visible but it was like they had been turned into a black and white photograph, and they were now the playground and goal posts and bike rack of the Kennedy assassination day. They continued sitting and listening, and when the radio voice reported the police had a suspect in custody, Sister said the first words she had spoken since she had responded to the knock: "Good! Good! I hope they get him!"

And that was it. They continued sitting until the bell rang at 3:00 and they started packing up their book bags, retrieving their jackets from the cloak room at the back of the classroom, and getting into their usual bus or car or bike or walking lines, still in silence. Paul walked home with Gerry who ultimately spoke first: "Shit. He was like our dads." Which was true. The first and only other president they could remember was Eisenhower, who always looked more grandfatherly, or like Father Ellis, while JFK was the same age and generation as their World War Two vet fathers (Paul seemed to recall that everyone's dad on their street had served), and while they didn't generally think of their dads as "young" they did recognize that they were fit and vital enough to do yard work and throw baseballs and footballs and even run the base paths and after fly balls a little at 4th of July neighborhood softball games. "Yeah," Paul said, adding that he was tough, a war hero, recalling his courage related to the well-advertised and eventually memorialized in movie and song PT 109 incident in the Pacific Theater (Paul had sent away to the White House for the "official" account). He also reminded Gerry of how JFK had stood up to Russia during the Cuban Missile Crisis. Even at that age they knew enough to recognize the Soviet Union as a threat, and seen images of Khrushchev banging his shoe at the UN and saying "We will bury you." President Kennedy had held his ground and Khrushchev had backed off. He also wanted Americans to be energetic, to have "vigor" which he pronounced VIG-uh in his Boston r-dropping dialect that translated into St. Anthony students having to occasionally do organized calisthenics in the schoolyard, presumably because they'd never beat the Russians if they weren't able to do jumping jacks and touch their left toes with their right hands while their feet were spread apart.

When Paul got home he thought he was going to be the first to share the news, but his brother was already home from high school and he and their mother were sitting on the couch staring at the TV, so Paul just sat on an ottoman and joined their watching. Just as in school, they were all quiet, except at one point Paul's mother just shook her head and asked, a few times "Why?" They went to a prayer service at church that night and said a rosary for President Kennedy's soul and to ask God's help for his family and their country and their new President Johnson. Some women and girls in the congregation—maybe even a lot of them—were sobbing. Paul's mother wiped a few tears as well. And for a few days afterwards there was talk of a possible Russian plot to strike America now, at its weakest and most vulnerable time, and Paul recalled little shivers of fear whenever he heard a siren or a jet flying overhead, thinking it might be an air raid, remembering the under-the-desk drills they did in the younger grades preparing for a possible nuclear attack. Paul's mother washed out a few of the empty Sealtest milk bottles the milkman delivered every week, filled them with water, and stored them on the shelf next to the dryer in the basement.

V
Christmas (Thanksgiving to January 2nd)

It was either a shame or a blessing and probably both that we didn't have much time to mourn JFK, because Thanksgiving was the very next week only six days after the assassination and three following the funeral, and Advent only 72 hours later on the first day of and the first Sunday in December. I'm not sure I agreed with Biggsy that the Christmas season should be considered to begin on Thanksgiving, but unquestionably once December started our hearts and minds locked tenaciously onto the coming holidays and approaching winter. I couldn't articulate it at the time, but after what we as a country and we as Catholics and we as hero-missing early teen-year boys had just been through, the thoughts of cold and snow and precious days off from school had something of a cleansing, even purifying effect. We all needed a break.

Predictably, Father Galvin scheduled Biggsy and me to serve the 9:00 Mass for the First Sunday of Advent on December 1st. I remember that while we were garbing up in the sacristy I asked Biggsy why he hadn't given Advent its own season in his little system. When he seemed a little puzzled I reminded him of all that revised calendar *stuff* (I might have said "bullshit," or maybe not, since we were in the sacristy) he had talked about the first week of school—the new names for the seasons and all that. I said something about Lent having its own season, so why not Advent since they were both church seasons, and here we were kicking off the whole liturgical year with the First Sunday of Advent Mass. He was probably a little surprised that I remembered all that (and I may have been surprised as well); but since Biggsy wasn't one to be caught off guard, ever, whether he had really thought this through three months ago or had made it up on the spot, either way he dove right in and said something about Lent needing its own season since it was almost two months long and felt even longer with going to Mass every day and Stations of the Cross every Friday. Advent, on the other hand was very short—four weeks at most and sometimes even shorter if the 4th Sunday comes close to Christmas. And besides, he argued, once Thanksgiving comes, nobody thinks about Advent, only about Christmas.

I said Okay or nothing and we served the Mass as usual and that was that. The next day, Monday, Bernie asked us (which was the same as ordered us) to ask our parents if they would support the building of the sisters' new convent—not the house across the schoolyard where all St. Anthony's nuns went after school and lived and ate and slept and prayed, but the bigger building in nearby Glen Riddle where they planned to build a convent and school for training new nuns. But rather than just asking for money, they were selling an album of Christmas music, performed by the novices and postulates in their existing facility. My mom said OK so a couple of days later I brought in the money (it was like five dollars, maybe less) and brought home the album. It was called *In Sweet Rejoicing* and I know because I still have it. When I looked at the song titles, I recognized some such as "Away in a Manger," "O Come All Ye Faithful," "Joy to the World," and "The Friendly Beasts." Some titles were in Latin and generally unrecognizable, although when I looked at the first song on the first side—"In Dulci Jubilo"—I knew enough Latin from being an altar boy and even before that from following along in my missal that had the English and Latin in side-by-side columns on the same page to figure out that the album title had come from that song because that same part of the word *dulce* was in the prayer "Salve Regina" also known as "Hail Holy Queen"—*vita dulcedo et spes nostra* (our life, our sweetness and our hope). I guess Biggsy's lesson the year before about etymologies had stayed with me to some degree. I put the album on the turntable and listened to the first couple of songs—very high voices singing to a solo piano—then went to put it away in the cabinet where our family stored its records near my mom's Sinatra and Judy Garland and Broadway musical albums and my older brother's Joan Baez and Kingston Trio when I noticed the *West Side Story* album was sitting outside the cabinet, leaning against the cabinet door, and remembered the time my mother persuaded my father to take us all to New York to see the show when I was only eight.

I stared at the album cover for a few minutes. It was the original 1957 soundtrack of the Broadway cast, and I read the names of the leads as I had many times over the six years since we'd seen the show—Carol Lawrence, Chita Rivera, Russ Tamblyn and Larry Kert—and saw the image on the cover of the characters Tony and Maria running down a New York street, looking absolutely and deliriously joyful. On that trip we had stayed at the Roosevelt Hotel, and in my memory I could still see the towels with the hotel name on them in big blue block letters. I put on that album and listened to the opening instrumental pieces, then the "Jet Song" which I had always liked, especially the line "*The Jets are in gear, our cylinders are clicking.*" The song after that—"Something's Coming"—I only vaguely remembered, but when I went to lift the needle and move it to another track I stopped when I heard this line: "*There's something due any day, I will know right away soon as it shows.*" I kept listening:

The air is humming. And something great is coming.

One of the prayers the altar boys say with the priest at Mass in Latin popped into my head—the "Pater Noster" ("Our Father")—and especially the phrase "adveniat regnum tuum" ("thy kingdom come"). Then Advent and Adveniat and West Side Story all got tossed together in my head. Something's coming. Christmas was certainly something we all looked forward to, mostly to be off, get presents, usher in winter to play outside and possibly miss school on snow days, and most of my life, perhaps presaging Biggy's revised season system, I had considered Advent as an annoying delay, making us wait four long weeks instead of moving right into the holidays as soon as Thanksgiving was over. But then I thought about Tony sensing, intimating that something wonderful was coming into his life. He didn't know, couldn't have known, that it would be Maria, and that soon after that life-changing arrival he would be running down the street with her in sweet rejoicing. But as he sang that song it almost seemed that he was experiencing a *different* kind of rejoicing—the unbridled joy of anticipation. The joy when what you want and what you expect is still out there, still waiting to happen, still whole and entire and unbroken until the time it finally arrives, after which the other kind of joy, the joy of having and experiencing what you were waiting for begins.

I had to serve the 6:30 AM Mass some weekday mornings in Advent, and riding my bike in the dark of the continually shortening day as the streetlight shadows crept up behind and finally overtook me as I rode I could also see and feel the early December frosty mornings and the just-rising sun, backlighting the trees whose bare branches seemed to be scratching, tickling, prodding, nudging awake the orange stripes on the horizon. The air was crisp. Humming. Something great was coming. Winter. Christmas. Mary into Bethlehem. The virgin birth. The Son of God into that humble stable surrounded by even humbler friendly beasts the ox and ass the nuns sang about, and angels and shepherds, yes, yes all of that. But something else, too. Could it be? Yes it could. Something's coming, something good. If I can wait. If I can wait.

Holiday Hiatus

Nancy sent an email to the Reunion Committee the week after Thanksgiving saying, simply, "I think it's safe to say we probably won't be able to get together consistently until after the new year, so let's take a planning break and pick it up again in January. For any of us that can get to Buddy's these next few Fridays, great, but no pressure. Let's just relax and enjoy the season. Actually though, reunion-wise, I think we're in pretty good shape, in terms of what we've done and still need to do and how much time we have left etc. I've already reserved the room and Paul tells me the memory booklet and song list are well under control so a little hiatus will probably do us all some good." (Actually, Nancy would essentially be the only one benefitting from a hiatus and actually taking and needing a break because she was the only one doing any consistent work.)

Paul hit "Reply All" and wrote, simply, "Sounds good."

Robbie Hannum responded to Paul's message copying the rest of the group saying, "Ditto for me. Merry Christmas everyone CU next year ;)" referencing their little joke from back in the day.

After a few more seasons greetings flew back and forth, Paul replied just to Nancy saying, "How's that list shaping up?"

An hour or so later Nancy wrote back with "What do you mean?"

As soon as Paul's phone pinged he read Nancy's message and wrote back, "You know, like who have you heard from so far, who's coming (I mean outside our core group of regulars)? That kind of thing."

Nancy responded, "Thinking of anyone in particular? ;)" after which Paul wrote "???" so Nancy responded, "No, Paul; Mary Liz has not yet responded to any of the social media invitations and I don't even know any other way to get ahold of her.

Now it was his turn to ask, "What do you mean?" but Nancy came back with, "God, Paul! You are so transparent. Everyone assumes you want to know if we've heard from Mary Liz and whether or not she's coming."

Before Paul responded, and he wasn't sure he was going to, Nancy wrote back, "You never had to say anything. We all knew. Then and now."

Paul didn't comment on her assumptions, but a few hours later wrote back, simply, "Merry Christmas."

The book on Mary Elizabeth Albarelli back in the day was that she was just way too much girl for any of the boys in her class. She started developing what Paul later learned in medical school were called her "secondary sex characteristics" as early as fifth grade, but back then her classmates just noticed more roundness around her hips and of course some telltale symmetric bulging on the right and left sides of her upper chest, but way ahead of any of the other girls in the class. Her dark brown wavy hair had always come to just above her shoulders, but by sixth grade when she had briefly been Gerry Giordano's girlfriend right after the first-ever boy-girl party for their St. Anthony's class and the little bit of spin-the-bottle kissing that went on there, the time she had shown up with that prominent dark brown eyeliner (a couple of the girls in the class had started wearing eye makeup at that age, but on Mary Liz it made her already dark eyes look even darker, more exotic), she had let it grow until it reached the middle part of her back.

For a short while at the end of seventh grade she had a little thing with Robbie Hannum that pretty much culminated in their making out at her infamous birthday party, albeit briefly. But it was almost as if in the confusion and clamor of the scene that ended her party she decided to repudiate the boys at St. Anthony's and the small potatoes of love at the elementary school level, because during the summer between seventh and eighth grades a few of the girls heard that she was dating guys in high school who undoubtedly assumed based on her appearance that she must also be 15 or 16 or maybe even 17, which was more or less confirmed at a July splash party at the Springhaven Township Swim Club when someone had even seen her walk off into the shadows behind the snack bar with Tommy Crocker who was going into his sophomore year at Springhaven High, which was even more scandalous because after leaving St. Anthony's Tommy hadn't taken the usual and preferred Catholic diocesan pathway to Bishop Keenan's, so she was fooling around with a "public."

Anyway, they sort of counted her out of their league, assuming they would never be able to handle her after she'd done God knows what with Tommy Crocker and God knows who else, which was just as well, because reports from Gerry and Robbie were that Mary Liz was a real tease. She apparently would feign affection, then drop you, then want you back, especially if someone else liked you at the same time, presumably to prove that she could have any boy she wanted at any time even if it meant stealing him from another girl (which was generally true and the beginning of some combination of admiration, resentment and estrangement on the part of Nancy and a few of the other girls in the class), and on and on until she ended things for good. At the same time, reportedly, when things were good, they were very good, which only increased the desire to touch that roundness or even be close to it. Paul was just as attracted as any other boy in the class (or at least any boy with sufficient testosterone because it was almost impossible not to be, as she was literally head and rounded shoulders above the other girls in the class in pure magnetic sexual energy), but maybe even more than most of the others because of that time at the St. Eugene's dance. And knowing some of the Mary Liz's lovelife history/mythology as it existed at the time he wasn't completely unprepared when he was drawn even more forcefully into the Mary Liz gravitational field that Christmas of 1963, not that it necessarily helped him handle it particularly well.

Season of Giving

Paul didn't ask "What time?" or even "Why?" He just said "OK." When Mary Elizabeth Albarelli says "Come over tonight" and you are Paul Perdu who is attracted to her as are most other sexually-awakened boys in the class, but even more than that thinks about her when he gets up in the morning and all day at school and before he goes to bed at night and whenever he hears almost any love song on the radio that's all you can say. And she didn't ask "CAN you come over" because she knew without even having to think about it or having to wonder if he could that he most certainly would find a way even if he technically couldn't, so she didn't ask that and answered the questions he was too dumbstruck to ask himself. "After dinner. About 7:00. Come to the side door." Mary Liz's house on Cedar Street across Timberline and past the church on the way to MacNamee's drug store had the usual front and back doors but her dad had built a little den off the side of the house, a detail Paul had memorized along with the location of the window dormers that always made him wonder which bedroom might be hers and the dark brown shingles that matched a number of other houses on that part of the street (years later when he learned that the shingles were made of cedar he had a "Duh" moment when he realized or suspected but was never able to confirm that the street took its name from some original house with the same exterior) and every other detail of that house whenever he walked by it on the way to MacNamee's. And then finally, "I have something for you."

He didn't even hear that. He was already thinking ahead, realizing he might actually have some trouble getting there. It was Monday, December 23rd, and they had just gotten out of school for the holiday after the usual half day the day before Christmas Eve. That half day always ended at the church, more specifically in the church basement, the only room large enough to hold the whole student body since the school didn't have an auditorium or any large indoor gathering spaces after they had converted the former lunchroom (not a cafeteria, not a place to serve food, just a large room with long green tables where the students from every grade would line up their lunch bags or lunch boxes—all labeled with their names—on their designated grade tables at the beginning of the school day, and walk down during lunch period around noon pick up their bags and boxes and sit at those same designated tables and eat quickly to leave more time for recess, and where on Fridays which were still meatless in those pre-Vatican II days and you would walk into that room around noon when the lunches had been sitting out at room temperature for over three hours and the smell of tuna fish curled up like a cartoon vapor cloud fist and punched them in their noses) into two new first grade classrooms way back when he was in third grade to accommodate the burgeoning baby boomer population, which was fine with Paul given the bad memory of that room when he was in second grade and some boy in the school had shit his pants and stuffed them in the trashcan in the boys' lavatory and Hiram the janitor had found them and reported it to Sr. Marcellina the principal at the time and she made every boy in every class march down to the lunchroom and line up along the wall and reach into his pants and pull up the elastic band of his underpants to show her to prove his innocence and Paul remembered feeling shame, not wanting anyone and least of all a fearsome black-habited white-starched-cloth-face-framed nun to see his underwear and he remembered sweating, even shaking, even though he had an elastic band to show (the guilty boy was Joseph Carlino in fourth grade, poor kid with a bad case of the runs that got in trouble with teacher, principal, and later on would be in worse trouble with his parents, but every kid in the school old enough to wonder what it would have been like to sit in those poop-filled shorts all day, not to mention what it would have smelled like in the classroom, actually felt sorry for him, even though he was kind of a queer—their word for a dork back in those days).

And where Father Ellis always made a little speech about the true meaning of Christmas, and that even though he knew they were all looking forward to being out of school for a week and getting presents they needed to remember that it was the birthday of Jesus and they needed to give him the present of their worship and devotion and good behavior—the same little speech that had been part of his sermon at the 9 o'clock Children's Mass the day before—and how they shouldn't get too comfortable being off and to remember to study because they would have mid-term exams when they returned just after New Year's, but he hoped they would have a merry and holy Christmas just the same, a major buzzkill decades before that term existed, and then every kid in the school would march up to the stage/altar and Fr. Ellis would hand out a little box of hard candy that had a holly leaf print on the outside, and from there they were free to either walk home or head back to the school to get the bus, a bike, or into a waiting parent's car. Paul and Gerry Giordano and some of the guys were getting ready to cross Timberline on Cedar to head up to Sycamore together with some of the girls, but before Mary Liz peeled away to go in the opposite direction on Cedar to go home she came up to Paul and said, "Come here a minute," and as they walked away from the group she continued, "Come over tonight."

The trouble he might have was that his family was supposed to get and decorate their Christmas tree that night. Usually they did this on Christmas Eve, but this year they were going to his Aunt Josephine's in South Philly for Christmas Eve dinner and the seven fishes which Paul hated but he liked the spaghetti so there wouldn't be time to do the tree the next day since his dad had to work. So how could he get out of that? He had also decided to ask Gerry to go with him, partly because he was scared—he still had no idea why Mary Liz wanted him to come over—and also Gerry would help add credence to whatever lie he would have to tell his parents to be able to go out while the family was starting to put up the tree and the trains since Paul was not usually just a part of that but now at age 13 he would be an integral part with some of the heavier lifting and always liked setting up the train platform in their knotty pine-paneled finished basement—the 4-foot-by-8-foot sheet of plywood covered in green felt and on which the track was permanently nailed—on top of the two sawhorses and putting out the small fake trees around the track while his dad carefully took out the train cars from their boxes and then loading the little oil pellets into the locomotive stack where they would later make smoke when the engine got hot, so he said he and Gerry just had to stop at Biggsy's house to see his trains and the Biggs family had never had trains before and everyone knew how poor they were so it was a big deal and Paul's mom said they had all week between Christmas and New Year's to see those trains, what was the rush, and Paul thinking fast said, I don't know, he wanted us to come and see them tonight, we won't be out that long, and Paul felt secure that his mom would never talk to Biggsy's mom to verify that story, so she just said OK, but don't be long, so he was free for an hour or so, and he walked to Gerry's who was already waiting outside.

As they walked Gerry said, "What do you think she wants?" and Paul said he didn't know, but she had said she had something to give him. Gerry wondered if it might be a Christmas present and asked if Paul had anything for her. Why would she give him a Christmas present? They weren't going steady. In fact the rumor was she was dating a high school kid, consistent with the usual understanding about her lovelife practices. But what if it were a present? He didn't have anything for her. But why would he? They had never exchanged gifts before. As they approached her house on Cedar they saw the outdoor Christmas lights. Paul's dad just put a few strings of lights on the blue spruce tree in their front yard and had installed a spotlight on their front porch to shine on the door wreath, and both the tree lights and the spotlight were plugged into a small light bulb-holder-extender with two electrical outlets that screwed into the bulb socket on the front door light, but Mary Liz's dad went all out with lights on trees, bushes, around and framing the porch, and even a Santa and reindeer up on the roof.

Paul looked at the side door where Mary Liz told him to come. It was all dark so he and Gerry just stared at it a minute or two until Gerry said, "Go ahead." Paul started walking to the door by himself. Gerry wanted to stand on the sidewalk, figuring it wouldn't be long, predicting Mary Liz wouldn't have much to say and that even if Paul had a lot to say he would be too anxious to say it. Paul walked up to the side door, after first checking to see that lights were on in the front room—guessing or hoping her dad would be in there watching TV after dinner, although maybe the TV was in that den he had built—and also on in the kitchen where her mom was probably doing the dishes. Would Mary Liz be helping her, and not be ready to greet him at the side door? The side room looked dark and Paul's heart began to sink. Did she forget? She had said after dinner, about 7:00. It had to be at least 7:00 based on when Paul had left his house. Did he mishear her? Was it a different night? It couldn't be tomorrow, that was Christmas Eve.

These thoughts raced through his head as he kept walking, and as he stepped over some dry autumn leftover oak leaves that crunched underfoot he heard a dog start barking inside. He didn't know they had a dog; he didn't remember ever seeing one outside whenever he walked by. He stopped walking but the dog kept barking, and then he saw a silhouette move in the front room. Was that her dad? Paul stood frozen on her lawn, midway between the sidewalk and the side door, when a light came on in the side room, and then the lantern outside the door. Paul could hear the dog, then a low faint voice from inside (almost certainly her dad, saying, "Shut up... Shut UP!"). Then the side door opened and he saw her dad illuminated from behind by the room light who shouted, "Who is that? Who's out there?" Paul was thinking he should turn back but he was still frozen there when Mary Liz appeared in the doorway, holding the neck collar of a large black dog that was trying to jump and lunge forward saying, "It's OK. It's

OK." With the dog still yelping and lunging her dad said again, "Who is it?" and Mary Liz responded, "It's OK. It's for me. Go back upstairs."

As her dad turned and walked out of the doorway after delivering one more "Shut up" Mary Liz said to Paul, "It's OK. Come on up." As Paul continued to stand there she said again, "Come on. He won't bite." As Paul started walking toward the door the dog was jumping, trying to free himself from Mary Liz's grip as she said, softly, "It's OK, Atlas. It's OK. It's just Paul. It's OK." As he got to the door the dog leaped as if to jump up on him and Paul instinctively stepped back. Mary Liz said, first to the dog, "It's OK, Atlas; it's OK" then to Paul "Do you like my new puppy?" Looking at the dog that stood thigh-high next to Mary Liz when it wasn't jumping Paul blurted out, "That's a puppy?" Looking back at the dog she said in a softer cooing baby-talk sort of voice, "He's just a baby, aren't you. Aren't you my little baby?" Then to Paul, "This is my Christmas puppy. His name is Atlas."

"Atlas?" Paul repeated, attempting gingerly to pat the dog on the head and not appear too outwardly cowardly in front of Mary Liz since, for the moment at least, the "puppy" was sitting calmly.

"Like the strong man," Mary Liz said, then to the dog in that baby-talk voice again, "Aren't you my strong man? Aren't you? It's OK. Go inside, baby; go inside, Atlas. Good boy. Good baby."

"What kind of dog is that?" Paul asked. Mary Liz said it was a Black Lab. "Is he going to get bigger than that?" Paul asked. "Oh yeah," Mary Liz said. "He's just a puppy."

She had stepped out onto the lawn and closed the storm door behind her, and Paul could see Atlas sitting there by the lower glass pane. Paul looked at her in the half light from the lantern, and when she smiled it was as if another light from somewhere were illuminating her face. "Here," she said, handing him a small wrapped box. "Merry Christmas." Paul just said, instinctively, "Thanks," then starting to stammer a little, "I didn't know this was why…I didn't…I don't have anything for you…I didn't…" but she cut him off, "That's OK. You don't have to get me anything. I just wanted you to have this. Go ahead; open it."

Paul started to unwrap the gift, fumbling a little in the half darkness until he could feel as it moved and almost see that it was a bottle with a liquid inside. "It's Jade East," she said.

"Jade East?" Paul repeated.

"Yes, Jade East," Mary Liz said. "It's a cologne. Have you ever heard of

"'Atlas?'" Paul repeated, attempting gingerly to pat the dog on the head and not appear too outwardly cowardly in front of Mary Liz..."

it?"

Gathering his wits Paul said, "Yeah, sure." In fact Paul did know about Jade East, as it was one of the four most popular colognes boys his age were wearing, besides English Leather, Aqua de Selva, and Canoe, and along with Right Guard underarm spray to cover whatever off-smells were arising from their churning sweat glands to hopefully attract (and not repel) the opposite sex.

"I had smelled this on a guy I was dancing with at the St. James dance (a Catholic high school in Chester to which Paul would have gone the following year if the more proximal Bishop Keenan hadn't opened the previous year) a few weeks ago and asked him what it was. It smelled nice on him and I thought it would smell nice on you."

"Thanks," Paul said again, "but I don't have anything..."

"It's fine," Mary Liz interrupted again. "You don't have to get me anything. Merry Christmas. See you tomorrow night."

And with that she turned and went back inside through the side door as the dog started barking and jumping again and Mary Liz said, her voice muffled now from behind the glass, "It's OK, baby. It's OK" and her dad, even more muffled from behind glass and a floor up in the front room, "Shut up!"

Paul tried to analyze and discuss all of this with Gerry as they walked home briskly to be able to help with the Christmas tree setup and decorating without raising too many suspicions. What did it mean? Had she wanted him to dance with her that night back in the fall at St. Eugene's when he so much wanted to too when "Forever" played but was too timid to ask? Did she want him to ask her to dance the next time he went if she went too if grade school dances weren't too tame for her? Would she ask him? Did she want to go steady? Or was it too late? She was already going to dances at St. James so maybe it was true that she was dating an older kid with whom she obviously danced close enough to smell his Jade East. Maybe they were even making out, or doing something in the backseat of a car. Was she saying that he had no chance with her, but if he ever wanted to get a girl anything like her this is what he would need to wear? And what did she mean by "See you tomorrow night?"

"Tomorrow night is Christmas Eve, you idiot," Gerry said. "Midnight Mass."

In the excitement Paul had forgotten that he and a number of other altar boys would be serving at Midnight Mass and of course the school choir would be there with Mary Liz in her usual spot on the right side of the choir loft (Paul's left looking from the altar) with the rest of the sopranos.

Paul had nothing for her, but there was still time to get something to give to her after Mass. But what? He couldn't ask his mom. And he had no money, except those silver dollars his parents' friend Phil Avery had been giving him and his brother every Christmas for the last five years and about which his dad had said never to spend them but to keep collecting and someday maybe each one would be worth more than one dollar, but this was kind of an emergency. So with the Christmas tree having gone up the night before and Paul's dad working a half day so they could drive to South Philly to his Aunt Jo's for an early dinner (like 4:30), Paul had most of Christmas Eve morning free. He had to tell another lie—that he was going over to Gerry's—which was pretty normal for him to do so his Mom accepted it as such and only said to be back by 2:00 so he could get cleaned up for dinner. He decided to walk up to the Strawbridge and Clothier department store on Springhaven Road and wandered among the last-minute shoppers, the crush of people, music, gold and red banners and ribbons, and perfume counter smells on the ground floor. What should he get? Perfume? He had no idea what she might like, and he hadn't danced with any girls recently (or actually ever) that might have clued him in to what was popular. He took the escalator to the third floor which left him off right at the jewelry counter, the same one where Richie Brennan said he had bought a "friendship ring" in seventh grade for Nancy Hendrick for two dollars, but they were going steady and Paul couldn't do the same with Mary Liz, at least not yet. Except what did it mean that she had given him a gift?

The glass cases had watches, bracelets, rings, necklaces, earrings, and on top of the counter there was a 3-sided rotating vertical display of rings inserted into small felt slots covered with glass doors. Paul was staring at it when he heard a woman's voice say, "Can I help you?" Paul looked up to see a woman about his mother's age, maybe a little younger, smiling, wearing a red sweater and a green and red checked scarf.

"Need a friendship ring for someone? I'm sure whoever the girl is she would love one of these as a Christmas present?"

"I don't know," Paul stammered. "I just..." but the saleswoman interrupted him.

"We have a lot of other lovely pieces of jewelry she might like, too.

Earrings, bracelets…how about a little charm bracelet?"

She directed Paul's attention to one of the glass cases. There were so many bracelets. Too many. Then he noticed a small chain-link bracelet with one charm—a dog.

"What about this one?" Paul asked, pointing.

"Oh that's a sweet little bracelet and there's already a charm on there. Does she have a little puppy?" Paul nodded. "Let me take it out and show you."

She reached into the case and took out the bracelet and laid it on a small piece of black felt. The dog charm didn't look like Atlas, but at least it was a dog. Paul wasn't sure but he didn't have a whole lot of time so he also wanted to get something quickly and get out. He had never been in here by himself before and was very uncomfortable. He could feel his palms and armpits sweating.

"How much?" Paul asked.

"Let's look at the price tag," she said, turning over the bracelet to look at and show him the small piece of cardboard attached by a string to one of the bracelet links.

"$3.50," she said.

Paul had five silver dollars in his pocket. "You really think she'll like it?" he asked.

"Of course," she said, "What girl wouldn't? Does she have a dog?"

"Yeah," Paul said, "she just got one for Christmas."

"Perfect" she said.

Paul walked briskly home from Strawbridge's, having stuffed the wrapped box into his right pea coat pocket (luckily it was small enough to fit where he usually stored his right glove so he had stuffed the right glove in with the left glove in the left pocket which now bulged). When he walked in the door his mother was getting the dough ready for the fried bread/doughnuts they always made on Christmas Eve (some would be stuffed with olives, some with anchovies which Paul hated and some dusted with powdered sugar like a real doughnut which Paul loved). He stayed in full stride when he walked in the kitchen door so as not to attract any undue attention and it worked because his mother called out to him as he breezed by only to say "You'd better get upstairs and get cleaned up; we have to leave at quarter to 4:00."

With the charm bracelet still sitting safely and snugly in his overcoat pocket, Paul went into the one upstairs bathroom he shared with his older brother. He had been experimenting with shaving the past few months, shearing off the wispy whiskers on his upper lip and straightening out his sideburn edges every few weeks or so (maybe in preparation for a dance or party) with the old safety razor his dad had given him and shown him how to use and how to use his tongue to puff out his lip to ensure a cleaner shave. This seemed like a fitting occasion for another shave, and would also serve as a built-in excuse to use the Jade East. His brother kept pounding on the bathroom door saying, "Come on! What's taking so long? I have to get in there." Finally the door opened and Paul emerged out of the steam looking and feeling cleaner and smoother-faced than he ever had, even as his brother waved his towel to clear the air saying, "It stinks in here."

When Paul walked into the kitchen to ask his mother again what time they were leaving she asked, "What's that smell?"

Paul replied, "After shave."

"Well," his mom said, "I sure hope you showered first, 'cause stink on top of stink is a bad combination."

"What time?" Paul repeated.

"Quarter to four," his mother responded.

"I have to be at church by 11" Paul said, "Fr. Galvin said even a few minutes earlier if possible."

His mother said, "We'll have plenty of time. We're eating at 5:00 and we can't stay down there all night."

All the way to Aunt Jo's Paul underwent gentle teasing from his brother and even his father about the "after shave." "Who do you need to smell so special for?" his brother taunted. "I'll bet it's Mary Liz Albarelli." "Shutup," Paul came back, while his brother laughed and even his father chuckled. And all through dinner Paul kept wondering if they would leave in enough time, and twice he had gone into his Aunt Jo's bedroom where all their coats had been placed on the bed to check the pocket of his pea coat to be sure the gift was still in there, that it hadn't fallen out or been taken out. Paul ate quickly and probably overdid the sugared fried dough (which might have been responsible for some the abdominal rumbles that were emanating from the back seat of the car on the way home), and asked his mother every 20 minutes or so "What time are we leaving?" After the third or fourth time she just said "We'll leave when we leave, now stop asking." They left around 8:00 and were home by about 8:45. As his mother had said, plenty of time.

The usual hectic mix of cars pulling up to the front entrance of the church on Timberline Avenue, dropping off altar boys each toting a cassock and surplice plus choir girls plus older parishioners who couldn't easily walk from the street-only parking on Cedar and wanted to get there an hour ahead of time to get a good seat was only made worse by the darkness. Fortunately for Paul's dad they were able to pull up to the side entrance by the sacristy and didn't have to deal with the craziness in front.

"Thanks, Dad" Paul said as he clambered out of the front seat, his one hand in the pocket securing the gift still sitting in there that he had guarded from the walk home from Strawbridge's, all the way in the car to Aunt Jo's, as it sat in his coat pocket on the bed in Aunt Jo's guest room, all the way home, and now on the ride to church.

"I'll be back at 1:00" his father said, "so be sure you're out here and ready."

"Better make it 1:15," Paul said, not only because Midnight Mass often ran over an hour, but he also wanted to pad the time a little to be able to give Mary Liz her gift in case he couldn't deliver it ahead of time, which was the original plan to ensure it was delivered safely so he wouldn't have to carry it in his pants pocket at Mass, although the cassock would certainly obscure it.

"Do you know what time I got up this morning?" Paul's father asked. It was true; his dad had been up at 6:00, worked a full day at his appliance store, came home to pick up the family and drive to South Philly to Aunt Jo's, then back again, and now to church and after 1:00 AM back to church again.

"Sorry," Paul said, mostly to himself as he closed the door and watched his dad pull out to make the U-turn and head back down Cedar.

Paul watched from the top of the side entrance steps until his dad had gone through the light at Cedar and Timberline before scampering down the steps again and running to the front entrance where he hoped to accidentally run into Mary Liz and give her the gift. Car after car pulled up and practically every choir girl except Mary Liz filed past him and up the front steps. Finally he had to desert his post and head to the sacristy where Biggsy was already garbed up and waiting.

"You're late," Biggsy chirped, "Let's go."

"Just a second," Paul said, "I have to check something."

"Let's GO!" Biggsy repeated, "Galvin said he wanted the candles lit by quarter after 11 and it's past 10 after. What do you have to check?"

Paul just ignored him and stepped into the narrow walkway behind the altar between the altar boys' sacristy and the priest's sacristy, where he was mostly obscured by the wooden wall at the back of the altar but could peek out the lattice work to see out into the church. The place was already packed. He scanned the pews and saw the faces of neighbors, and other schoolchildren that would be allowed to stay up late. He gazed up to the choir loft to make sure Mary Liz was in her usual spot where she could look down at the congregation, but she wasn't there. That was odd. He didn't see her get dropped off, so he had assumed she was already up there. Shifting his gaze slightly to the right he saw Sr. Sanctissima, the choir director and organist, from the back, wondering if maybe Mary Liz was talking to her. But no. Sanctissima's skinny frame was bustling around with music books and getting the organ ready. He looked over the rest of the choir area to see if Mary Liz might be talking to someone else, but no sign of her. From behind him Biggsy barked again, "Come on now or else I'll do them all myself." Finally he saw her enter the frame and make her way across the loft from right to left. Maybe she had arrived later than he thought. He watched her a few more seconds, wondering if she knew he was looking up at her, and if there was a chance she was looking and trying to find his eyes behind the lattice. As he was about to turn back he noticed Fr. Galvin walking quickly up the side aisle heading for the priest's sacristy. He was running late too.

Paul walked back inside the sacristy, hung up his coat on the coat rack and took his cassock and surplice off the hanger where his mother had put them after ironing them about an hour before. There was enough of a bustle inside the sacristy with other altar boys getting ready (they would be the acolytes for the procession and stand by the sides of the aisles, while Paul and Biggsy would be serving the Mass) for Paul to slip the gift box under his shirt and quickly button up the cassock and slip on the surplice which was loose and billowy enough that no one would notice the bulge. It was too risky to leave it inside his coat; other items had been stolen out of the sacristy over the years. Then he and Biggsy grabbed the candlelighters, advanced the wicks just enough to hold a flame without going out but also not burning out too quickly—they were pros—and walked out onto the altar holding the candle lighters in their right hands and their left hands against their chests. After bowing at the foot of the altar (genuflecting with the candle lighters was dicey so Fr. Galvin had said a bow was enough) they walked up and to the top step and Biggsy took the three candles on the left and Paul the three candles on the right—their usual routine. After each was done (and they almost always finished if not exactly at the same time then within a second or two of each other), they turned and walked back down the steps. Paul cast a quick glance up at the loft and just barely caught sight of Mary Liz and just as quickly looked down to be sure he didn't trip on his cassock (that had happened once in sixth grade when he was a newbie and he went down the steps on the side of the altar and dropped and broke the cruets, spilling wine on the green altar carpet. Once was enough to teach him to take the steps with care), got to the bottom, bowed again, and walked back into the sacristy.

At exactly 11:30 Fr. Ellis, the pastor, started switching off the church lights from the electrical panel in the priest's sacristy, that loud familiar click of those old circuit switches until the church was in almost total darkness. Then Fr. Galvin, Biggsy and Paul walked out of the priest's sacristy and into the sanctuary—Biggsy holding the large candle to lead the procession and Paul holding the censer and incense-container with the flip lid and spoon, the frankincense smoke wafting up into his face which he liked, to walk behind Fr. Galvin with the rest of the acolyte altar boys following the priest. Fr. Galvin bowed and the procession went through the open gate of the altar rail, across the right side of the front aisle and down the right side aisle to line up at the back of the church. As soon as they were in place, Sister Sanctissima (who had been leaning over the choir loft half wall so she could see when he was ready, and even in the near-total darkness she could see Fr. Galvin nod) raised her black baggy-sleeved arms, and as she brought them down the choir started "Adeste Fidelis," the great welcoming song of Christmas, and the procession began. Across the back, up the left side aisle, across the front, down the center aisle, across the back and finally up the same right side aisle they had walked down and across the front and up onto the altar as the choir kept singing and Fr. Ellis in the sacristy started switching on the lights again. By this time the choir was into the third English verse, "O yea, Lord we greet thee, born this happy morning..." Fr. Galvin and all the altar boys waited at the foot of the altar for the singing to stop. Then the acolytes walked back to the center aisle to take their places next to the first seven pews on each side (where the first seat in each of those pews was reserved for them, marked by a strand of red ribbon tied to the pew set back and draped into the first seat space.

Paul didn't typically pay a lot of attention at Mass, not even when he was serving (unlike back in 5th grade when he followed along in his missal, reading every one of the priest's words in Latin even before he knew what he was saying, all the way up to the first half of sixth grade when he was memorizing the Latin prayers and understood them and said them so fervently and was entertaining thoughts about becoming a priest until the second half of that year when the testosterone started flowing and that was the end of that), having served so many times that every "et cum spiritu tuo," every bow, every genuflect was on autopilot. Usually this left him ample time for his mind to wander, which usually meant imagining the choir girls and especially Mary Liz looking at him, thinking he must look pretty cool up there, in costume, knowing all the right moves and even a foreign language. But this time when he wasn't fidgeting to keep the gift box in the right position inside his shirt he was thinking about the moment he would give Mary Liz the gift and wondering what he would say.

The Mass dragged on: Confiteor, Gospel, Credo, Orate Fratres, Pater Noster, Communion (at least here he could distract himself by this performance part of the service, where he would walk next to the priest, holding the paten under each communicant's chin to catch the host should it fall off the person's tongue or not make contact in the first place. Then the clean up of the chalice, the reassembly with paten and drape into that perfect trapezoid shape, and finally the closing prayers and the "Ite missa est" (Go, the Mass is ended) and the final song, "Joy to the World," with Mary Liz driving the soprano parts, the first "heaven and nature sing" quiet, the next one a little louder, and the third one louder still leading up to the final, triumphant, melismatic "CHRII-IIST, THE LORD!"

He and Biggsy and Fr. Galvin walked back into the sacristy where the priest said "Merry Christmas, Boys" and they replied, almost in unison, "Merry Christmas, Father," and Galvin again, "It's pretty late so I'll take care of my vestments, just put out the candles and you can go."

"Thank you Father" they said, again almost perfectly in sync, and they walked quickly behind the altar to the other sacristy, grabbed the candle lighters and twisted them to the other side with the big bell shaped candle snuffer, walked quickly back out, bowed, and walked up to the top step, snuffed the candles, walked back down and into the altar boys sacristy where Paul practically ripped off his cassock and surplice, rolled them into a ball, went back to the wooden wall and looked through the lattice to confirm that Mary Liz was still up in the choir loft (she was, helping Sister cover the organ), walked back and said "See ya" to Biggsy and grabbed his pea coat and in one smooth motion grabbed the gift box from inside his shirt and put it back in its former coat pocket home and ran to the side door after glancing quickly up at the clock on the sacristy wall that said about five after one.

Stepping outside he could see that his dad was already waiting, parked across Timberline along the curb on Cedar, so Paul went back inside and walked down the side aisle while looking up and seeing the choir girls starting to file out, with Mary Liz pulling up the rear. He quickened his pace and got to the vestibule just as she was coming down the steps from the choir loft so that she almost ran into him. Stopping short and looking startled to see him at first, she quickly relaxed and smiled that beautiful half smile of hers that lifted her eyebrows and seemed to light up her whole face.

"Merry Christmas," she said.

"Merry Christmas," Paul responded.

They were alone in the vestibule. Paul's heart was pounding. He reached into his coat pocket and pulled out the box and extended it towards her saying, "Here. This is for you."

Mary Liz took it and said, warmly, "Oh, you didn't have to get me anything."

"I know," Paul said. "I wanted to."

"That's so sweet. Thank you." Then screwing up her nose slightly she said, "You're wearing the Jade East, aren't you?" Paul just nodded. "That's good," Mary Liz said; "it smells good on you. I knew it would."

For an instant Paul thought maybe she was going to kiss him, or wondered whether he should kiss her, but they were in church and it was late and his dad was waiting so he just blurted out, "I have to go."

"Merry Christmas," Mary Liz said again. "See ya next week."

But Paul was already out the doors and walking to the light at Timberline and Cedar to cross the street and get to his dad's car.

"Paul's heart was pounding. He reached into his coat pocket
and pulled out the box and extended it towards her..."

VI

Winter (January 2nd to Ash Wednesday)

Biggsy had said that the worst day of the year was Labor Day night with its sick sinking stomach pit feeling about the end of the long languid summer break and not New Year's Day night, because even though there was some of that same deep abdominal drop about returning to school, it wasn't as bad because it ended a shorter Christmas break compared to summer's much longer hiatus, but I disagreed. New Year's was much worse. Labor Day was bad, I will give him that, but at least there was autumn to look forward to as the gateway to a holiday season that started with Halloween and went on into Thanksgiving and Christmas. And I'll grudgingly admit that my mom was right that the early September preschool depression the night before and day of school restarting would usually lift as soon as I saw my classmates and friends in the school yard buzzing around before the first bell, and that was actually more true as I got into the later grades, and even truer still in 1963 when it included seeing Mary Liz again.

But the view ahead from a New Year's Day dark and cold evening was bleak, when the televised west coast Rose Bowl rubbed our noses into winter's chill with sights of golden sunshine in what was still a California afternoon, and the even golder pants and deep cardinal red uniforms of the USC football Trojans that had played in the previous year's game. I might have also suggested that Biggsy change the name of this season from "Winter" to "Winter Desert" for the period stretching from New Year's to Ash Wednesday because the skies always seemed gray and dreary and just about to snow, when all we could see ahead was a literally and figuratively barren terrain, cold and cold and snow and the only bright spots were the occasional (and in those pre-global-warming times, more frequent) reprieves of snow days and maybe to some degree the fun of sledding the big hill by the library and ice skating (either indoors at the Lansdowne Ice and Coal or, when it was cold enough long enough, outdoors on the pond that formed near the Crum Creek Dam) which were, in those days, the only available winter sports, but otherwise empty, and Ash Wednesday and spring were too far away to see.

The new year of 1964 held an unexpected bright spot that paralleled simply seeing Mary Liz when school started—seeing her again after New Year's and hopefully hearing how she liked the charm bracelet. I had not seen her since handing her the gift after Midnight Mass, so I had no idea how she felt about it. Did she appreciate that I had even included the dog charm, in honor of her new puppy? Did she wear it over the Christmas break? Did she show it off to family and friends? Did she say who had given it to her? Was it "some kid at school" or even "some boy" or maybe did she even mention my name? Would she have been coy in a way only she could be coy and say nothing, so that a cousin or an aunt might have said, "Who gave you that? Was it your boyfriend?" (because who else would give her such a gift?) and would they then have teased her about it "Ooooh, Mary Liz has a BOYfriend") and would she blush and look away grinning, proud that she did indeed have a real boyfriend who would have given her a real and nice gift? Would she have admitted that she had started it, the whole gift giving at Christmas thing, the kind of thing boyfriends and girlfriends do, and that it hadn't been just ANY gift to him but a bottle of cologne, a personal gift, something she wanted her boyfriend to wear when they were dancing close or making out, something she could smell to give her pleasure or to enhance the pleasure she already had just by being close enough dancing or kissing to smell it? Or would she have denied it ("No No No! He's NOT my boyfriend, just a boy in my class, I don't know, maybe he likes me but I don't like him, not as a boyfriend," or worse, "No No No, I have no idea why he gave it to me, I don't like it and I don't like him, he's gross," but then why was she wearing it)?

So even as depressing as it was to get through New Year's Day evening, dinner over, the company gone, my dad already asleep on the couch as the college football game played on, the clack of helmets banging in that bright TV screen Pasadena sunshine (but no USC this year), and the desire to stay up as long as I could because I knew, I always knew, that as soon as I went to sleep, vacation would be over, I felt that little bit of sun just knowing that the next day I would see Mary Liz. Would she wear the bracelet to school? Could she even? Were students (girls mostly, I guess) even allowed to wear jewelry like that to school? I don't remember any girls ever wearing any jewelry, or at least not anything that nice. It wouldn't take long to find out. After a toss-turn mostly sleepless night I eventually got up, washed up and dressed and splashed on some Jade East and headed for school, waving off the scrambled egg sandwich my mom had just thrown together in her tousled hair and blue plaid robe.

Mary Liz was not in the schoolyard, so after the second bell rang I ran to get in line. She didn't join the line as we waited, but as we were milling around in the hall outside the classrooms, Mary Liz finally sauntered in, black hair blacker than ever it seemed and dark brown eyes as soulful as ever. I glanced at her wrist—no bracelet that I could see, but it wasn't a perfect angle for seeing it. I never saw the bracelet, but I couldn't confirm, at least not for sure, that she WASN'T wearing it. She didn't really talk to anyone at recess, went home for lunch and right home by herself after school. Walking home myself that day winter became a winter desert again while that little bright oasis I had created in my head faded further and further into view behind me.

Reunion planning resumes

The Reunion Committee had decided that they would begin planning in earnest after the 2018-2019 Christmas-New Year's holidays. After she and Paul met with the manager at the Locust Crest Tavern, Nancy had signed the agreement and booked the banquet room for Saturday night, June 15th, 2019, two days after the actual feast day of St. Anthony of Padua therefore conforming as closely as possible to the old tradition but conceding to the logistical challenges of a Friday night social event considering work and travel schedules, and within three calendar dates of the actual date of the actual eighth-grade graduation party almost 55 years earlier which had been on Friday June 12, 1964 (the last day of school that year and their class's last day of elementary school before summer and before the wild wide world of high school ahead).

Locust Crest was a late 18th century tavern/inn selling alcoholic libations and offering lodging on what had been an old drover's road between Philadelphia and the farms to the west. It was one of the oldest buildings in Delaware County, built just before the American Revolution and still operating. Locust Crest had a reputation for being not just old but somewhat stodgy (and more than a little musty), a place for blue-haired older women to go for lunch, but in the past 4-5 years it had come under new ownership that had tried to preserve some of its historical character by repainting the interior with the familiar colonial grays and blues and tans and including menu items that could have been or were described in a way to suggest they actually were early American favorites such as "Brandywine" duck, "colonial" chicken pot pie, and "tavern" stew, along with more modern fare such as short ribs, salmon, fish tacos with mango salsa, hummus (in a "colonial crock," of course) and even a rotating seasonal vegan entree with quinoa. They had also added an outdoor seating area which they could use into later October and even early November if they turned on the outside gas heaters.

But the Committee still needed to finalize the menu, create the invitation and decide whether to send via US mail vs an email evite vs social media vs all of the above, and finally the music. They knew that once January hit the party would only be six months away, so Nancy's email to Paul and the other Reunion Committee members at 8:00 AM on January 2nd was right on schedule, short and to the point. The subject line said simply, "Reunion," and the message was, "Hope everyone had a good holiday, but time to get back to work. Buddy's on Thursday night at 7:00 for another planning session?" Paul's response was similarly short and direct: "Working 7p to 7a so can't get to Buddy's, but I am already working on the music and the memory booklet, so you guys can do what you want with the rest. p. "

Regarding the booklet, Paul's "working on" included what he had already written or at least sketched out in the fall, plus a single entry in January relating to Fr. Galvin's getting "canned" as Paul's father had said that Sunday in early January 1964, reading the story in the *Inquirer* about the allegedly "illegal" Mass Galvin had celebrated outside the formal structure of the Roman Catholic Latin rite. Paul decided not to get into Biggsy's theory at the time—that Galvin's dismissal was somehow linked to Janitor Hiram's death. Biggsy said he had befriended the new janitor, an indeterminately-aged older man named Leonard Schmidt (whom the nuns said to address as "Mr. Schmidt" but the boys usually called either Schmitty or just Leonard or even Lenny which often provoked him to say something like, "I'm gonna tell Sister Bernadette you called me that and you'll be in trouble, you'll see"), who always wore what appeared to be and smelled to be the same khaki shirt and pants every day, who had the same length of stubble every time they saw him—never shorter as if shaved and grown back, but never any longer either.

Leonard used to brag that he got his shoes for nothing at Donovan's Funeral Home and didn't care that they were dead men's shoes as long as they had decent soles and heels, and that back in the early 30's as a teenager he'd been in a vaudeville magic act as the magician's assistant and that he could get his hands out of being tied up in rope or handcuffed—any kind of binding up, just like Houdini—which Gerry Giordano and Robbie Hannum decided to test one afternoon in December on the football field at recess when Robbie had gone home for lunch and come back with a short length of rope from his garage, and to the delight of a gathering small crowd they grabbed Leonard's hands and started wrestling him down to the ground where Gerry sat on him and Robbie tied his hands behind him, laughing and saying "C'mon, Mr. Schmidt, let's see you get out of this, like the Great Leondini" and Leonard saying, repeatedly, "You sonofabitches, I'm gonna tell Sister, I'm gonna tell, you sonofabitches" even after the bell rang so almost everyone in the school yard could hear it, until Biggsy untied him and said that if Leonard didn't tell the nuns he would get him some cigarettes (which he probably stole from his older brother) and which is how he struck up a kind of relationship with him and was able to get inside the boiler room on a couple of occasions, which as far as Biggsy could tell looked pretty much as it did when Hiram lived there, and even asked him about the rat poison and where he kept it and could he see what it looked like, but Leonard said he wouldn't show him, couldn't show him, saying it was "too dangerous to even show a little kid," to which Biggsy replied "Well can you at least tell me how it works?" and Leonard said "It makes the rats bleed inside, and they lose so much blood they get so thirsty they have to run outside like they're crazy looking for something to drink and then they die looking and still bleeding or jump into water and drown."

"So you see" Biggsy told his chums, "Hiram could have bled to death, just like I said, and it could have been the rat poison."

"But what does that have to do with Galvin?" Paul had asked him.

"I don't know," Biggsy said, "or at least I don't know yet, but that's what I intend to find out. I still think Hiram knew something, and somebody wanted him out of the way, to keep him quiet forever."

"Galvin?" Paul exclaimed, incredulously.

"Why not?" Biggsy responded. "It's possible."

Instead Paul just included this simple statement in the booklet: "In early January, 1964, Fr. James Galvin, our assistant pastor and the supervisor of the altar boys was reassigned out of and far away from St. Anthony's. The papers said he'd had some conflict with diocesan authorities over celebrating an illegal guitar Mass in a motel room, although the very next year a lot of us repeatedly experienced guitar Masses in our high school auditorium, and all of it strictly legit. Go figure."

But the memory project didn't really get any traction until Paul started researching some of the media coverage from February 2014 which had been the 50th anniversary of the Beatles first visit to America. Paul found some newspaper articles; CBS-TV's *Sunday Morning* ran a story; the Grammy Awards did a tribute. Some of the commentators connected the Beatles to JFK, saying the country was in a deep depression and the Beatles brought them out of it. Maybe that was true, but Paul didn't remember it that way, which provided the memory spark he needed to start writing. Aiming and hoping to straighten out some of the revisionist history about the mood of the country in the wake of the JFK assassination and at the time the Beatles arrived, at least for those who were 13 and 14 years old at the time (and assuming, of course, that his mood was representative), he wrote the following:

"We were all really upset about JFK around the time he was assassinated, or at least I know I was. I had a scrapbook with pix of him, and was very interested in the whole PT 109 story because we were ALL (at least the boys) interested in World War Two (most of our dads had served, or at least I can't remember a neighbor my age or classmate whose dad hadn't, and distinctly recall that Gerry's dad had been a bombardier in the European theater and Robbie's dad had been at Iwo Jima), we watched *Combat* and *The Gallant Men* and *The Longest Day* on TV and at the movies etc. etc. And of course, JFK held a special appeal for Catholics. So yeah, we were upset, some more than others, since I remember that on that Monday Nov 25, the day of his funeral and the national day of mourning, we were all off from school which was always great for whatever reason. But when Gerry and Robbie knocked on my door to invite me to participate in a football game at 'the football field' (remember, that was what we called St. Anthony's field where we played CYO-league games on Saturday mornings and pick-up games at other weekend times and where the boys spent almost every school day recess in favorable weather playing touch football or fox-chase-the-geese or ball tag or whatever, thinking in our idiosyncratic way that *our* football field, the one owned and maintained by our school and used by its students was THE football field, the only football field that existed, and while we're on that subject, guys, do you believe we played tackle in full equipment—helmets, shoulder pads, thigh pads and spikes—just for casual pick-up games?), I had the vague sense that it somehow wouldn't be right. That it would be irreverent (although that word and concept weren't in my head). But my mom settled it for us— no football for me on the day we were burying our fallen youthful Catholic president."

Paul continued:

"But I don't remember brooding about JFK or obsessing over the assassination except for those few days and weeks around the end of November '63. The news in 2014, 50 years later, said we all were and did, but it doesn't ring true, at least not for me. Life went on. Thanksgiving came and went. Christmas came and went. Winter arrived. Then February and the Beatles. And I definitely don't recall any conscious thought that, hey, the feel-good of their music and the arrival on American soil of John Paul George and Ringo is helping me over my JFK depression. That was not part of my sensibility at age 13-14. I don't think I was capable of that kind of reflective hypothesis or conclusion at that age. Maybe older and more mature folks were aware of it. I only know I loved their music and its energy and their personalities and the whole frenzy for reasons I can't articulate except that I was drawn into the mass hysteria, and it was impossible for me to tease out any single facet except for the ultimate effect on me which was the desire and drive to dive into it and even imitate it. So I made a replica of Paul McCartney's Hofner violin bass out of one of the rectangular cardboard sheets that came in my dad's laundered shirts and attached it to an old sawed-off broomstick and practiced being Paul the way I had seen him on *Ed Sullivan* as "All My Loving" and "I Saw Her Standing There" and "She Loves You" blasted out of my little fold-down turntable with the fold-out speakers, playing left-handed (I was partially left-handed in reality—not for sports since I threw and batted right although a lot of guys liked to bat left once in a while for fun and challenge, but I wrote left and ate left so I was at least a little like Paul and yes, there, I admit it, Paul was my first favorite just like he was Nancy Hendrick's favorite and only later was I attracted to the more literate and brooding Lennon). What I DO remember was that I wanted that ability to attract girls the way they did. When I was pretending to be Paul in front of my bedroom mirror, the screaming girls in the imaginary audience included the girls in our class. So for me, the Beatles collision was not with JFK, but with testosterone.

Satisfied that he was off to a good start with the memory booklet, Paul turned to the music. There was never really any question about Paul handling that; in fact, back at that post-Labor Day meeting at Buddy's when he had volunteered for that job in addition to the memory project, everyone else more or less just said "OK." No additional comments. No discussion. Back in the day Paul had the largest collection of 45's he used to bring to parties, each with one of his mom's return address mailing labels pasted on (before self-adhesive when each one had to be licked or sponged to activate the glue) so they wouldn't get mixed in with the records others kids might have brought. And after 1964 he had the most albums, after the Beatles made listening to whole albums common when you knew every song would be great and could have been a single in its own right (and often was) and not just filler. And what no one else knew by way of firsthand direct evidence or having asked about it and found out to be true but had more or less assumed without asking and would more or less shrug off as predictable or say "tell me something I DIDN'T know," Paul still had every one of those records, including the original album covers and original paper sleeves inside the covers with the ads for other records and recording artists on the same label (such as the Dean Martin or Trini Lopez or Tom Jones promos) and the paper sleeves the 45's came in, including the original for the very first Beatles record he ever owned—the 45 version of "I Saw Her Standing There" and "I Want to Hold Your Hand" on the A and B sides of the Capitol Records release with that familiar orange and yellow label and no one would dare say which side was A or B, it was like they were both A, and the black-and-white photo of the lads' in their Edwardian collared jackets and Paul holding a cigarette (imagine that in 2019). Finally, although Nancy and George said they didn't remember, Paul had been the DJ at the actual graduation party in 1964.

He and his ex-wife had fought repeatedly about the records, she wanting them out of the apartment and later the house, sold to collectors or vintage records stores or donated to Goodwill (or just "pitched" as she liked to say, she didn't care where, she just wanted them gone), and he resisting, keeping them right where they were in the two heavy pine wood bookcases that ended up in the unfinished section of the finished basement in their suburban home, eventually amassing almost as many cassette tapes and after resisting CDs for years finally gave in and started collecting those as well, then carefully and painstakingly transferring them to the boxes and milk crates when they split up and sold the house and he moved to his current apartment and then back into the bookcases he got when they divided the property in the settlement since she didn't care, she had always hated those bookcases anyway ("those old gross things") feeling they looked too primitive. And he still played them, too; back in 2011 when the previously shuttered shoe polish company Shinola re-launched with a line of high end audio turntables Paul had dropped a couple thousand dollars he really didn't have to spare and bought one (creating the opportunity for jokes with his friends who only listened to digital downloads of songs in mp3 format or some maybe still on CDs that they didn't know shit music from Shinola), along with a software program that allowed him to transfer analog to digital so he could create CDs from the records and play them in his car.

After the Beatles arrived in 1964 he had tried to teach himself guitar on his older brother's Sears Silvertone electric. While he never really developed any serious skills as a player, he was the undisputed authority on what was good or worthwhile. Paul probably could have put together a playlist from his own vinyl collection, but that would have meant digitizing from the turntable which would have been very time-consuming since he would have to sit and mark each track individually (because of all the scratches on the records, letting the system mark them automatically often led to multiple marked tracks for a single song), which would have meant listening to every album all the way through and that seemed like it would be just too much work and take way too much time. He also could have just downloaded what he needed but that would have meant not just work and time but also money (four hours of music at 2-3 minutes and over a dollar or more per song on one of the music download platforms would have been about $100 plus all the time and why go through all that when a DJ probably already had exactly what he wanted—the top hits from 1963 and 1964 with a preponderance of Beatles, other British Invasion bands, Beach Boys, Four Seasons and Motown—so to save time and avoid download costs he Googled "DJ Springhaven PA" and found "Premier Entertainment Group" with an office in nearby King of Prussia that said they serviced southeastern Pennsylvania, the Lehigh Valley, Northern Delaware and South Jersey with music for weddings, bar and bat mitzvahs, corporate events and parties so he emailed them through their contact page:

Hi. I am in charge of securing the music for an upcoming 50th elementary school reunion on Saturday June 15, 2019 in Springhaven PA and wondered if you had a DJ available. We are looking for music from 1963 and 1964. Please let me know, and how much it would cost for about 4 hours. Thank you. Paul P

The next day someone named Mike wrote back:

Dear Paul P. Thank you for contacting the Premier Entertainment Group, LTD. School reunions from that era are one of our specialties, so I'm sure that PEG can meet your needs and provide you and your friends with a very enjoyable and memorable evening. I will check our schedule and see which of our DJs might be available for that night. We charge $110 an hour, so four hours would be $440 plus an extra $55 for set up and breakdown and other incidental expenses. I am attaching a sample contract and our pricing sheet and a sample playlist we use at school reunions from the 60s, so please take a look and I will get back to you when I can confirm that I have a DJ and then we can execute an agreement. Thank you again for contacting Premier.

Mike DiLello

Paul looked at the songs on the PEG list and realized that they spanned a couple of decades from 50s doo-wop through 70s soft rock and even some punk. So he wrote back:

Hey Mike. I will wait to hear if you have someone available. But while you're looking, I should let you know that the playlist you sent is not exactly what we're looking for. I needed just 1963 and 1964. Do you have anything like that? Thanks again. P

Mike from Premier wrote back and said they already had a couple of other events that evening (June was a busy time for weddings and graduation parties) so he was checking with one other person, but "in the meantime here's another playlist that should be more of what you want." Paul looked at those songs. More Beatles, Temptations and Supremes, but still some tunes from the 50s: "In the Still of the Night" by The Five Satins from 1956; "The Twist" by Chubby Checker from 1960 and "What's Your Name" by Don and Juan from 1962 (a little closer but still not what Paul wanted); all the way up to "I Can't Stand Losing You" by the Police from 1978 (Oh, come on!). Paul was getting a little frustrated. What was it about "just 1963 and 1964" that was unclear? Didn't these people even know when the songs on their playlists were recorded? It wasn't hard to figure out. So he Googled and found the *Billboard Hot 100* singles (both the year-end and chronological lists by weeks and months from those years, copied and pasted them into a Word document, and sent it back to PEG saying, "These are the songs we want. Do you have them in your files? Can you create a playlist just drawing from this?" Mike wrote back and said he was "pretty sure" they had most (but not all) of the songs, but they didn't have anything exactly like that, and while they could always add a few custom songs to any list and include it in the price, if Paul wanted the whole playlist customized (such as the *Billboard* list reproduced exactly) there would be an additional charge of $150 for the time and downloading costs.

That's when Paul decided to just do it himself, according to the digitize-download plan he had originally considered and rejected. More time and some money but less than paying a DJ and this way Nancy could lower the ticket price and he could get exactly what he wanted.

Beatle flu

February 1964 was Beatles month. Starting with stepping off that Pan American plane at JFK airport (recently renamed from Idlewild) on Friday February 7, 1964, through their first appearance on *Ed Sullivan* two days later until their third appearance on February 23rd the TV news and especially the radio airwaves were full of Beatles stories and playing Beatles music. WIBG was the primary popular radio station in the Philadelphia area. Biggsy who always knew such things, probably from his older brother, told Paul that "WIBBAGE" as the WIBG DJs called it was formerly a religious station (and that the "IBG" after the "W" stood for "I Believe in God" which Paul assumed Biggsy had made up; but for as long as Paul could remember it had played the music he and his friends liked, and was how he and his friends first learned about and heard the music they would eventually like. So in the week leading up to Beatle Day from Rockin' Bird Joe Niagara in the morning to Hy Lit at night the DJs played Beatles music what seemed like constantly, especially "She Loves You" and "I Want to Hold Your Hand," with maybe a few other British invasion bands such as the Dave Clark Five thrown in here and there.

And Paul got to hear them all over and over again because he was sick most of the month, with little else to do but listen to the radio, and little else he could do because reading made him dizzy. That Friday the Beatles arrived Paul awoke and knew he was sick. He had tried to get up and the room spun so wildly he felt he was going to throw up so he just lay back down and tried to keep very still. "Mom…Mom" he called/groaned from his bedroom but she was already bustling downstairs, so Paul's brother who was in the hall bathroom yelled downstairs "Paul's calling you." Paul whispered something and his brother shouted again, "He says he doesn't feel good." Paul's mother was upstairs within seconds (those hard wired early-life influenza memories meant that ANY child's illness no matter how seemingly trivial always felt like a crisis to her; today she would have probably been diagnosed with PTSD). She came into Paul's room and put the palm of her right hand on his forehead. Then she leaned over and put her lips on his forehead and said "Oh dear; you're burning up. I'm calling Salatucci."

Dr. Salatucci was their pediatrician and of course in those days he made house calls, so he came over around lunch time and came up to Paul's bedroom and examined him and announced that Paul had the flu and would be pretty sick for a few days but would be alright after that, and there was nothing to do but give him plenty of liquids and baby aspirin for his fever and aches and pains. And Paul had plenty of those—arms, legs, back, eyes, even his hair—they all hurt; and the fever made him feel he was out of his mind some of the time. So that when the radio played "She Loves You" it was images of Mary Liz that swirled in his head, with him believing, Yeah yeah yeah I know she loves me. And in "I Want to Hold Your Hand" when Paul heard "And when I touch you I feel happy inside" he was thinking Yes, yes, I want to touch you, I want to feel happy inside. And with the high fever Paul could feel and hear his heart beating loud and fast in his ear so in "I Saw Her Standing There" when Paul heard "Well my heart went boom" he thought his own heart might explode.

So that Sunday Paul had to watch the Beatles their first time on *Ed Sullivan* from the living room couch in his PJs and with a blanket since he still had fever and chills and he was never sure whether or not it was the show or the fever or both but the night seemed like a dream, including his father's occasional comments like "What are those girls all screaming about?" and "You call this music?"

He didn't get better as quickly as Salatucci predicted; in fact, by the following Wednesday he still had a fever plus his chest hurt and he had a really bad cough. So Salatucci came back and examined him again in his bedroom but this time he announced that Paul had pneumonia and would have to go into the hospital for a few days. Paul was too sick to care but his mother started saying "Oh no. Oh dear. Oh No" because she remembered those stories about 1918 and how it had gone with so many young people at the time—fever, cough, pneumonia, death—but Salatucci tried to reassure her saying Paul should be fine but he just needed a chest x-ray to confirm the diagnosis and some antibiotics (which didn't exist in 1918) and he should be back home in a few days. Paul was also too sick to realize he might miss the Beatles' second *Ed Sullivan* appearance on February 16th, but in fact he was improved enough to come home that Sunday morning so was able to see the show that night, this time with less delirium but no new acceptance or encouragement from his father. Salatucci had said that while Paul was a little better he still needed a lot of rest so he would need to take off the rest of the week. By this time Paul was feeling well enough to realize he had just been given a get-out-of-school-free card for another week, except that by Tuesday Gerry Giordano brought over some homework so his freedom was incomplete.

By the third *Sullivan* appearance Paul was out of the PJs and off the couch. His mother planned to send him back to school Monday the 24th, but Paul pleaded for more time and got his mom to agree to keep him home that Monday, and was even able to stretch it to Tuesday the 25th by using a little trick Biggsy (of course) had told him about when boasting he could get out of school whenever he wanted by putting the thermometer on top of a heat-generating tube radio. Paul tried it and saw the mercury zoom up to 106. It took him some time to perfect it, leaving it on the radio just long enough to get the temperature up just enough—to a believable 101 plus or minus, although he sometimes had to shake it down from 104, then reheat a little when he had shaken too much and the grey strip fell below the 98.6 arrow. And of course he played on and took advantage of his mother's anxiety, her deadly fear of influenza and any febrile and/or respiratory illness knowing she would always err on the side of more time off, more time to recover, more time to hover over him helicopter-like, although the term wouldn't be coined for several more decades. But that night while listening to the Clay-Liston fight on the radio and his mom came in and he showed her the thermometer saying "It's still a little high" (with heating, shaking, re-heating and re-shaking just a little he had deftly gotten it exactly to 101.2), his mom surprised him by denying the result with her palm and lips and re-took his temp in person. It was 98 and he was good to go for Wednesday the 26th, so even his mom's health-anxiety had limits. He had missed most of February at school, Valentine's Day had come and gone and with that any opportunity to exchange candy hearts with Mary Liz (if such a thing would have even been possible), but thanks to the Beatles music and a waxing and waning fever Mary Liz had been in his head the whole time anyway.

VII

Lent (Ash Wednesday to Holy Saturday/Easter Eve)

Since Easter is a movable feast linked to the equinox and lunar cycle, there would inevitably be some years when Biggsy's new system that had the season of Lent follow the season of winter would get into a little trouble when the Biggsy calendar and the regular calendar had significant overlap. Ash Wednesday—the start of Lent for both the Christian world and Biggsy—was usually a symbolic and some years a literal oasis, a warm fertile spot in the middle of the winter desert that foretold the coming of Easter and spring. But in 1964 with Easter coming really early—March 29th—Ash Wednesday fell on February 12th, not only still part of the calendar winter but even in a Biggsy calendar there was no way to deny that it still felt wintry cold with temperatures in the 30s and 40s. I remember that on Ash Wednesday Biggsy wished everyone a "Happy Lent" on our way into school, when Gerry, the one who had gotten Biggsy thinking about the seasons way back in September once again challenged him by pointing out that it still felt very much like winter, kind of the reverse of the conversation they'd had when school started. Biggsy, as agile-minded as ever deflected it as easily as one might blow away a floating dandelion seed by pointing out that just because it was cold didn't mean it was winter, and that Lent starts off cold and ends up warm. Of course he was right.

Actually getting the forehead ashes provoked distinctly different reactions in me during my eight years at St. Anthony's. In grades 1-3 it was a duty, something we had to do as we had to do everything else our teachers commanded as part of our faith whether we understood it or not, same as attending Mass every Sunday. In grades 4 and 5 when I was starting to better understand and appreciate my Catholicism I was happy and even proud to wear the mark of my faith, and also appreciated getting the accompanying bolus of grace and maybe even drawing down a little on my purgatory time. In grades 6-8 when testosterone was starting to trickle and then surge in my bloodstream, lowering my voice and foresting my underarms and wisping my upper lip with hair, it was an annoying embarrassing literal smudge on any sense of cool I might have been cultivating. But the rule with ashes, per the nuns, was that you could not wipe them off. You had to let them fall off or fade away on their own. The more devout members of our class might have ash remnants for a week or more (leading to some personal hygiene questions, naturally), and one year Carol Curley still had them for her class picture. I remember wanting to think she looked ridiculous, memorialized that way, but hesitated knowing her place in heaven was probably guaranteed.

By seventh grade I had perfected a process for having the ashes gone by the time we returned to class after the lunchtime/long recess: first, when heading up to the altar at 7:30 Mass to get the ashes, as the priest came at me with that black thumb I would pull back ever so slightly so he couldn't get a full-pressure hit on me, such that the ashes stuck, but ever so flimsily; second, while saying the grace before meals at lunchtime there were two opportunities to "accidentally" remove some of the ashes with each sign of the cross, meaning that for the forehead touch at "In the Name of the Father" I used a bundled index middle and ring finger instead of just an index as we often did when blessing ourselves quickly and really lingered there a nanosecond or two longer and rubbed and twisted quickly and deftly rather than the usual light tap, after which I would furtively glance down at my fingers, looking for the telltale black to tell me how successful I'd been; and third, to finish the job, I always made sure to be as active as I could at recess to work up a little brow sweat that I would then have to wipe, and for insurance I would pull my zippered jacket over my head rather than unzipping and removing it the usual way, and ensure there was plenty of forehead contact with the inside of my coat. If the teacher later asked what happened to my ashes, I could register genuine surprise since, blackened fingertips notwithstanding, I hadn't looked at myself in a mirror and so really didn't know the status of my ashes (although I confirmed it in the bathroom as soon as I got home), and also honestly report that they may have come off during recess and not have to also report that as a lie the next time at confession.

Unlike other parishes we visited for football games where the church and the school were on the same campus, at St. Anthony's the school was on Sycamore Street and the church a half mile away at the corner of Cedar and Timberline Roads. To get there from school we had to turn right on Sycamore out of the school driveway, turn left on Cedar, and cross at the light at Cedar and Timberline to get to the church. Instead of reporting to school every morning, all during Lent we reported to church for 7:30 Mass. And since in those days fasting before Communion was three hours and Mass was so early, there was no time to eat beforehand, so when we got back to school we had to eat breakfast at our desks before starting classes. It ate up class time and so by definition was wonderful. My breakfast was either a scrambled egg sandwich on toast my mother would make quickly while I dressed for school, wrapped in aluminum foil and so still warm by the time I got to my desk, and by then the melted butter on the toast would have completely saturated the bread and eggs creating a soft and creamy delight; or cold cereal in one of those small variety pack boxes where the box face had an H-shaped perforation so you could cut through it and the waxed paper underneath and pour the milk right into the box turning it into a de facto bowl (the breakfast milk was in the thermos in my lunch box—lunchtime milk was delivered late mornings by Wawa Dairy Farms to be in time for the noon meal).

Lent was supposed to be about repentance, sackcloth and ashes and fasting and extra meat abstinence and giving up something you liked such as desserts (foregoing green beans or spinach or something else you didn't particularly care for were not considered true penance) and deprivation and mortification as the cleansing preparation for the great feast of Easter and Resurrection and rebirth, but I saw it as a welcomed break in the routine, something to interrupt the monotony of the winter white desert and to allow all those Lenten obligations to change up the daily drudgery of school. In addition to morning Mass every weekday, on Wednesday afternoons we left school early to go to Confession, and every Friday afternoon we got out early again to attend Stations of the Cross. So overall we got to start our school day a little later every day, and end it a little earlier on Wednesdays and Fridays. And all those earliers were even earlier for me on days when I was assigned to Stations as an altar boy, usually with Biggsy, since we had to get there before everyone else to suit-up and help setup—we were never as punctual as we were when it meant an earlier school dismissal. And all those earliers that were even earlier were earlier still because of the 10-minute walk to church.

All those walks from school to church and church to school as a class and student body were in our usual two by two lines and no talking. What we thought was such a cruel and unnecessary constraint—not being able to talk while walking outside—was in retrospect actually a wonderful gift because it forced us to see more, smell more, hear more, feel more, notice more. Maybe a few more cardinals and robins are vocalizing, marking territory. Maybe the first hint of a balmy breeze on an end-of-Lent Friday afternoon. Maybe as we stopped at the light at Cedar and Timberline there'd be the sound of car radios coming out of open car windows which meant it had to be getting warmer. As we moved into later February, when the daytime temperatures creep above freezing but the nights still dip below it, not only does the maple sap go through its diurnal rising and falling but the snowpack melts a little during the day and refreezes overnight, creating little channels under the edges of the snow lining the sidewalks and curbs which becomes a kind of roof or shelf over those spaces. One of my perennial pleasures walking back and forth between church and school was stepping on those shelves of ice to snap them off the rest of the snowpack. Every step was another crunch and crack, and in my wake all those broken pieces looked like so many ice floes in a sidewalk sea, and every inch off the snowpack was another piece of the effort to hasten spring. And something about stepping onto that ice and hearing that loud CRACK or CRUNCH or POP and seeing that chunk of ice now separated from the hard snow and doomed to melt to a drippy dribble by day's end almost conferred a sense of power. As if I were calving a 2-story Arctic Ocean iceberg, which nowadays the environmental video clips on TV and the Internet employ to warn and frighten about climate change, but back then I wanted the weather to change, to bring on spring.

And it worked because every day and every week that we walked every morning to school from Mass and every Wednesday from school to church for Confession and every Friday from school to church for Stations from Ash Wednesday to the Wednesday of Holy Week (the last half day of school before Easter break) there'd be a little less snow and a little more grass as winter slowly but inexorably receded in those pre-global-warming mid-March marches until at one point there was no snow anywhere except that shrinking pile of black cinder and gray exhaust smoke-colored crystals in the A&P parking lot where the plows had piled it way back in January but so high there'd be some hanging around until April and the ground became sopping sponge wet as the gradually melting snow turned our backyard lawns and the school football field and the curbside grass next to the sidewalk on the walking way between school and church into marshlands and made a delightful squish when you stepped on it.

There was a small stream, a tributary of Rock Creek that ran under Cedar so we had to walk over the sidewalk that crossed the water where a short iron rail kept folks from tumbling down the embankment. Sometimes when the marching line stopped for some reason (usually when the front of the line was stopped at the Cedar-Timberline light) my part of the line was at or near the creek so I got a chance to look over the railing for a longer time than when we just marched by. In early Lent the stream was frozen and the ground was hard and often snow covered on those early morning walks from church back to school, but by the afternoons at the end of March walking to church from school for Confession or Stations it was warm and wet and the grass already greening and a few crocuses were poking up their purple heads. That year one time when the marching line paused by the creek railing allowed me more creek-view time I saw a tadpole who seeing me darted under a rock, and one time on a particularly sunny day I even saw a garter snake stretched out on a rock in the creek reminding me of something Biggsy told me when we were nine or ten and we were walking in The Woods in late winter and I was looking around and wondering when the brown grasses and frozen creek water would be filled with tadpoles, frogs, salamanders, crayfish (we called them "CRAW-fish") turtles and snakes, and Biggsy said that snakes always come out around Good Friday which I just accepted as true at the time assuming that whenever Good Friday fell it would be spring, snakes would know it, and come out and even thought maybe it had something to do with Satan and evil and what was happening to poor Jesus and only later wondered how could the snakes know when Good Friday was since it might fall several weeks earlier or later in any given year so maybe it was more about the temperature and the fact that the creek was flowing again and there might be a fly or mouse or flightless fledgling to eat, but that year in 1964 it all seemed right because when it was close to Good Friday I actually did see that garter snake so with the snake and the wet sponge earth and the ever-so-slowly-greening grass and the crocuses I knew that Easter and spring were upon us. And walking over the water every day was like walking from winter to spring, like the Easter metaphor literalized and writ large in front of our eyes: the stiff and hard and seemingly dead becoming fluid and alive. And even more so that year because Easter arrived just as spring arrived, just as it is supposed to if you really want to talk about all the heavy rebirth symbolism.

And like any spring pre-climate-change when the seasons seemed more defined, just as Biggsy had noticed with summer gradually slipping away spring wasn't just there one day where winter had been the day before and then gone another day three months later when the calendar changed to summer, because there was wind to dry that sponge earth and winds know no calendars and have no clocks but their own. And not just winds, not just some haphazard moving air from north or south or east or west but coming in with March like the King of the Jungle, mane marvelous and magnificent stalking the heavens until the right time then rearing back, jaws wide, teeth bared, howling, roaring, scattering seeds and pods across that quickly drying sponge but not before they had thrown down anchor roots.

And never a subdued beast, never a beaten or tamed lion, it merely left with the same flawless timing which brought it in then went out transformed, like a lamb, that sacrificial symbol that will offer its snowy fleece to Something in the sky, rising with the fire and incense smoke and prayers, and that Something in the sky will be moved by the display and want to help the helpless people and so will send tears to earth and it will rain and rain and be April.

With apologies to Biggsy and his clever reboot of the seasons, Good Friday was like a season all to itself, embodying in one day so much of what the long season of Lent was all about—the fasting, abstaining from meat, and the quiet. There was so much quiet. We were off from school, but the day had a decidedly different feel, very unlike the Friday after Thanksgiving. At the feet washing service on Holy Thursday night Father Ellis had reminded us in his homily that Good Friday was a solemn day, not a day to play or be loud or boisterous. If the weather were nice he admonished the boys not to give in to the temptation to go outside and play baseball, and to the girls it was not a day to play the radio loud and maybe practice new dance moves. It was a day to think about what was coming, the awful suffering that Jesus had endured about which we were reminded every Friday at Stations of the Cross. When I awoke that day my mother was typically already bustling in the kitchen—making Easter breads, biscotti filled with a delicious chocolate and apple butter filling that I never knew were Italian because we pronounced it biss-KUT so it was kind a of a neutral word and I never made any connection to the English word "biscuit" either—but it was a kind of quiet bustle, only broken here and there as when she might call me and say something like "Can you get me the butter in the fridge?" or "I need your height" (I was already about five foot ten by then) to get a baking dish off the top shelf of a wall cabinet.

As Father Ellis had said, there was no playing outside. And no TV. Just kind of sitting around the house, maybe wandering room to room, maybe a little reading. And from noon to 3:00 it was complete silence to commemorate (now there's a good liturgical word) the suffering on the cross. No talking at all except for essentials. Some years I had actually read my missal during that time. That year I just lay on my bed, and if God were not distracted enough by other more pressing concerns he might have noticed that I was not thinking so much about Jesus and his Passion, but about Nancy Hendrick's party scheduled for the next day—Holy Saturday afternoon. I may have drifted off to sleep for a bit, because at one point I heard my mother calling me from downstairs, reminding me we had to get to church early since I was altar boying for the 3:00 P.M. Good Friday Cross Veneration service.

I barely made it to church in time to put on my cassock and surplice before Biggsy and I walked from the altar boys' sacristy to the priests' sacristy, our transit behind the altar mostly obscured by the woodwork except for our heads which were visible through the carved lattice work. The priests were already garbed up—just the long white alb and the cincture but no chasuble—and holding the pillows they would throw down on the floor in front of the altar steps and then prostrate themselves, their heads and forearms on those pillows. What a sight, the three priests just lying there in front of us while we stood. The altar was stripped bare—no cloth, no flowers; just stark white. It was obvious there was something very sad going on, and then the organ and the choir drowned us with melancholy and minor chords singing, "O come and mourn with me awhile...Jesus our love is crucified" and "O sacred head surrounded by crown of piercing thorns, O bleeding head so wounded, reviled and put to scorn." You can't help noticing that something or someone has died.

But not just Christ. The whole world had started dying back in November. Flowers, grasses (actually just dormant), flies in the attic on their backs with stiff legs, trees sleeping in suspended animation. And part of you too. Dead and buried all winter under flannel and wool shirts, coats, long johns, wool cap, scarf, gloves, boots, wrapped tight and barely able to move. But Christ's death changes everything. It redeems. All those poor souls waiting in purgatory will soon be able to rise up and float to heaven, where the gates had been shut ever since Adam and Eve sinned. But soon they'll be open, and in three days when the stone is rolled away to open the tomb and Jesus emerges glorious and risen and alive it will be like the world opening and you and everything around you suddenly emerging and awakened from hibernation, in a lighter jacket and your skin can touch the air again. And the few crocuses you saw in the creek bed will be joined by 10, 30, 50 more, some in your backyard attended by groggy bees, creating a little humming patch of purple.

And the priests have come alive again, getting up, extending their arms and starting to pray while I whisk away the pillows as Biggsy holds the big missal they read from. And the next night at the Easter vigil there will be darkness then a gradual illumination as we start lighting the candles of all the altar boys and choir girls who will walk in processions up and down the church aisles, walking us from darkness to light, from winter to spring, from death to resurrection. But I am getting a little ahead of myself: first there will be Nancy's party on Holy Saturday afternoon.

Trivia Quiz

Paul still had the music playlist to put together, but since he already had some fairly concrete plans about that and only had to execute on it, he decided to start at least getting something written down on the trivia quiz. After firing up his laptop on his kitchen table "desk" and starting to reflect on some of the everyday and better-known characteristics of the school and church that many former classmates might know or would be amused to remember and would therefore be suitable fodder for the quiz, he came upon an organizing theme: he would ask some simple, relatively straightforward questions that had similarly simple, straightforward answers; while others would be questions that were more like invitations to remember certain stories that had more detail and nuance. He could also link some of these stories to different school years, starting with first grade and working his way up to eighth.

First the generic/miscellaneous:

Q: What were the three dismissal calls at the end of the school day?
A: (1) First bus (it was the first of three 20-minute bus runs, but second and third were never called, the riders just knew to wait); (2) Sycamore Road and Cedar Avenue (for walkers, who all had to start out on Sycamore, but some took it to Cedar and turned right or left); and (3) Car and Bicycle Line (self-explanatory).

Q: What was the inexpensive way the nuns made us wax the floors before summer break?
A: Asking us to save bread wrappers which were made of waxed paper back in the day and bring two of them to school then put one under each foot while seated at our desks and rub the wrappers back and forth on the floor. Paul could add, "We had to admit it did impart a kind of shine, and it certainly helped us pass the time sitting in the building before being cut loose for the summer, besides giving us permission to make some noise and opportunities to pretend we were running or even driving a Flintstones car."

Q: How much were the chances we had to sell to our parents, grandparents, aunts, uncles and/or in front of the A&P, and how many to a strip?
A: One for a dime, three for a quarter, 12 to a strip.

Q: What color were our vocabulary cards?
A: A kind of pale green, with the words printed in black.

Q: What was the crayon brand sold in our school store (and essentially the only acceptable brand)?
A: Perma (a kind a chalky alternative to the waxier and better known Crayola).

Q: What was the name of our Poetry books?
A: Poems for the Grades.

Q: And our wannabe art history books?
A: Picture Studies

Q: What is "S'ter, S'ter, S'ter!"?
A: Squirming in and lifting partially out of your seat, arm raised and hand flapping when you knew the answer and were trying to get called on.

Q: What were the St. Anthony Mass times?
A: 6:30, 7:30, 9:00, 10:00, 11:00, 12:00 (all in the main church), and 12:15 in the church basement.

Q: What was church thunder?
A: The sound of the movements of the larger congregation at the 12:00 Mass in the upstairs church as heard by the smaller congregation at the 12:15 in the church basement (since the two masses were out of sync, the downstairs folks would hear a loud rumbling whenever the folks upstairs would stand, sit, march up to the communion rail and ultimately file out of the church, all of which occurred 15 minutes earlier than it happened downstairs).

Q: What color was the "candy table" used at lunch time?
A: A really ugly dark green, same color as the benches that encircled the large oak in the middle of the playground.

Q: What did safeties say when they were about to take another student to the principal?
A: "You're reported!"

Then the stories linked to particular grades:

First grade: "What question about meals and eating" he started, "freaked out some of us (or at least me) during the first few days of first grade?" Paul suspected that probably no one would get this one, especially since he was probably the only one impacted, but it was still a great story. Since St. Anthony's was located in the middle of a suburban neighborhood with multiple parish homes within a 5-10-minute walk and several actually abutting the school property, a fairly large number of students went home for lunch every day. To get a general idea how many were going and how many staying, their first grade nun, Sister Pauline Agnes (who at the time they could only describe as "talked funny" and only later realized had a thick Irish brogue, whom Biggsy would eventually describe as being "right off the boat," as usual a phrase he had probably picked up listening to older siblings and/or parents) asked on either Day 2 or Day 3 of that first week, "How many are going home for dinner?" In addition to her accent, the class didn't know that by "dinner" she meant the midday meal (and that she would call the evening meal "supper"). More accustomed to using "lunch" for the meal they ate at school and "dinner" for the family-shared repast in the evening, at home, after she asked that question even at the tender age of six Paul distinctly remembered thinking, "Aren't we ALL going home for dinner? How long is this day going to be?"

First grade: Recite the first two chapters of our first-grade reader in their entirety:

Chapter 1: "See, see."

Chapter 2: "See David, See Ann."

And what was the name of David's and Ann's dog? Zip.

Second grade: What was the underwear scandal? One of the boys in one of the grades put his poop-soiled underpants in the trashcan, Hiram found it and took it to the principal, after which every boy in every grade was marched down to the lunch room which we still had at the time and had to pull up the elastic band on his underpants to prove it wasn't him, and presumably the boy who couldn't do it was the culprit and then probably had another reason to shit his pants.

Third grade: What was the name of Alexander the Great's horse that we learned about in our history class that year? Bucephalus. Paul and Gerry had matching satiny Phillies jackets, and Paul wrote "Bucephalus

I" under the back collar of his and Gerry "Bucephalus II" on his, and they took turns riding piggyback on each other, attacking some of their male classmates as they pretended to be the storied Greek conqueror.

Fourth grade: What was Mrs. Lynch's side job? Selling World Book Encyclopedias. And what was the motto of the "Look-It-Up Club" whose members regularly read those encyclopedias? "We never guess, we look it up." And what did we save for Mrs. Lynch? Betty Crocker box tops (although Paul couldn't remember whether she redeemed them for school-related or personal items). And why did Mrs. Lynch need to have a side job and make a little extra money? No one knew exactly.

Fifth grade: Paul couldn't come up with much of anything for fifth grade, except that at ages 10-11 it was a kind of a transitional year between little boy and adolescent, getting old enough to understand some things, such as his faith, and he could recall really getting into reading his missal at Mass, going back and forth between the Latin and English on different sides of the page, at the same time he was studying the Latin altar boy responses so he felt...sort of...holy, and even remembered being somewhat drawn to the priesthood that year. In the end he wrote a question for altar boys only: What is the response to "Introibo ad altare Dei." ("I will go in to the altar of God")"? "Ad Deum qui lætíficat juventútem meam." ("To God, the joy of my youth.")

Sixth grade: What teacher flipped us the bird every day? Sister Mary Agatha, who had the odd habit of pointing to the blackboard, and even occasionally banging on it, then pointing to the class, with her right third finger. Stifling laughter was particularly challenging.

Seventh grade: Why did a well-known player on St. Anthony's CYO football team have to stay after school for a solid week in seventh grade? Gerry Giordano, for running up to random male classmates at recess time yelling "Geography quiz! What's the capital of Thailand?" and before they could answer yelling "Bangkok!" and whacking them in the groin.

Eighth grade:

At that point Paul stopped typing, leaned back in his chair and looked out the french doors that opened onto the small balcony in his third floor apartment. He had already been reflecting a lot about their eighth grade year ever since they started planning the reunion, but didn't think it would be appropriate to write about or talk about the topics that were more or less esoteric or too personal. Again, he wanted to keep the trivia quiz as general as possible. It was late March so his bike sat there on the balcony, unused since early December, next to the charcoal grill he rarely used at any time of year, under the plastic cover. The stand of hardwood trees on the apartment complex property—a mix of red maple, northern red oak, ash and poplar—were still bare from a distance, although he would have probably seen a few buds if he could have looked more closely. Back in 1964 this was the same time of year as Nancy Kendrick's birthday party, the one on Holy Saturday afternoon. Should he have an entry about that? Probably not, since not everyone in the class was invited, and probably only 20 or so kids were there. Still, out of everything that happened that year, Nancy's party was…what word did he even want to use himself? "Memorable" seemed too tame, but "life-changing" was definitely hyperbolic. At the very least, of all the various stops along the St. Anthony's journey from September to June, eighth-grader to rising high school freshman, boy to man, Lent to Easter, winter to spring, lost to found, Nancy's party was an important one, a literal milestone—a place to pile up a few rocks to say "I was here" and recall what happened.

Nancy's Party

Paul was barely 14 years old (had just turned earlier that month). When he sees kids that age now he thinks they are like babies, barely out of the toddler years. But as he remembers it now, 55 years later, it feels that the mind he had then is the same mind he has now.

The invitation to Nancy's party was not really a surprise. Younger boy-girl birthday parties in 60s-era knotty pine finished basements with suits and stiff crinoline dresses, pin-the-tail-on-the donkey and/or musical chairs games and cake and ice cream had stopped around second or third grade, ages 8'ish or 9'ish, replaced by slumber/pajama parties for the girls, and maybe movie theater outings or nothing for the boys. But two-gender parties in the age of pubescence, of breast buds and thin hair wisps on upper lips, had actually started up again in sixth grade, awkwardly and tentatively. Paul was invited to that first one in sixth grade at Dolores Kolowski's house, and when word got around that it might be a "kissing party," perhaps in his abject guilelessness or due to uncertainty and anxiety about what that might mean or entail he blathered that news to his parents. And for some reason, the same parents that would later try to reign in his wildness with curfews and groundings did not forbid him to go. In fact, they said almost nothing about it until the night before when Paul's father sat him down behind the closed door of his bedroom and said he needed to tell him "a story" which Paul soon learned was the time-honored "facts of life/birds and bees" talk. Just like that. He didn't use any cutesy faunal metaphors or abstract illusions, just the *Dragnet* TV detective Joe-Friday-like facts. And his introduction to the topic, his rationale, was that if there would be any kissing at the party, he wanted Paul to be prepared for what might happen and how he might feel. It turned out to be both a huge overreaction on his father's part, at least as it related to that particular party because nothing more than kissing occurred, and simultaneously a huge underestimation because Paul could never have been adequately prepared for a what a simple closed mouth kiss with Mary Elizabeth Albarelli would later do to him emotionally.

His dad didn't provide many details, but surprisingly and despite his usual black-and-white businessman's demeanor, he waxed almost poetic, saying again and again that love was a beautiful thing. That love between a man and a woman had a magical quality to it that was hard to describe. Years later after his dad died and he and his brother were helping their mother clean out his father's dresser drawers, buried under socks and handkerchiefs and the German luger his dad's cousin had plucked from the belt of a dead Nazi soldier Paul found a short paperback book titled *How to discuss the facts of life with your son*. After paging through it and skimming the text Paul smiled as he realized his father must have lifted a couple of talking points directly from this early "How to" genre book, and saw from the old receipt still inside revealing that his dad had purchased it four decades earlier at the Malvern Retreat House bookstore at the men-only Catholic weekend getaway he attended every year.

The kissing at that sixth grade party had been pretty tame—just a simple game of Spin the Bottle—but when it was Mary Liz's turn to spin and that long-necked 16-oz soda bottle stopped spinning with the bottle mouth pointing to Paul, he gulped hard and immediately began to sweat as Mary Liz leaned across the small circle heading in his direction. But before he even realized he should also be leaning in to meet her halfway she was already three-quarters of the way across the center of the circle and their lips met so roughly it felt as if Paul had been punched in the mouth, his upper lip hitting his teeth so hard he sensed it was already starting to swell, although he was nonetheless electrified. Mary Liz giggled and said "Sorry" and resumed her place in the circle. Paul longed for another chance to do better, but her subsequent spins never stopped at him, and his spins never stopped at her. And even though with each kiss he became a little more competent, none had the literal force or the sparks of that first one with Mary Liz. Still, the subsequent buzz notwithstanding, Paul never counted that as his official "first kiss" with Mary Liz, as it was more a collision of lips—not really an accident, technically, but lacking much thought or intention on his part. In fact, it happened so quickly that, in the moment, he barely registered what had occurred; and the buzz he later recalled feeling may have been nothing more than the usual tingling of compressed tissues and nerves as his lip puffed up.

By seventh grade the parties had no organized kissing games, but there was plenty of kissing by a few defined "couples" that would pair off and make out in a dark corner. This is what was going on at Mary Liz's party at the end of seventh grade that eventually caused the boys and girls to be split into separate classrooms in eighth grade. By the time they got to Nancy's eighth-grade party, there was only one defined couple (Robbie and Dolores, each of whom had recently broken up with Gerry and Susan—lots of trading and switch-offs in those years), so Nancy kind of got the word out that for sentimental reasons maybe they would go back to playing games as they did when they were younger, a somewhat cryptic message that could have referred to Musical Chairs or Spin the Bottle.

After the busyness of Good Friday the day before, Holy Saturday, the day of the party, had a more relaxed and less solemn feel. It was more or less as if the hardcore suffering was behind them, the church was quiet what with Jesus being in the tomb and all, and the big liturgical party (as it were) was coming later that night with the Easter vigil. The smaller, afternoon party for Nancy's birthday came first and started slowly, with kids wandering in, the boys gravitating to the other boys and the same on the girls' side of the basement. The recently-released *Meet the Beatles* album was playing on Nancy's portable record player (the same kind Paul had with the pull-out fold-down turntable and the swing-out speakers on hinges). At final count there were 19 kids—11 girls and eight boys, and Paul could still name everyone who was there. Nancy's mother had bought hoagies from Donatello's deli, so after they were downed, a few sodas drunk, and even the birthday cake candle-lit, sung at, cut and eaten, Mrs. Kendrick cleaned up as Nancy told her they wanted to dance a little as she put on side 1 of the Beatles album again. At that point the boys and girls were still separated like the positive and negative charges in a thunderstorm sky, so as soon as the sound of Mrs. Kendrick's shoes on the stairs disappeared and Nancy confirmed that her mom was safely upstairs, she decided it was time to make some lightning by announcing that they were going to play Post Office.

None of the guys knew exactly what this meant, except that kissing was somehow involved. Here's how Nancy explained it: She had already written the numbers 1-22 on small pieces of paper, folded them, and put all the odd numbers in one bag (a standard brown lunch bag) and the even numbers in another. Girls were even, boys were odd, and before putting the papers in the bag she had already discarded numbers 17, 19, and 21 because of the unequal numbers of boys and girls. Each of them took a number out of their respective gender-specific bags, and whoever started the game would stand in the bathroom (most houses in the suburban communities of the day had basement bathrooms), call out a number for someone from the other gender, and the two of them would go behind the closed door of the bathroom, kiss, then the first person who had started the game would walk out, and the person who had been called in would in turn call another number from the opposite gender, and on and on. Pretty simple really.

The Beatles album kept playing. When one side finished, Nancy would turn it over to play the other, then when that side finished she would turn it over again to play the first side, and on and on. That album played throughout the whole game.

Since it was Nancy's house and Nancy's party and Nancy's idea, she started the game. No one knew what number she was, but she called out number 1 and Gerry Giordano got up, unfolded his paper to show everyone he was #1, and pumped his fists over his head and repeated "Num-ber-1" several times before disappearing behind the bathroom door. After about 10 seconds there were some cat calls and hoots since it was taking so long, then the door opened and Nancy walked out, saw everyone and started laughing. Then Gerry called "Number 6 for sex" to more hoots and hollers, and Nancy got up, giggling. Then Nancy called "Lucky 7" and it was Robbie, and Robbie called 18 and this time HE got lucky, because it was Mary Liz. Paul prayed hard that Mary Liz would call his number, 5. "This Boy" was playing ("This Boy, would be happy, just to love you, but oh my…"), but she called 3—Stephen Berry. Once the word was out that Mary Liz was #18, the circle could have closed pretty quickly with every boy calling for her every time, and it seemed to be headed that way when after Stephen finished with her he just called #18 again to more hoots and hollers. Nancy, the official and unofficial referee got up and told the boys "You can't keep calling Mary Liz's number." At that point Robbie stood up and said "I'll do a full minute without taking a breath with anyone who calls number 3!" As everyone was laughing Mary Liz got up to go kiss Stephen as the game demanded, then making it clear that she wanted no parts of any of the boys' numbers called so far, she tried a number that hadn't yet been called—5. Paul's. He got up and started walking slowly toward the bathroom. Nancy yelled "Show us your number," as if Mary Liz had demanded that anyone going in with her had to show proof that it was legitimate. Paul obliged, showing her his unfolded paper and she said, "OK, go in." Robbie yelled "Put in a good word for number 3 in there!"

Paul walked into the bathroom, so flummoxed that he had forgotten to close the door so Mary Liz reached behind him and closed it. Thoughts raced. Their awkward Christmas gift exchange. The time at the St. Eugene's dance when "Forever" was playing and Paul so wanted to slow dance with her but didn't have the courage. This time it was "All I've Got to Do" ("Whenever I want to kiss you, yeah, all I've got to do…"). Mary Liz didn't say a word, but smiled and came towards him. He seemed to recall that she

"Paul prayed hard that Mary Liz would call his number, 5."

had put her arms around his neck but he wasn't sure, although he was fairly sure his arms stayed by his sides. Paul leaned in with his eyes open, then closed them when their lips met. Unlike that awkward moment with Spin the Bottle two years earlier and that dry lip punch, this was softer, gentler, and even moist as Paul could feel her starting to open her mouth, but he didn't know what she was doing or how to respond so he still kept his mouth closed, and after a few seconds that felt immeasurably longer she pulled away and it was over. He opened his eyes and saw Mary Liz smiling. Then she walked out.

Paul just stood there in the bathroom until he heard Nancy yelling "Call a number, and it can't be Mary Liz's number again" along with some muffled laughter. But of course that was exactly whose number Paul wanted to call. But when Nancy yelled again, "C'mon, Paul, call a number" he called #6 and heard Nancy say, "OK, who's 6?" then laughing "Oh that's me" and more laughing and then she came in and they must have kissed but he didn't remember anything about it, and after he walked out of the bathroom the song had changed to "All My Loving" ("*Close your eyes, and I'll kiss you, tomorrow I'll miss you, remember I'll always be true*") at the end of Side 1, and after that song ended the record player tone-arm kept knocking against the metal spindle until Nancy came out and flipped it again to Side 2 and "Don't Bother Me" came on ("*Since she's been gone I want no one to talk to me.*").

Number 5 wasn't called again for the rest of the game, but neither was 18. Paul must have subconsciously, involuntarily absorbed all the songs from that album that played over and over, because every time after that whenever he has heard "This Boy" or "All My Loving" or "Hold Me Tight" ("*tell me I'm the only one*") or "It Won't Be Long" ("*yeah yeah, till I belong to you*") he can't not think of that day and of Mary Liz and that feeling of being terrified flushed alive and utterly somewhere else.

VIII

Spring (Easter Sunday to June 13th)

Between the A&P's back parking lot and the backyards on Clover Lane was a wooded area we called, simply, "The Woods." When we weren't at each other's houses playing games inside or one-on-one wiffle ball in driveways (where a hit on the ground or in the air past the pitcher was a single, in the air past the dogwood tree on our front lawn six feet behind the pitcher a double, to the sidewalk a triple and in the street a homerun) or stepball at the front steps of someone's house (usually ours because we had the three steps near the sidewalk and where the "batters" throwing the ball against the steps had worn a bare spot on the grass by the bottom step) or building snow forts on January snow days with secret snowball caches in case of attack or ball tag in July over several contiguous unfenced yards or wireball over the telephone wires between my backward and Gerry Giordano's or flashlight tag in our front yard after dark on long summer nights because the big yew bushes flanking the front porch and in front of the dining room bay windows were perfect temporary hiding spots to crawl behind (hiding from the flashlight's beam, that is, not from mosquitoes), we were in The Woods, accessing it through the backyard of an older couple named Woolsey who yelled at us for cutting through whenever they saw us but we did it anyway, assuming any path to The Woods belonged to everyone.

A branch of Rock Creek ran through The Woods before exiting to flow behind the backyards on Clover Lane and then crossing Taylor's Ford Road to run behind yet another set of backyards and so on and so on making its meandering way through still more southwest Delaware County backyards and occasionally under streets through sewer pipes until it joined a branch of Darby Creek in Upland and emptied into the Delaware River, but as with The Woods we simply called it The Creek, like the Native Americans whom others might have called Cheyenne or Lakota Sioux or, in our area, Lenni Lenape, more simply referred to themselves as The People (or as in the 1971 movie *Little Big Man*, The Human Beings) as if there were no other people so the trees in our development were The Woods and water flowing through it was The Creek, as if there were no others, and truly for us there weren't.

Whenever we walked into The Woods and started getting farther and deeper into the trees losing sight of the Woolsey backyard, we never got lost because we knew the way and had a number of markers we always looked for—a tree trunk with a large knob, the ruins of the old Taylor mansion with its crumbling, dilapidated stone wall—until eventually we would hear The Creek. We would hear it before we could see it, and we could smell it before we could hear it, that rich, sweet, earthy, musky, moist smell of decay. We could catch frogs and salamanders and crayfish in The Creek. Once I brought home a blob of frog eggs and kept them in creek water and

150

they actually hatched into what looked like hundreds of tadpoles, one of which we used for our "outer space" experiment at a time when a few years before the Apollo moon missions NASA was sending animals into space to extrapolate their experiences to what might happen to humans, putting him or her or it in a small medicine bottle inside some creek water with foam rubber around the outside and throwing it into the air as high as we could and letting it fall to the ground to see if he or she or it would survive, which he or she or it seemed to at the time but he or she and all the others eventually died.

We played army, imitating our dads who had all been in World War II in one capacity or another (I was jealous of Biggsy yet again because his dad had been a bomber pilot and mine had a desk job in London) or maybe Vic Morrow as Sergeant Chip Saunders on the TV show *Combat* or maybe barking orders like John Wayne or Robert Mitchum in the movie *The Longest Day*, picking up sticks that had one prominent straight and long branch and two shorter sub-branches coming off it at nearly right angles so they looked and felt like tommy guns (there were always plenty of those) or thicker broken branches that looked like bazookas, throwing pine cones or rocks like grenades often into The Creek because the splash looked like a real explosion. But the special secret place in The Woods was a circular patch of land probably no more than 15 feet in diameter surrounded by water in a spot where The Creek divided and flowed around it, and where inexplicably a small patch of bamboo grew so we called it Bamboo Island. I would find out later that anyone could grow bamboo in our area because as an older teen and adult I would see it here and there in gardens or maybe on roadsides or in wooded areas after having "escaped cultivation" as gardening books might say. But it was nowhere else in our neighborhood and we had never seen it before so it made Bamboo Island magical and exotic.

We made campfires there, smoked our first stolen cigarettes there, looked at our first Playboy centerfolds there, pilfered by Gerry out of his father's sock drawer where it lay buried under the dark blacks and where he stealthily returned it. We were Tom Sawyer and his gang, escaping the bounds of Aunt Polly and polite society. We were Peter Pan's lost boys before Wendy arrived with her civilizing ways. We were soldiers, pirates, explorers, shipwrecked sailors, anything we'd just read in comic books or "real" books or seen on TV or in movies. The Creek was never more than three feet wide at any point around the island, and in some spots usually only two so it was easy to jump across from the "mainland." Once in a while someone would try to swing across on the overhead vines, but since the timing to let go was tricky and we would just as often wind up back

"…where inexplicably a small patch of bamboo grew so we called it Bamboo Island."

where we started or in the foot to foot and a half of water, and since the makeshift bridges of oak, maple, cherry, hickory or whatever other broken logs might be scattered around, while innovative and resourceful, felt less adventurous, most times we jumped.

Playlist

As April turned to later April Paul realized he had better start working harder and more intentionally on the music, so he went back and looked at the *Billboard* top 100 lists he had originally pulled up off the internet when he was still looking for a DJ and before he had decided to create the reunion playlist himself. There were actually two lists: one for the top 100 songs for 1963 and 1964 in terms of sales, radio airplay, and jukebox play for a given year; and the other was the week-by-week number 1 songs. There was a lot of overlap between the two lists, but also many on one list that were not on the other. His initial plan was to only look at the songs between September 1963 and June 1964, and make the list of songs conform exactly to the actual school months from eighth grade, which would mean picking songs on *Billboard*'s weekly list starting with the week of September 1, 1963 (which had been a Sunday, and they would have started classes that Tuesday September 3rd, the day after Labor Day) and ending June 13, 1964, the feast of St. Anthony (which had been a Saturday, and per the usual routine the last official day of school and the graduation party would have been the day before, Friday, June 12th). However, when he started looking at the actual lists, he realized he might have to adjust that plan, partly because the *Billboard* weeks started on Saturdays rather than Sundays so the school weeks and *Billboard* weeks didn't match cleanly; but mostly because some of the songs that had been popular earlier in 1963 (the second semester of 7th grade and the summer between 7th and 8th) and later in 1964 (the first semester of freshman year in high school) were just too good to leave off the list.

That was when he also decided he would include the song lists in the memory booklet, along with a 1-2 sentence blurb about each one and why he included it and a general justification about wanting to capture the songs they were listening to before they entered eighth grade, when thoughts of finally finishing elementary school and getting ready for the next big step up to high school were starting to swirl in their heads, plus the ones they were listening to after they graduated and had already started high school, when perhaps they might still be experiencing the occasional final memory flickers of what they had just left behind. It did occur to him that he may have been the only one attending the reunion who thought as deeply about this subject and felt those feelings, and seriously doubted that anyone might take him to task for including some songs that they technically could not and would not have heard until they had left St. Anthony's (and probably the same folks that would have accepted the professional DJ's playlists that included songs from the 50s and 70s and thought they were just fine), but it didn't matter; he mostly needed to justify it to and satisfy himself.

Paul didn't have to look very far for inspiration and affirmation that his broader date range was the right way to go, because the very first song on the charts in January 1963 was "Telstar" by the Tornadoes, named after the first communications satellite launched in the early 60s that enabled broadcasting telephone calls and television shows across the ocean. He remembered the song but didn't own it in his personal record collection, so he downloaded it and played it immediately, listening to the clear digital signal in his ear buds, and there it was just as he remembered it. That primitive electronic guitar squeak undoubtedly meant to sound like something space age, capturing the energy and enthusiasm for space travel and space exploration that President Kennedy promised to make a priority during his inaugural address in January 1961 signaling a reach for another aspect of the "New Frontier." The song almost sounded like signals from outer space or from another world, before synthesized sounds were widespread. Paul knew he had to include that song, since it represented such an important ferment of the times, after which he wrote his first playlist blurb, using a spreadsheet template he had created:

Song	*Billboard* week	Artist	Comment
Telstar	January 5, 1963	Tornadoes	Notice the low-tech attempts to create a seemingly other-worldly sound that evoked being in the "outer space" milieu into which that communications satellite had been launched in 1962 (per Wikipedia, no longer functional, but still orbiting the earth), and maybe even capture some of the optimism from the early Kennedy administration—about conquering space and putting a man on the moon before the end of the decade, and of course, beat the Russians at doing it since they had gotten a man in space before we did. Later in 1963 there'd be some desperate grasping for a bright spot, something to lift the American spirit after the assassination.

And so began Paul's romp of joy through the *Billboard* lists, music downloads and his own record collection. He realized that many if not most of his classmates might not notice or care about the almost academic rigor with which he undertook the project, and also might not even remember some of the songs, let alone be able to relate to his commentary. But Paul didn't care: This literal labor of love was more for himself than for anyone else, as even just sitting back and reading what he had written about "Telstar" brought a kind of deep peace and contentment he didn't typically feel much in his current life.

The next #1 hit after "Telstar" in later January was "Go Away Little Girl" by Steve Lawrence, but he left that off the playlist as something that probably would have appealed more to his parents and their generation. Then came "Walk Right In" by the Rooftop Singers in early February, but he left that one off too, as he recalled it as more of a folksy Hootenanny, Kingston-trio-ish kind of song that college students and young adults were listening to at the time, but not so much kids in elementary school, or at least he wasn't, and never heard it at parties. But then he found four solid inclusions in a row from March through May: "Walk Like A Man" by the Four Seasons (his spreadsheet comment—"Inspired some of us boys to consider acting on our hormonal surges"); "Our Day Will Come" by Ruby and the Romantics ("Notice that lush, dreamy organ that almost sounds as if it's underwater. And didn't some of us want this prediction to be true about our own adolescent love affair dreams?"); "He's So Fine" by the Chiffons and "I Will Follow Him" by Little Peggy March. Paul's comment for "He's So Fine" actually became another trivia question: "Which famous/infamous George Harrison song whose refrain sounded a lot like (or almost exactly like) the one in this song resulted in a lawsuit for the ex-Beatle? Give up? It was "My Sweet Lord" (sing it or hum it or pull it up on the internet and see what you think."). For "I Will Follow Him" he wrote "Some of you may recall that Peggy March hailed from nearby Lansdale, something WIBG's morning DJ Joe Niagara mentioned almost every time he played that song."

Actually, Paul had very specific personal memories for both of those songs whenever he heard them later in 1963 and into 1964 and anytime after that, including when he downloaded them for the reunion party playlist. He remembered thinking wishing hoping dreaming that Mary Liz might be singing those songs for him, thinking that Paul, that handsome, shy, soft-spoken guy, was so fine, and someone she would want to make hers, sooner or later (and hope it's not later) and that she would follow him anywhere, over deep oceans and high mountains. Same thing with "My Guy" by Mary Wells from 1964, which also unsurprisingly made the list. As with the other two, how wonderful it would be if Mary Liz was proudly telling anyone and everyone in her orbit—friends, family, even strangers— that nothing anyone could ever say would ever tear her away from her guy, Paul, that they were birds of a feather and would stick together.

"Forever" by the Marvelettes had to be there; although technically not a #1, and not on the *Billboard* Top 100 list either, but released in early 1963, it was permanently etched in Paul's memory as the dreamy ballad he heard that night in October 1963 when he attended the dance at St. Eugene's for the one and only time, saw Mary Liz, Nancy and Dolores standing in a small circle in the dark gym when that song came on, and Nancy and Dolores both peeled off to slow dance with two guys he didn't know, leaving Mary Liz standing there alone, the lyrics so loud in that dark and suddenly quiet gym, seeping into a part of his brain to be stored and never discarded (*"Darling...forever...forever...you can break my heart...take my love for granted...I'll always be just a fool...if I, if I, could be with you"*) and he wanted so badly to go over and ask her to dance, heart pounding, face flushed, but his legs wouldn't move, and finally another guy he didn't know, very tall (maybe in high school?) came over to her and she went off to slow dance with him. He always imagined (and would have given anything to actually hear) Mary Liz singing all those songs to him, especially "Forever." But he didn't dare write anything like that on the spreadsheet. Mental notes only.

Paul was surprised by the number of what he had considered "novelty songs" that had had enough popularity to make the *Billboard* lists, such as "If You Want to Be Happy" by Jimmy Soul (not included; he wasn't sure if the repeated references to "ugly girl" had offended some of his female classmates back in the day, and might stir up uncomfortable memories 55 years later), and "Dominique" by the Singing Nun (included, with the comment "I will confess to a smidge of Catholic pride that a song by a nun could get to #1 with that little touch of melodic sunshine at the darkened and darkening end of the year). "Dominique" held that position from mid-December 1963 through mid-January 1964 when Bobby Vinton's "There! I've Said It Again" knocked it out. He wanted to capture that transition zone, that fertile time between the last of the pre-Beatles songs from the autumn and early winter of 1963, and the post-Beatles explosion that followed, when from early February through early May it was all Beatles commanding the #1 spots with "I Want To Hold Your Hand," "She Loves You," and "Can't Buy Me Love." Paul wrote one comment for all three songs: "There's not much to add to what so many of us felt then and perhaps still feel now in memory about early 1964 when the Beatles arrived sonically and visually in and on our radios, televisions, newspapers and magazines, and emotionally in our hearts and minds with an energy, enthusiasm and optimism we longed for and so sorely needed after the darkness of November 1963, even if we weren't consciously making that connection." This latter sentiment doubled down on Paul's earlier assertion in the memory booklet that, commentators' and pundits' assertions in 2014 notwithstanding, he wasn't making any conscious connections between JFK and the Beatles in early 1964 (such as thinking they were all sinking, their optimistic JFK-inspired space-age hopes dashed until the Beatles came to the rescue), and he assumed nobody else was either.

Paul went a little "off list" by including every song from the Beatles' inaugural American album *Meet the Beatles*, the one that was playing in Nancy's basement in late March of that year when he and Mary Liz had their Post Office moment, but he kept the comment rather flat and relatively impersonal by simply writing "Some of the class may recall that this album was played in its entirety and repeatedly at Nancy Hendrick's birthday party on Holy Saturday afternoon in 1964." There was a lot to unpack in there, but he left it packed.

Mary Liz was gone

Paul didn't learn about English literature's examples of April ambivalence—such as Chaucer's sweet showers signaling a time of awakening, to begin a journey, as a pilgrim in *The Canterbury Tales,* vs. Eliot's bleaker description in "The Waste Land"—until senior year of college; but as far back as eighth grade he knew the sting of the latter's "cruelest month" version, and that cruelty had nothing to do with any bone-chilling rains or surprise late snow falls or long long stretches of gray gray skies, but with one simple observable reality—Mary Liz was gone.

Gone.

She had been there on their last day of class before Easter break, the Wednesday of Holy Week (a.k.a. "Spy Wednesday" because those who sought to arrest Jesus were spying on him), March 25th, and since Paul had altar boy assignments that whole long weekend—the feet washing Mass on Holy Thursday, the Good Friday veneration of the cross at 3:00 in the afternoon then Stations of the Cross at 7:00 (Nancy's party Saturday afternoon, a Holy Week service of another sort), and the Easter Vigil service on Holy Saturday night that culminated in Easter Mass—he got to see her at every one of those events in her usual place in the right front row of the choir loft, half sitting half leaning on the half wall that, like a guard rail, made the loft a safe space. Paul didn't talk to her on any of those church occasions, but he saw her, and of course he saw her and they kissed at Nancy's party. They were off from school Easter Monday, but when they returned the next day, Tuesday March 31st she just wasn't there. One day of absence was no big deal, especially the first day of school after a holiday break, so no one speculated or drew any conclusions beyond the guess or assumption that perhaps she had eaten a little too much of her mom's ham, lasagna, or Easter bread, or of the inevitable chocolate bunny or coconut cream chocolate egg she bought as we all did from the school for their Easter fundraiser. But when Tuesday March 31st became Wednesday April 1st and April kept moving along into its second and third week with still no Mary Liz, kids did start to wonder.

If anyone knew what had happened, no one was talking. Nancy and most of the girls in their crowd were as perplexed as Paul was; any of them who might have been in a position to know something said they didn't know anything, or if they did they weren't talking. They also wondered if wherever she went and whatever she was doing came upon her as abruptly as it had come upon them; how else could she have kept it so quiet from even her closest companions, even though, given how aloof she could be, and her tendency (at least rumored) to hang out with older kids and even be dating boys in high school, she really wasn't all that close to the girls in her class at St. Anthony's. She had seemed so relaxed and lighthearted at Nancy's party. Someone even wondered if Mary Liz had died but that was crazy. She was just gone. At first Bernie said nothing, but Nancy eventually called and spoke to Mary Liz's mom who said she had to move to Pittsburgh for a few months to help a sick aunt and would finish eighth grade there, so that was the official story and the nuns backed it up and of course asked us to pray for Mary Liz and her aunt.

Paul had started to do what decades later would be called "visualization." When he walked onto the school grounds and looked over to where Nancy and Dolores were talking, he imagined a phantom Mary Liz standing there with them. When they were settling into their desks before class started he would look over to where her seat had been in seventh grade near the front of the fourth row and imagine her sitting there. When serving the 9:00 Mass he would stand at his little spying spot behind the altar, peeking through the lattice woodwork up at the choir loft imagining her walking to the organ area to pick up her music folder then walking to her spot on the right with the rest of the sopranos, saying in his head, "Please, Mary Liz. Please. Where are you? Please come back."

He even resorted to the St. Anthony prayer they had all learned back in first grade, silently asking please, please find her and bring her back. After what she and Paul had just exchanged at Nancy's party he felt a little hole had opened in his chest. Once when he and Biggsy were discussing the prayer that made their school's namesake so well-known, Biggsy said he thought it was ridiculous that Anthony of Padua, the 13th-century priest and teacher and actual colleague of Francis of Assisi would take time out of his busy heavenly schedule of intercessory prayer for healing and world peace and an end to famine and poverty and other lofty objectives to help someone find a misplaced set of car keys or a pencil case. Regardless, growing up, whenever anyone lost anything—from a missing sock to homework or even a pet that had run away—a parent or teacher or even some devout classmates would invariably chant "Please St. Anthony come around, for something's lost that can't be found." And despite Biggsy's skepticism, students at St. Anthony's fancied themselves as having something of an inside track to get quicker and surer results. This may have been in Paul's mind when he resorted to the prayer himself, perhaps feeling somewhat desperate, or it may have just been a reflex.

After a while most everyone settled back into their routines, all except Paul who kept wondering and wishing and visualizing. And so that was how the April wasteland would go. Empty. With Easter over so early there was nothing to look forward to generally; the end of Lent that culminated with that concentrated number and intensity of services seemed to be building to something—yes, the clerics would say, building to the Resurrection, the greatest feast of the Church—but after that was over and the students realized the end of school and summer were still two months away, it felt like a huge letdown, even a bit of a tease. And with Mary Liz gone there was definitely very little for Paul to look forward to in school. The weather didn't help—mostly a gray wasteland rain and only occasionally that sweetness of a warmer shower. And the kids in eighth grade were getting even more impatient, starting to feel the itch of not just wanting to be done with school for the year, but with St. Anthony's forever.

Then around the middle of the third week of April at first recess Biggsy told Paul, Gerry and Robbie that he wanted to have a meeting under Hannum's oak tree at second recess. Once they had gathered, he started in usual Biggsy fashion.

"Well, chums," he started, "I may have solved our little mystery."

Paul closed his eyes and shook his head and said to himself, "Here we go," then aloud, "It was YOUR little mystery, Biggsy, not ours."

Ignoring Paul's comment Biggsy continued, "Doesn't it seem a little strange that in November Hiram dies, mysteriously, two months later Father Galvin is sent away, also mysteriously, and three months after that Mary Liz Albarelli disappears?"

"What's strange," Paul said, "is that you're probably about to tell us that they're all connected."

"That's right," Biggsy said, but before he could start to elaborate Paul broke in.

"Christ, Biggsy, you've dreamed up and said some crazy shit before, but this is really crazy."

"You really think it's crazy?" Biggsy came back. "I'm just putting two and two together. There was just no logical reason for Hiram to die. He was young and healthy and strong. This may not be as easy for the rest of you to understand but I'm studying to be a doctor so I know his death could not have been from "natural causes" as people like to say. Something had to happen to him, and from the clues I saw in the boiler room when I found him I figured out that somebody had to have poisoned him, probably because he knew something or saw something, and now that Galvin and Mary Liz are gone I've put together the other pieces of the puzzle."

"I can't wait," Paul said under his breath but Biggsy kept going.

"The way I see it, Galvin may have started screwing Mary Liz right around when school started this year, and Hiram may have caught them, then Hiram may have threatened to blab to Ellis and Bernie and may have wanted to blackmail Galvin, but Galvin didn't have any money so he may have decided he had to just make Hiram go away. So he may have gone down to the boiler room one time when Hiram wasn't there, and he may have put the rat poison into some of Hiram's food. And now Mary Liz was sent away because she may be pregnant."

"Pregnant!" Paul exclaimed. "By Galvin? Are you nuts?!"

"What else could it be?" Biggsy asked.

"Oh, about a million other things, maybe like Hiram dying of natural causes and Galvin saying the illegal Mass and Mary Liz moving to Pittsburgh to help her aunt like her mom said. And besides, she didn't look pregnant a couple of weeks ago."

"Oh really?" Biggsy said. "You are so gullible. Did you know that some girls don't look pregnant until the very end? I read that. And it's been winter and early spring and she's had to wear a coat a lot of the time you've seen her, and didn't you notice she was wearing a big bulky sweater over her uniform a lot lately, one that goes pretty far down her legs but at least covers her belly?"

When Biggsy mentioned the sweater Paul did have to admit that she had been wearing that sweater what seemed like almost every day leading up to Easter, and a couple of times he saw her wrap it loosely around herself, crossing her arms so that it covered her chest and belly and saying, "It's FREEZing in here" when it wasn't really even that cold.

"But what about Galvin and that illegal Mass?" Paul asked.

"A decoy," Biggsy said, "meant to distract everyone from what was REALLY going on. He may have said that Mass, but it probably wasn't that big a deal and by itself didn't mean he had to go away."

"So Ellis is in on this, too? And the archbishop?" Paul asked, incredulously.

"Of course," Biggsy said. "Jesus, you are so naive. Haven't you ever heard of a conspiracy?"

"So now what?" Paul asked. "What are you going to do with this information?"

"Yeah," said Robbie Hannum, who was completely taken in by the tale Biggsy was weaving, "are you gonna tell Randy about this?" Randall Stanton whom friends and colleagues and even the kids called "Randy" was a member of Springhaven's small police squad but also drove St. Anthony's one and only school bus on three separate runs that together with the walking, bike riding and car pick-ups got everyone home from school every day, so he would be easy to find and was already very easy to talk to since everyone knew him, he had two nephews and a niece in St. Anthony's (he was still unmarried), and helped coach CYO basketball.

"I'm still thinking about it," Biggsy said. "I'm still thinking about it."

*   *   *

In the meantime, spring inched and then jumped along and with it the period of daylight, and with that the St. Anthony students could spend more time outside, both at recess, after school and on weekends. April crept and slipped into May which was Mary's month at St. Anthony's, and presumably at every Catholic elementary school in the diocese, the region, and for all they knew maybe even the country and the whole Catholic world. Years later in his college hippie years Paul would conflate this early devotion to the Virgin Mother of God with more pagan, earth-energy-centered sensibilities that honored Mother Earth—the time after April's cruel hard cold rains that softened the ground and allowed the out-leafing and out-budding of trees and buttercups and clover and wild rose—but back at St. Anthony's May was all about honoring Mary of Nazareth, of singing to her everyday after lunch as a different student who had been assigned the duty for the day would craft and place a crown of flowers (Paul made his with his mother's help from the pink azaleas that grew in the flower bed along the fence that enclosed their backyard) atop the 2-foot high statue that sat on the bookshelf at the front of the classroom, singing "Immaculate Mary, our hearts are on fire. That title so wondrous fills all our desire. Ave, Ave, Ave Ma-ri-AH; Ave, Ave, Ave Ma-ri-i-ah."

And each daily ritual culminated in the grand May procession on the next-to-last Sunday in May that coincided with the First Communion Day for the second graders, they processing (the girls in their white dresses and veils and white shoes like little brides, and the boys in white suits and ties and also in white shoes) with all the other grades out of the school yard and into the street as Randy and another policeman controlled the traffic, turning right on Sycamore and walking down to the corner at Cedar then looping back on Sycamore and into the school where they lined up for prayers, more hymns (such as "Ave Maria! O Maiden, O mother" that switches in the refrain to the Latin "Ave Sanctissima! Ave purissima!" before crescendoing on "Sinless and beautiful Star of the Sea!" out of *The St. Gregory Hymnal*), then finally in sync with the last hymn "Hail Virgin, dearest Mary," just as the choir sings "We haste to crown thee now" their eighth grade May Queen does just that with a wreath of flowers large enough to fit on the head of the 8-foot statue in the little courtyard outside the convent, before Fr. Ellis made his usual brief congratulatory remarks, saying how beautiful, what a fitting tribute to Mary, how lovely the choir, and on and on. Practicing for the May procession and standing in the heat of middle and late May was torture for some, but as Paul knew from altar boy duties, anything that gets you out of class is a blessing, no matter how hot or how seemingly boring, and especially if it ends (as it always did) on the actual May Procession day with Fr. Ellis giving them the next day off amid the usual hoots and hollers.

All of this for the Church's Mary, Jesus' Mary, the Mary of all Catholics, while Paul's Mary, his Mary Liz was still missing, absent, gone. He didn't know if she would have been the May Queen or even a contender as the nuns thought she was too wild, and maybe not even chaste, but she was Paul's May Queen and he was singing in his heart for her to come back, maybe not a *St. Gregory Hymnal* hymn, maybe more like the Beatles' "This boy, wants you back again."

IX

School Year Stops (June 13th*)
(*or 12th or 14th if 13th falls on
a Saturday or Sunday)

Although Biggsy felt that the season at the start of the school year lasted a few weeks, to give both teachers and students enough time to fully disengage from summer and fully immerse in the new school year (although both disengagement and immersion were relative concepts, perhaps better characterized by degrees than absolutes), he felt the school year could stop more or less abruptly, and that at least the students could disengage more or less immediately and step effortlessly into summer. That had probably been true for us in seventh grade, and all the years before that as well. And maybe other eighth grade classes before in previous years could have walked into the church two-by-two no talking for the graduation service and sat through all the prayers and speeches and singing and awards ceremony daydreaming, maybe mapping out exactly what he or she would do as soon as they were dismissed and could go home and reverse the process that had occurred just nine months earlier—trading stiff white collared shirts and ties and uniforms for shorts and tee shirts and sneakers or maybe bathing suits and diving headlong into the swim club pool and summer without the need for any adjustment period or decompression. But THAT year, the September 1963 to June 1964 school year, with all that happened—not just in school but in the larger world outside of school—I won't speak for anyone else but as I tried to look past that day and that night into the summer that lay ahead I got stuck. How could I disengage fully or even partially from the school year when there was still so much unfinished business between me and Biggsy, or between me and Mary Liz? And there was still the graduation party that night, and no way of knowing what would happen there. I guess it was possible that Biggsy was right, that I would be able to turn the school year off and turn summer on like a spigot. Maybe he could. But I don't know. I could see myself walking out of the graduation service that day and even the party that night still carrying a lot in my head and my heart that would take me more than a day to shake off.

A lot more.

If ever.

Graduation

Friday June 12, 1964 finally arrived. The feast day of Saint Anthony of Padua was technically the next day, Saturday June 13th, but per the usual custom since the feast day fell on Saturday the school year officially ended the day before with a graduation ceremony at the church in the morning and a party for the eighth-grade graduates that night. It was a Friday but there was no school in the school building that day for those graduating (going to church for the service was the substitute for going to school, while grades 1-7 would still have to show up at school for a half day), just as there would be no school on Monday June 15th or Tuesday June 16th or on any more days in June July or August and not again until high school started after Labor Day. The day before had been blue sky sunny and crisp, the afternoon temperature only hitting the upper 70's, but Friday dawned with wispy clouds graying the sun and the humidity was already creeping in as if to presage what Paul and his classmates were in for during the long summer ahead. At 8:45 A.M. the eighth grade class at St. Anthony's elementary school gathered at the base of their parish church steps, where their teacher and principal (soon to be ex-both) Sister Bernadette Marie formed them into two parallel lines, first girls then boys, the students in each line placed by height so that the shortest boys followed the tallest girls and the whole line when formed resembled a 2-toothed saw blade, in advance of their procession two by two up the steps and into the first 15 pews to start the graduation ceremony marking and celebrating their final day in grade school.

By then Biggsy had still not shared any of his murder-blackmail theories concerning their deceased janitor, banished priest, and missing classmate with the police (when asked about it by Robbie Hannum a day or two earlier Biggsy had said he still wasn't quite ready to "go to the authorities," such a Biggsy phrase, because he still had more investigating to do on his own, and when Paul heard that from Robbie he remarked that even Biggsy must have had limits to how much bullshit was too much), the latter issue having been diminished somewhat, for Paul anyway, since Mary Liz had returned. She was standing in line with her classmates outside of church and after processing/marching in ultimately sitting in the second pew for the graduation festivities, having reappeared the day before when the class was practicing for the ceremony—reappeared as unexpectedly as she had gone missing. She was just back, as if she had never left, and seemingly trying to reinforce that impression by consistently deflecting any and all questions her friends asked about where she'd been what happened with her aunt did she really finish eighth grade in Pittsburgh and if so why was she back at St. Anthony's for graduation by saying repeatedly, simply, "I really don't wanna talk about it."

The eighth graders who had been altar boys and choir girls had already surrendered those duties to the then-seventh/rising-eighth graders, instead occupying seats in the pews and feeling slightly awkward there, as if they shouldn't have been there and didn't belong and instead should have been on the altar or in the choir loft, not yet accustomed to this first of many changes still to come.

As one of the taller students in the class Paul was in the second to last pew, and two pews behind him the parents and grandparents had filled in the rest of the seating until there was literally standing room only, up along the side aisles as always happened at the crowded Christmas and Easter Masses. He could have and perhaps should have been thinking any number of thoughts, such as of the past eventful year and the significance of this milestone—completing eight years of elementary school education (his mother, that morning kept saying, repeatedly, "We're so proud of you" with his dad usually completing that sentiment with "Yeah, but there's still a lot ahead of you in high school and college and all the rest so you can enjoy today but you can't sit back on your laurels" whatever that meant)— speculation about what it would be like to start high school at Archbishop Keenan's, but before that enjoying the summer, finishing little league in the next week or two with playoffs and then All Stars, his summer job in his dad's business helping on the delivery truck as he had started doing on Saturdays the last couple of months, their family summer vacation in Wildwood Crest, but instead his head was filled with the last few months since the time he kissed Mary Liz at Nancy's party, and how sad he had been when she was gone the next week, and how happy now that she was back. So unsettled before, and so peaceful now. Ever since she had shown up at practice the day before she was all he could think about, wondering if he were really seeing her or if it was just more of the kind of imagining and visualizing he had been doing since the week after Easter, thinking that if she showed up at the actual ceremony it would confirm the reality, and now that he was in the same general space with her, in church with her again, and instead of him on the altar and she in the choir loft they were now only a few pews apart, as if the fact that they had rejoined each other in time and were moving closer to each other in space might also mean closer in affection. And now feeling even more confident that after seeing her at practice and now again at the ceremony that his luck would hold out and she would attend the graduation party that night, and that if he were really lucky maybe he would be able to talk to her, maybe even dance with her, and if really REALLY lucky maybe, just maybe, another kiss, even if it were a kiss goodbye because they probably wouldn't see each other over the summer and she had announced months before (and before she had vanished) that she would be going to Springhaven High, not Keenan, but the luckiest thing of all would be a kiss hello, a good to be back I've missed you kiss, and before we have to go to high school we will have a wonderful summer of more kisses kind of kiss.

As a result of that distraction the Graduation Mass came and went almost without Paul noticing. The Father Ellis homily which he rarely barely listened to anyway at other Masses was like a hum or buzz or drone. And when Biggsy went up to the altar rail to collect his eighth of eight highest average awards Paul barely noticed, wasn't even annoyed or frustrated. And he only found out it was time to file out when he heard and felt and saw everyone around him stand up and he snapped to to some degree, vaguely peripherally aware of the choir singing (all sixth and seventh graders) *"God's...bless-ing sends us forth* (Where is Mary Liz's voice?), *strengthened for our task on earth* (that soprano soar in every song I listen for and love to hear?), *reee-FRESHED in soul, re-ee-new-ewed in, mi-i-i-nd.* (Oh wait. She's here. Getting ready to exit the pew on the other side of the aisle and walk right by me.) *May...God with us remain* (Will she turn to look at me?), *through...us His Spirit reign* (Will I see her tonight? Will we dance? Kiss?), *that Christ be known to all mankind."*

*   *   *

By 21st century standards it was a pretty low tech audio operation— Paul up on the altar/stage in the basement of the church with his box-record player with speakers that swung out on hinges and could even be taken off the hinges and placed as far out as the wire length (about 3-4 feet) for maximal stereo effect, using the microphone from the lectern to mike one of the speakers to amplify the sound, which wouldn't have worked very well if the stereo mix on the record really separated the instruments and voices, but didn't matter in this case since all the records were mono.

Speaking of which, Paul had brought his own records, the ones on which he had squandered most of the money he made working for his dad—mostly British invasions bands such as the Beatles, Searchers, Dave Clark Five, Rolling Stones—while Nancy complemented that with her Motown, Beach Boys, Four Seasons, and other American bands. Paul had one special 45 he was saving for the dance he hoped he would get with Mary Liz—"Forever" by the Marvelettes, hoping he would be able to finally fix the mistake he had made back in October at the St. Eugene's dance when he had let the opportunity to dance with her pass him by.

There were long tables on one side of the room against the wall with a narrow row behind it for volunteer parents working the food and beverages stations—bowls of pretzels and potato chips, some hoagies from Donatello's deli cut into 3-4 inch manageable pieces, a selection of chocolate cupcakes and a few pies such as apple, French apple with the raisins and vanilla icing, and lemon, and finally a 2-foot diameter metal tub filled with ice and sodas (with more wooden cases of soda behind the table along the wall so the parents could keep refilling the tub).

Mostly the boys and girls stood in their separate groups, but mixed a little, and eventually some started dancing together. When Paul put on *Meet the Beatles* he decided to let the whole album play through rather than picking individual tracks, just as it had at Nancy's party. When "I Saw Her Standing There" came on, more and more boys and girls started dancing together in a kind of group dance rather than paired off, so Paul came down off the stage and joined them for that fast and raucous number. Mary Liz was standing off on the side, actually talking to Sister Bernadette which struck Paul as odd. All those years taught and pestered and hounded by nuns and now here she was on the night she was officially being released from that prison (even more significant since she wouldn't be continuing in Catholic school) and she was talking to a nun. Then "This Boy" came on, a slow dance. Some of the chaperoning parents scowled and glared as they watched their innocent 13- and 14-year olds adopt the slow dance style of the day—the embrace with the girl's arms and hands behind the boy's neck and the boy's arms and hands around the girl's waist and maybe even slipping/inching ever so slightly towards her back side, chests close enough to touch, and if groins still slightly separated, still close enough for electric arcs. Just as Paul was deciding he would save his chance to ask Mary Liz to dance to "Forever" he saw Biggsy go over to where she was standing, then take her by the hand and go out into the middle of the dance floor. Biggsy? Biggsy who thought girls were a distraction and had no time for them, THAT BOY now dancing with HIS GIRL? What the hell was going on? Paul went back to the stage as "This Boy" was ending and "All My Loving" coming on, looking up to see Biggsy and Mary Liz separate, thumbing through his 45's until he found "Forever" and putting that one on as soon as side 1 of *Meet the Beatles* ended, then hurrying down to the dance floor and over to Mary Liz (he wasn't going to miss his chance this time), but getting there and looking at her he was tongue-tied so they just looked at each other a few seconds (that felt like minutes), not smiling, not scowling, more or less expressionless until Mary Liz said, "I'm hot. Let's go somewhere."

Gerry and Nancy were still making out in the corner when Sister Bernadette Marie saw them before they realized they had been caught and she started walking over to where they were standing, her brisk walk, with robes flying and rosary beads swinging wildly, just like the day she went to check out what had happened to Hiram, but she stopped short as they broke apart, perhaps realizing she no longer had any authority over them—they had graduated, they were done—and perhaps just saving her energy for the next Gerry and the next Nancy coming up the ranks she would have to tangle with come September.

Biggsy walked briskly too, right up to Paul and said, "Let's go!"

"Where?"

"The Woods."

"Now?"

"Yes, now. Why? When else? What else do you have to do? This party blows. Let's go."

Paul began, "Well, I was thinking…" but Biggsy cut him off.

"What? Going somewhere with Mary Liz? I knew it. You are such a pussy, and so pussy-whipped."

"She said she was hot and wanted to go somewhere" he told Biggsy.

After she had said that to Paul he had mumbled something about needing to get Nancy to play the records for him, but he'd be right back. Nancy was talking to Gerry at the time, so Paul went up to her to ask her to take over the DJ duties, and when she asked why and he told her what Mary Liz had said, adding that, yes, the room was a little warm so maybe they would go outside and get some fresh air for a little bit (and thinking maybe that's where he might get his kiss) at which point Nancy started laughing.

"Oh Paul you are such a queer. She didn't mean hot-hot as in the temperature in the room or outside, but LOVE hot, hot FOR YOU. She wants to make out with you, and maybe more than that."

Paul was incredulous; dumbfounded. But on the off chance that Nancy might be right and it might be true he hurried up to the stage and put on side 2 of "Meet the Beatles" to buy some time as Nancy and Gerry started going at it again in one of the corners of the room.

"And that's what I'm saying, too," Biggsy continued, "let's go somewhere, except not just somewhere or anywhere, but to The Woods, to Bamboo Island. Come on, man. It's our last night together."

"What are you talking about? We'll be in the same high school the next four years."

"No, asshole, I mean the last night like this. At St. Anthony's. As grade schoolers. Who knows what will happen to us over the summer or once we start high school and we get mixed with all the other kids from all the other schools? Let's have one more night as we are now, and do it in our hideout. Time to get lost, man, let's GO!"

"But..." Paul stammered, "the records...my record player...Mary Liz..." but Biggsy cut him off.

"We'll come back and get it later. We'll only be gone an hour. We'll get back before the party's over. Somebody else can play the goddamn records or there can be an hour with no music. What's the big deal? Let's go. Let's disappear and reappear and make everyone think we have super powers, that we stepped into a different dimension and then stepped back."

Reluctantly, Paul went over to Mary Liz and told her he had to do something with Biggsy and the guys for just a couple minutes and would be back soon, but she just said "Pussy!" and turned and walked away. Paul wanted to follow her but could feel Biggsy behind him, waiting, probably glaring.

Paul, Biggsy and Gerry and Robbie walked up the stairs from the church basement into the vestibule and out, out past the small stone wall that encircled St. Anthony's, down Cedar Street to left on Sycamore to left on Taylor's Ford to right on Clover Lane through Woolsey's backyard and into The Woods, walking in the dark so the Woolseys couldn't see them and yell, and the ground was soft with no dry crackling leaves so they probably couldn't hear them either and they weren't talking, just walking, without flashlights or matches or cigarette lighters to illuminate the way but they had done it so many times including at night they could have walked in blindfolded and never gotten lost, especially since they knew certain markers (such as the tree trunk with the gnarly knob that was somewhat visible even in darkness), and anyway within a few minutes their eyes got accustomed to the dark plus under the stars and the tiniest sliver of a waxing crescent moon they were able to see just fine, down the path, past the ruins of the old Taylor mansion and its crumbling stone wall, following their own well-worn footsteps from days and weeks and months and years before till they saw the light tan colored wood of the 6-foot length of 1X6 Biggsy had picked up from the construction site next to the A&P a few weeks earlier and placed it as a bridge over The Creek, feeling justified taking it because the excavation that would soon bring a new Kiddie City to that small shopping center was starting to eat up part of The Woods, their Woods, and kept walking across the makeshift bridge in single file as it bent and bounced from their combined weight and motion, almost touching the water and mud below with each step, and finally onto the other side, onto Bamboo Island.

The rocks and charcoals from their last fire were still there—the sixth and seventh graders and other neighborhood kids who played there knew not to touch them. Biggsy asked, "Does anyone have matches or a cigarette lighter?" but no one did so he said, "Then I'll make a fire myself" as he started squatting and trying to find some dried grass or twigs or other tinder and rocks he could try striking to make the spark until Paul interrupted him.

"We don't have time for that. We have to get back. My record player and all my records are still there. People will wonder where we are."

Biggsy stood up holding a small stick and a baseball sized rock and looked at Paul as much in the eye as he could in the dark.

"Man, you just don't get it. We're *never* going back, or at least I'm not. *We* know where we are and that's all that matters. If you go back now you'll be stuck there forever. Lost there forever and never found, even with all the prayers in the world to Saint Anthony."

Then Biggsy threw the stick and rock into The Creek and they all heard the splashes.

"There ya go, mateys," Biggsy said, "Bury them all in the depths of the sea."

Then Gerry and Robbie started throwing sticks and whatever else they could find into The Creek, making multiple splashes that kind of ran together into a prolonged whoosh blending with their laughing. Then they

"*If you go back now you'll be stuck there forever.*"

stopped and the splash noises from the last rocks and sticks subsided and it was quiet. The season's first fireflies were starting to light, off and on and off and on, down by the ground, then up up up into the trees. They all stared ahead and no one spoke.

Reunion

The Locust Hill Tavern had five separate banquet rooms accessed by a common entrance that had an opening to two of them and to a hallway that led to the other three. Because of its 18th century history, the rooms had always been named after American Revolution personages, even after the recent renovations, and there were signs at the entrance directing guests to their respective events. On June 15, 2019, St. Anthony's reunion was in the Lafayette Room, the first room off the hallway leading from the common entrance.

Nancy and Dolores had set up a table just inside the room entrance, where they were collecting the cash or checks from those who hadn't paid in advance, and there was also a stack of the memory booklets Paul had had printed but they were saving those for distribution later. Paul had arrived early to set up the sound system he had rented for the evening from Tyler's Music—two tall skinny speakers, an amplifier and two mikes. But before setting up he stopped in the men's room to see how he looked; that alone was evidence enough that this night would be different. Paul never (as in never EVER) paid any attention to what he wore or how he looked. But that night he had looked in his closet, since for a change he would need or want to be more thoughtful and intentional about what he would wear to the reunion. Usually he adhered to his uniform of jeans and a golf shirt (although he didn't golf) and maybe a hoodie or jacket depending on the weather, but that night he was thinking, thinking, what should I wear? He had a pair of khaki pants and a blue blazer, what he called his "high school prom uniform" based on so many friends' prom pictures he had looked at over the years. He thought that would work, and would harmonize with the notion that this was a school-related event, and even more specifically a Catholic school-related event. But what color shirt? Better to stick with white, like the uniform white shirts all the boys wore at Saint Anthony's.

Eventually there was that moment in front of the mirror. That moment almost all 20 somethings 30 somethings 40 somethings 50 somethings 60 somethings 70 somethings, and maybe even 80 and 90 somethings have when there is that stark and naked realization that you are as old as you are. Is my hair really that gray? And is my skin really that wrinkled? Are the bags under my eyes really that big, and that dark? Do the crow's feet at the edge of my eyes really look like they were made by real crows that dried in concrete rather than maybe a seagull's ephemeral prints in dry sand? Is there really that much overlap at the corners of my mouth or are my lips just drooping down? And even though you may not feel it at that particular time, for that instant at least you look it, and you know that you look it. And you say to yourself "I'm not [fill in the blank] anymore" and that blank might be 18 or 25 or 30 or 45 or even 50, when you think you may have been able to pull off still looking youthful. But in this case it was 14, the age he was in June 1964. Fortunately, it is only that instant, it passes, and for that moment or at least until you get in front of another mirror as he did in the men's room and have that thunderbolt realization again if you look too long which he didn't, you forget about it. The real problem though, was the unspoken question: What would Mary Liz think? Would she see me as old, or would she see something in my eyes that I expect to find in hers that makes us still 14? If she even comes.

Some classmates came up to say hello or talk to him as he was setting up, but the busyness he was creating and probably embellishing a little allowed him to keep those conversations short to get back to his task, every so often scanning the room, seeing who was there. Finally he pulled up the playlist on his phone, tapped "Shuffle" then "Play" and the Dave Clark Five's "Glad All Over" started the evening's music.

And then she walked in. She did come after all. She didn't pay in advance but at the door. While some students came with their spouses or significant others and some came alone, Mary Liz walked in with a younger man she introduced as her son Jimmy, saying they were both in town for an older cousin's 50th wedding anniversary the next day, so she thought they might stop in. Jimmy was tall with thick black hair he had cut relatively short and spiked, and while it was somewhat hard to see in the relatively low lights in the room (Nancy had specified that the lights be dimmed to give the effect of a St. Eugene's dance but also to minimize the visibility of all their various wrinkles, crow's feet and extra chins), his eyes were dark and set not only deep in his relatively narrow face but also somewhat close to his nose, almost giving him a somewhat puzzled look, but again it was not so easy to make out his features with much precision. And while most of the St. Anthony's class who had kids that ranged in ages from their late 20's to their mid 30's and early 40's, Mary Liz's son seemed older than that. From all his years as a physician and more recently as an ER tech, Paul had gotten pretty good—actually very good—at guessing ages, which he would usually express as a 5-year range. When he looked at Mary Liz's son, even in the dim light he registered a guess, and surprised himself a little to assign the range 43-48. But no big deal; he and most of his classmates had already turned 69; if he was right about Jimmy's age range, she could have had him when she was very young.

But no Biggsy. Not by advance registration, and after 30 minutes past the start time not at the door either. On one level Paul wanted him there since they hadn't seen each other for over 50 years—Biggsy left the area after high school to attend Princeton and never came back, and although he didn't really stay in touch with anyone in the class (he was closest to Paul and didn't even stay in touch with him), from word filtering back to the area via one or another of Biggsy's multiple siblings there was a general understanding that he never attended medical school as he had always planned, but did have a career in engineering, and the word on the street was that he eventually worked for NASA on the shuttle program, and had married, divorced and remarried with four children between the two wives (presumably he eventually found time to get interested in girls)—and there was so much to catch up on or at least a lot of history to acknowledge, and on another level Paul was also glad to have him out of the way.

After about 40 minutes Nancy assumed the emcee function, taking the microphone from Paul and after getting everyone's attention thanked them all for attending on behalf of the Reunion Committee. "St. Anthony's may be going away," she said, "but we are still here" at which the crowd roared and woo-hooed. "And now," she said, "I will turn things back over to the man with the 55-year DJ career (he says he did this back at our graduation party but naturally only he remembers that, as he remembers a lot more as you will soon see and hear), Paul Perduuuuu." More cheers as Paul took back the mike but instead of saying anything he simply re-started the playlist and "Telstar" started playing.

Predictably Paul didn't mingle much, mostly staying at his DJ post by the amp and speakers, busying himself with the technical tasks to avoid having to make small talk. He felt his main contribution was the memory booklet and the music so he didn't need to say much—his written words and his choice of songs were speaking for him—and anyway he would be addressing the crowd later for the trivia quiz. He did sit at a table for dinner, but played it safe and joined Nancy and her husband and Gerry and his wife at their table, familiar regulars from Fridays at Buddy's, picking at his Caesar salad and roll, and getting up when dessert was served to start the quiz. He never got around to creating the questions in the game show format, but after spending so much time and energy on the music and the memory booklet the best he could do was a simple series of questions, but no one knew the difference and what he did was enjoyable enough.

Paul started the trivia quiz and was surprised at how many classmates did NOT remember the answers or the stories (such as green being the color of the recess candy table and the 3-4 curved benches that encircled the huge oak in the schoolyard). Not too many recalled "church thunder" either or that Mrs. Lynch had asked them to save Betty Crocker box tops for her. After the trivia Paul led everyone in acapella versions of a few songs from their old music classes (from memory, of course) such as "Erie Canal" (substituting "lunger" for "lumber" as some of them sang back in the day), "Dr. Eisenbart" (of course singing "Eisen-FART") and "The Keeper" (making all the Nancy and Gerry salacious substitutions, such as "blow" for "bow," "bastard" for "master," "go to hell" for "very well" and "lay down" for "way down"—"among the leaves so green-o"). When they were done Paul brought out a stack of the memory booklets and directed everyone to take a copy (he hadn't made them available ahead of time since the trivia questions were in there and he wanted them to be a surprise). Then it was back to the music for the last hour or so of the party, but a little while later a man approached Paul whom he didn't know. "Nice job" he said, to which Paul perfunctorily replied "Thanks."

"I'm Ed Malloy. I grew up in Springhaven but went to Arthur Harvey Elementary, then Springhaven High. I'm married to Diane Harris." Diane had been in Paul's class all eight years at St. Anthony's, a kind of middle-of-the-road student overall who sang in the choir and as he recalled excelled in spelling (she might have represented St. Anthony's in a regional spelling bee), but he barely knew her since she wasn't friendly with Nancy or Dolores or Mary Liz or part of what Biggsy always called "the clique."

"Oh right, Diane" Paul said. "Nice."

"Hey I saw that little blurb in your booklet about Hiram, your old janitor."

"Yeah?" Paul said. "Did you know him?"

"Not exactly, but you said something about how his death might have been foul play or somebody thought it might have been."

"Oh right," Paul said smiling and half chuckling. "I threw that in there hoping this kid in our class named Ron Biggs might come, since that was his theory. He used to read a lot of Hardy Boys books back in the day and thought everything that was even the slightest bit mysterious might be part of some secret caper or criminal activity. He had a pretty vivid imagination."

"I knew Biggsy," Malloy said. "My dad was a doctor over in Media and Biggsy used to come to the office once in a while to sort of hang out and observe, thinking he might want to go to medical school someday."

"Dr. Malloy," Paul said, "I remember him."

"Did Biggsy ever become a doctor?" Malloy asked.

"No," Paul replied, "but I did."

"Really?" Malloy said. "Are you still practicing?"

"No," Paul said. It was a little hard to talk over the music and Paul didn't really want to get into it so he changed the subject and said, "How is your dad?"

"He passed away a couple of years ago," Malloy said, "but thanks for asking. I just wanted to say that my father was also the County Coroner, so I actually know something about how that janitor died. Since he was found dead at your school it was a coroner's case so my dad had to do his autopsy."

"Really?" Paul said. "And you remember that?"

"I do," Malloy said. "I'm a few years older than you and at the time I used to help my dad out in the morgue so I do remember that case, because it was so surprising that such a young man had died so suddenly. He was only 35 or 36 (Paul and his classmates had no idea how old Hiram had been, they just knew he was older than they were which could have meant 10 years older or 50 years older, but now at age 69 Paul realized how young Hiram had really been), and I'll never forget what I saw when my dad opened up his skull—all that blood."

"Really?" Paul said, again. "What was it? Ruptured aneurysm?"

"Exactly," Malloy said. "Maybe a mystery to you guys but not to my dad."

Paul smiled again, and actually laughed a little. "I can't believe it," he said. "All this time…all these years…I hadn't thought about it for over 50 years, but putting this party together…it popped into my head what Biggsy had thought at the time." Then shaking his head and chuckling again, "He was so nuts."

"Yeah, Malloy said, "He was definitely an odd kid."

Eventually the song "This Boy" came on as Paul hoped it would at some point (he had included it with the rest of *Meet the Beatles* on the playlist, but he had more than four hours of music so there was no guarantee it would play unless he abandoned the shuffle and specifically selected it). The first familiar chords strummed out. Mary Liz was over by the bar, talking to Nancy. Laughing. Throwing back her head as she always did back in the day when she laughed. She was oblivious to the song and what it had meant to Paul, to both of them. What did he expect? That she would hear the first chords and immediately turn to find him and they would meet and dance as she and Biggsy had done in 1964, to make right what had been so wrong 55 years earlier, especially with Biggsy not being there? He walked over and insinuated himself into the conversation. At one point he interjected "Do you remember this?"

"What?" Mary Liz asked.

"This song," Paul said. You and Biggsy danced to it at the graduation party and I was really upset."

"God, Paul," Mary Liz started, "Uh, that was like more than 50 years ago! Your memory is amazing."

At that point Nancy got pulled into another conversation, so Mary Liz and Paul were left facing each other. Above the din Paul blurted, "I know we were just kids, but I think I really loved you back then. At least it felt like that"

"Awww," Mary Liz said, "that's so sweet. But yes, we were just kids. We were...what? 14? You are too much."

He half smiled to cover his embarrassment then said, "Well, anyway, it felt real to me at the time, no matter how old we were."

She grabbed his face at his cheeks and growled, scowling. "Paaauuullll. Still so cute!" Then she smiled. He half-smiled back and they just stood there another few seconds.

"Well, I guess I should get back to the music," Paul finally started to say, but someone had already come over to say hello to and distracted Mary Liz. Paul didn't know who it was or if she had even heard him.

That was enough. He walked away.

Paul knew it was getting towards the end of the night but he hadn't checked the time in a while. Maybe unconsciously he didn't want to. Didn't want the whole affair to slip back into the world of time. He was scrolling through his playlist, off shuffle now, selecting specific songs. Sticking now with all Motown and other Soul or R&B singles for the girls to dance. The Ronettes' "Be My Baby." Martha and the Vandellas' "Quicksand," "Nowhere to Run" and "Heat Wave," and for that one Paul jumped out into the crowd, into the middle of the small circle some of the girls had made, dancing

"Awww," Mary Liz said, *"that's so sweet. But yes, we were just kids."*

with them the old "Heat Wave" line dance which he didn't remember that he knew. And even though he was aware it was the Locust Crest Tavern on June 15, 2019, for an instant, a nanosecond maybe, with the lights kind of low on the dance floor it was the St. Anthony church basement on June 13, 1964, where then just as now it was mostly the girls that danced, while the guys huddled hoping the vapor stew of English Leather and Jade East and Canoe would attract one of those girls and maybe, just maybe there'd be a slow and close slow dance in their future. "Heat Wave" had played that night too, part of Nancy's record collection, and at least a few boys (but definitely he) were wishing at least a few girls (but definitely he wishing Mary Liz) were thinking *"Whenever I'm with him, somethin' inside, starts to burning, and I'm filled with desire. Could it be a devil in me or is this the way love's supposed to be? It's like a heatwave, burnin' in my heart, I can't keep from cry-yin, it's tearin' me apart."* And for just that instant, that nanosecond, the parts of Paul's brain that see and hear and smell made the part of his brain that makes his feet move made his feet move so stiffly and awkwardly to anyone that might have been observing from the outside, his upper teeth curled over his lower lip, but it's OK since no one is old or stiff or awkward tonight as they glide through the song through time and into the arms of memory, the memory that is a fire burning in the heart.

After "Heat Wave" Paul exited the dance floor and went back to his DJ post, still playing mostly Motown and not so much British invasion or Beach Boys but he did slip in Manfred Mann's "Doo Wah Diddy" for that great *"Looked good, looked fine, walked on to my door then we kissed a little more"* call and response for which Nancy and Dolores went nuts. The girls wanted the mike and kept passing it around, each taking turns at verses and choruses. He could sense someone standing over him—the catering manager, knowing he wouldn't be able to be heard he held up his 10 fingers. Paul shouted back, "Ten minutes?" but the manager shook his head and shouted back, "No. It was supposed to be over at 10:00." Then pointing to his watch "It's 10:15." Paul nodded, then held up his own solo index finger and mouthed "One more song."

As "Mickey's Monkey" was fading out he leaned into the mike and said, "Last song. Ladies' choice" and hit "Play" on "Forever" and got up, looking for Mary Liz.

Nowhere.

He asked Nancy, Dolores, and a couple of other people. No one knew. Did she leave? Disappear? As before?

You can break my heart, forever (as before).
Take my love for granted (as before).
I'll always be, just a fool (as before).
If I, if I, could be with you.

He went back to the chair and picked up his phone, staring at the title, watching the scrolling timeline on that 2-minute song. Over so quickly. The song wound down and ended and the lights came up, just as at every dance he'd ever attended in grade school and even later in high school. Nancy grabbed the mike and thanked everyone for coming and said they were going to reconvene at Buddy's for anyone who wanted to come. Paul was packing up the equipment, winding the wires and cables when Nancy and Dolores were walking past, stopping to ask, "See you at Buddy's?" "Yeah," Paul said, "I'll be there after I get packed up."

He lifted the milk crate of cables and walked out into the humid mid-June evening. The smell of honeysuckle and crown vetch and wild roses from the hedges surrounding the parking lot blended into one aromatic cloud dissolved into the moist night air as if it had been misted out of a room air freshener. He saw a few fireflies, the first of the season, a sure sign that summer had arrived. He drove onto Taylor's Mill Road and pulled into the parallel parking spots in front of Buddy's, turned off the car and just sat.

It was so ridiculous, like a bad movie. Too pathetically the same as 1964. What was he thinking? That they would recover the feelings from back then, and finally slow dance the way he wanted to at the St. Eugene's dance and then at their graduation party? Finally pledge their love the way he thought they should have back then? It hadn't ended up well in 1964. She may never have had the feelings he had anyway. Did he think it would end up better now? He was divorced, and 69 years old; she was the same age and he didn't think she was married but maybe she had a boyfriend, and maybe just like back then she had an older boyfriend with whom Paul couldn't compete, although if her boyfriend were older than 69 maybe Paul would look pretty good, finally. Another car pulled in next to him and someone got out and walked into Buddy's. He didn't look to see who it was, but started his car and pulled out, driving back on Taylor's Mill, then right on Springhaven and left into the supermarket parking lot. It was the same footprint that formerly housed the A&P supermarket that was bought and sold and rebranded a number of times before it was eventually acquired by the Giant chain and a few years ago, torn down and rebuilt. The dry cleaners was still there, but the hobby-pet shop was long gone and a lot of new stores and been built, eating up more of what had been wooded, undeveloped land.

Paul parked and looked at the storefronts. Next to the dry cleaners was now a nail salon, and next to that the Ming Dynasty Chinese restaurant, and next to that and next to that and next to that, the water vapor in the air dancing like visible static under the parking lot flood lights shining down on the stores, and with the car windows down he could hear the air humming, the buzzing coming from the lights.

The situation wasn't just ridiculous—he *felt* ridiculous. Pathetic. Overall, his full-of-promise life—the practical career path his father wanted for him just because he was smart enough and that's what smart people did; the press-TEEGE his mother wanted for him, the respectability and aura of being a physician that would make heads turn and people look up whenever he walked in a room; and then the board certification and a stable, respectable medical practice and a comfortable living his ex-wife wanted for him—hadn't gone all that well. Was that part or all of the reason he had invested so much in this reunion, the recreating, finding and bringing back the people and the moods and the memories of that time, wanting to gather those people and those memories and those moods in the same space at the same time and hoping…for what? Some kind of chemical reaction? Some age- and time-reversing miracle? To find something they'd all had at the time that Nancy might say they still had but he felt was lost, had disappeared? To reconnect with Mary Liz and correct the mistake he'd made at the 1964 party going off with Biggsy when he could have gone somewhere with her when she had said she was "hot" and maybe that would have cemented their boyfriend-girlfriend relationship, but didn't, and the reunion party was his chance to recapture that? And now it was over, and it was gone, and she was gone; again. Lost again, from the party, from his life. And now what? Probably a moping day on Sunday punctuated by a few emails or text messages from Nancy and Gerry—about how great the party had been and SOOO nice to see so many classmates they hadn't seen in years, maybe even 55 years, and good God Paul, you really nailed it with the music and the trivia and the memory booklet and everything, awesome job, can't wait to rehash next week, so glad you pushed us to do this, so worth it. Would he be able to respond if he could even bring himself to read them? Then just back to work on Monday? Monday June 17th. Almost summer on the conventional calendar and early summer by

"…the water vapor in the air dancing like visible static under the parking lot flood lights…"

Biggsy's St. Anthony's seasons calendar but when you go to work instead of school it's the same as any other day in any other season except maybe no jacket and the windows down or A/C on in the car instead instead of windows up and heater on but otherwise indistinguishable. Khakis instead of corduroy, short sleeves instead of long but otherwise the same. And what after that? Would time bury the reunion party the way it had tried to bury their years at St Anthony's? Then another Friday rolls around and it's another in a 55-year series of after-work rip-roaring happy-hour get-togethers at Buddy's? For what? Another 10, 20, 30 years?

While he hated to admit it, Paul grudgingly acknowledged that the way Biggsy had recast the school year seasons had merit. There was something to be said after all for trying to mix and blend what was going on inside the building—with people, school subjects, Catholicism's peculiar systems and rituals and calendar-related rhythms—with what was going on outside the building—in the air, wind, sun, moon, trees, grasses, flowers, birds, bees, everything—into a coherent approach to marking time.

Paul wanted that back, but what could he do? Resume regular church attendance? He hadn't so much as set foot inside a Catholic sanctuary since his wedding over 40 years earlier, except for others' weddings and funerals. Take an adult education class at Springhaven High and re-experience the September-to-June school-year cadence? Not sustainable, since it would only last as long as he continued taking classes. Become a teacher and experience it every year with a new cast of characters? Perhaps it would be easy to get a state teaching certificate in light of all his higher education, although maybe a private school would accept him as is on the strength of his current C.V., if he wasn't already too old. But would it be enough to feel that school-year rhythm just experiencing the schedule, without having the same people around from 55 years ago? St. Anthony's had been an organic piece of whole cloth—yes, the movement of events against a homogenized natural and artificial calendar, but Biggsy, Gerry, Robbie, Nancy, Dolores and Mary Liz were inextricably woven into it. Could he get past that part? Could he get past Mary Liz? Was that all he really needed to do—no return to church, no adult education, no job or career change—the only leap he needed to make? And had the reunion party's expectation-reality mismatch already pushed him past it?

X

Summer (June 13th to August 15th)

After throwing all those rocks and sticks and enveloped by the dark and the quiet I don't remember whether we felt a familiar, comfortable sameness just being there, the four of us, in The Woods, on Bamboo Island, in the middle of The Creek that flowed around us, for an hour or so still connected to and forever connected by St. Anthony's and all we had ever done in that space; or already sensed, felt it was changing, moving on, flowing on the way The Creek flowed around and eventually beyond Bamboo Island, slipping away the way winter slips into spring into summer into fall as we stood in church clothes and shoes instead of play clothes and sneakers; or had already changed, inexorably; was lost, irretrievably. I only remember that as we stood there eyes darkness-adjusted looking at The Creek, across the water in the darkness to the "mainland" on the other side across that few-foot expanse of water that felt like miles, I had the feeling I had to move. To go.

It may have been a few seconds or a few minutes after all the rocks and sticks were thrown, after Biggsy had said we weren't going back when I turned away from the other three and walked the 15 or so feet to the farthest tip of the little island to get a running start, then took off. Reaching the other end where the three of them were still standing, ignoring the makeshift bridge and not wanting to chance the overhead vines knowing I risked landing in water and mud if I grabbed for them, I just jumped.

Off of Bamboo Island and over The Creek. Jumping for the other side and for the path that led out of The Woods and maybe back to the church and Mary Liz and my record player and records and maybe for whatever something else was out there in the dark I couldn't really see.

Suspended in the air for milliseconds that felt like minutes or like time out of time, out of calendars and clocks, jumping over the eight years at St Anthony's, our eighth-grade year, the last three months, the last three days, the last three hours, over the Latin altar boy responses the country and state capitals the imports and exports the catechism questions I had memorized the Drill and Mental complex fraction questions I couldn't solve in my head quickly enough to keep Biggsy from yelling "Too slow!" and besting me yet again jumping sailing over nuns priests prayers at Mass and before and after meals prayers for lost car keys and homework for lost souls in fanciful purgatories in the sky or real ones on earth jumping sailing over a dead janitor heroes singers fighters heartbreakers rivals Bernie Galvin Hiram JFK Beatles Cassius Clay Mary Liz Biggsy Mary Liz Biggsy Forever Forever the fool taken for granted eight years still jumping sailing flying

"...jumping sailing flying off of Bamboo Island over The Creek out of The Woods..."

suspended in air legs kicking furiously like Olympic long-jumpers to make sure I got across and cleared the water and the mud suspended in air milliseconds nanoseconds jumping sailing flying off of Bamboo Island over The Creek out of The Woods out of eighth grade and St. Anthony's and into whatever came next neck sticking out stretching craning jumping sailing flying diving headlong into summer.

Return

Paul sat in his car and looked at the nail salon, then at the Chinese restaurant, then at the bank and down the row of newer businesses, although "newer" since 1964 could have meant that by 2019 they were already long-established enterprises. Then he restarted his car and drove onto the narrow access road behind the row of storefronts. The back doors had the names of the businesses in 3-4-inch-high black stenciled letters, easy to read by the light of the caged security lamps outside the doors. He could drive over to Clover Lane to confirm it, but he was pretty sure, probably close enough just guessing they would have been right about there across from the backs of stores, on the other side of the access road— The Woods.

Paul turned off his car and got out to look. The farther he got from the back doors and their lights the harder it was to see, and there wasn't much residual ambient illumination from the parking lot floods on the other side of the building, but after a minute or two his eyes adjusted. At least he could see that there was barely anything left of The Woods but a thin, sparse remnant of contiguous trees on some undeveloped ground, along with a couple of trashed shopping carts turned upside down and an old car tire or two. Even in the dim light he could practically see through the wooded area to where it joined the backyards on Clover, some of which had back porch and deck lights on. The Woolsey's house was there where he and Biggsy and Gerry and Robbie used to walk in, although a couple that was already elderly in 1964 would have certainly died many years ago. He wondered what new family might be in there now; maybe the Woolsey's kids or grandkids moving back to the old neighborhood as some had done. He wondered if they ever walked from their backyard through the wooded area to the shopping center. Maybe to get a drink at the supermarket, if there were even a water fountain still inside in that store in an age when people—even preteens—walked around with water bottles permanently attached to their hands. Back in the day he would have never been able to see all the way through, The Woods were just too dense.

Paul walked over to the edge of the access road blacktop and stood by the dumpster that probably belonged to Ming Dynasty, as he could smell what was likely scorched wok-scraped sesame oil. He wondered what he might see and find if he were to walk off the blacktop and onto the ground among the trees. Maybe somewhere in and among those remaining trees was the very spot where 55 years earlier he and Biggsy and Gerry and Robbie had gathered after leaving the graduation party to have one last night as St. Anthony students on Bamboo Island. Although maybe the spot wasn't even in there anymore. Maybe it had been paved over and was sitting under the blacktop. Maybe he was standing over it right now.

He stepped onto the ground and started walking in, wondering if he would still know the way. Would any of the markers still be there? The tree trunk with the knob almost certainly would be gone, but maybe there would still be a few stones from the old Taylor mansion or its wall. Would he still be able to find The Creek? Would he be able to hear it, or smell it? Would he still be able to jump across it? Was it even still there? Had the excavators buried it when they added all the new stores and businesses?

He kept walking in, in short sleeves, khaki pants and loafers, having left his blazer in the car. There was a sweatshirt and an old pair of sneakers he kept in the trunk, but he was already committed, too far in to turn back and get them. The ground was uneven, but as it was only mid-June the grasses and weeds were low so he was sure-footed. For an instant he wondered if there were enough tree cover for deer to feel comfortable here, and if so there might also be blacklegged ticks and a risk of Lyme Disease. But the doctor's preoccupations were quickly suppressed by smelling the sweetness of the honeysuckle and crown vetch; he thought maybe he detected wild rose as well.

As he kept walking and bumped into some unfamiliar waist-level wildly branching obstacles, a low understory growth of something, he discovered he had been right: the unmistakable scent of wild rose, their pink-white blossoms easily visible despite the darkness. He stopped and inhaled deeply, then exhaled laughing, thinking, "I literally stopped to smell the roses. I have been reduced to a cliché." Yes, a sweet-smelling delight, but to touch also prickly, thorny—puncturing his bare arms in multiple spots and catching on his pants—thick, dense, all overgrown and tangled from decades of neglect. Obviously the shopping center owner didn't invest in maintaining a patch of undeveloped ground behind his commercial properties, visible to lessees and their vendors making deliveries, but out of sight to customers. A policy of let the invasives invade. But it still smelled sweet.

He looked up again, and ahead. Even in the half-dark half-light he still had his bearings—Clover Lane backyards in front, their back-porch and deck lights shining, and shopping center stores behind. So much of The

Woods and everything they imagined and played and dreamed there was gone, lost, without a prayer of recovery whether to Saint Anthony or any other celestial advocate that might have the bandwidth to be listening; but at least Paul felt sure that if he kept moving forward he would still find his way back to the dumpster, the access road, his car, and the way out. So he lifted his arms above the tangle of thorns and walked on.

"So he lifted his arms above the tangle of thorns and walked on."

ACKNOWLEDGMENTS

Rick and Joe thank

Leah, Kevin, Christen, Mimi and everyone at Finishing Line Press for saying "yes" (again) and delivering another fine product;

their classmates from the 1966 graduating class at Our Lady of Perpetual Help elementary school in Morton, Pennsylvania (too many to name and would risk missing some to try, but they know who they are) for keeping the memories alive at and in every reunion, party, picnic, happy hour get-together, text and email—whenever Rick and Joe see them or hear them or read their words, even now, the years melt away; and

graphic designer Nate Adams, for formatting the illustrations, studying old Hardy Boys books for fonts and styles, and creating the first dance of words and pictures.

Joe thanks

Donna, for the after-breakfast honey-do list that is always short and to the point: "Get upstairs and start painting."

Rick thanks

designer Matthew Evans, all the way from Belfast, for thinking a book about a prayer could look like an actual prayer book;

his grade school classmate and ever-since-then artist friend Joe, for tapping his own memories of that time in that place with those people to move his pen and brush to create the images that brought the words to life;

Elizabeth, her husband Greg, and all other English teachers past and present, inside and outside the family for showing their students life and the world through words and ideas, honoring former writers and inspiring a particular current fatherly one;

Sarah, the advertising executive for sacrificing precious night and weekend free time to gently suggest edits, brainstorm social media and website content, wrangle a designer, and just generally add polish and sparkle to the project, giving her dad some idea what a "Group Brand Director" does in her day gig; and

Kathy, for finding so many missed edits, but also for entering Rick's world as the girl from the neighboring Catholic parish—when his classmates pointed her out at the multi-school 8th-grader Safety Picnic it was a *South Pacific*'ish "Some Enchanted [Afternoon]" moment, seeing a stranger across a crowded amusement park and having a hard time taking his eyes off her, same way it's been ever since.

Joseph Cairone is an artist and former landscape architect. His early fascination with all things visual was initially inspired by the great comic book and graphic novel artists of the 1950s and 60s. It continued through his Rutgers University formal education and subsequent professionally completed projects throughout diverse regions of the country. Having concluded a successful 44-year career as a principal Landscape Architect of his own Philadelphia-based design firm, Joe now lives in Havertown, PA with his wife, Donna, and their rescue dogs, participating in regional art shows/exhibits and plein air events. The collection of illustrations for this novel is the product of a lifelong friendship with the author.

Richard Donze is a physician author whose poems and essays have appeared in medical journals and newsletters and four anthologies of physician poetry: *Blood and Bone, Primary Care, Uncharted Lines* and *Voices from the Front Lines: The Pandemic and the Humanities.* In 1998 Nova Science Publishers (Imprint, Kroshka Books) published his nonfiction book *Dinner Music: How to Compose the Permanently Perfect Diet,* a right-brained approach to nutrition advice. *The Natural Order of Things,* his first poetry collection, was published in November 2021 by Finishing Line Press. Dr. Donze was an undergraduate English major at the University of Pennsylvania before embarking on a medical career, and currently practices at Chester County Hospital in West Chester, PA, part of the University of Pennsylvania Health System, as Medical Director of the Hospital's Occupational Medicine Program. He lives in West Chester, PA with his wife Kathleen. *The Secret Saint Anthony Prayer* is his first published work of fiction.

www.ingramcontent.com/pod-product-compliance
Lightning Source LLC
Chambersburg PA
CBHW031102020726
47495CB00007B/2014